Also by Hilma Wolitzer

NOVELS

The Doctor's Daughter

Tunnel of Love

Silver

In the Palomar Arms

Hearts

In the Flesh

Ending

NONFICTION

The Company of Writers

FOR YOUNG READERS

Wish You Were Here

Toby Lived Here

Out of Love

Introducing Shirley Braverman

SUMMER READING

SUMMER READING

a novel

Hilma Wolitzer

BALLANTINE BOOKS NEW YORK

Published in the United States by Ballantine Books, an imprint of The Random House Publishing Group, a division of Random House, Inc., New York.

BALLANTINE and colophon are registered trademarks of Random House, Inc.

ISBN 978-0-345-48586-1

LIBRARY OF CONGRESS CATALOGING-IN-PUBLICATION DATA

Wolitzer, Hilma.
Summer reading : a novel / Hilma Wolitzer.
p. cm.
ISBN-13: 978-0-345-48586-1 (alk. paper)
ISBN-10: 0-345-48586-6 (alk. paper)
1. Book clubs (Discussion groups)—Fiction. 2. Female friendship—Fiction. 3. Hamptons (N.Y.)—Fiction. I. Title.
PS3573.0563S86 2007
813'.54—dc22   2006035771

Printed in the United States of America on acid-free paper

www.ballantinebooks.com

2 4 6 8 9 7 5 3 1

First Edition

Book design by Laurie Jewell

FOR MORTY

chief cook and reader,
with thanks and love

Emma sought to learn what was really meant in life
by the words "happiness," "passion," and "intoxication"—
words that had seemed so beautiful to her in books.

—GUSTAVE FLAUBERT, *Madame Bovary*

SUMMER READING

1.

Alyssa Snyder Is Troubled

Lissy Snyder hated nature, especially its lavish variety on the eastern end of Long Island. All those sudden winged or crawly creatures everywhere, feeding on one another and on you, too, if you weren't vigilant. Ants in the pantry, moths batting at the lamps, something living or dead plucked discreetly from the pool every day. And then there were the piano-tuner birds that shrieked or sang the same two notes incessantly, and the ones that seemed to be typing in the woods behind the house. Once in a while, Lissy stood at the spruce-lined border of the property and yelled "Shut up shut up shut up!" just to get a little peace and quiet. But they would begin again the moment she turned her back, like a rowdy junior high school class mocking a substitute teacher.

She had sweet-talked Jeffrey into buying a beach house while they were still on their honeymoon, a time he would have gladly agreed to anything. How gorgeous and powerful and canny she'd felt! But she hadn't bargained for the rampant flora and fauna in Sagaponack. That was supposed to be upstate somewhere, or in New England, where wildlife belonged, where rabid bats were as common as houseflies, and bears were said to be driven mad by menstruating women.

In Lissy's childhood memory of an idyllic Southampton summer, before her father left, before the death of her beloved nanny, there was a vast velveteen lawn skirting her cousins' house and, behind it, the sand dunes that led to the sea, and everything that lived there knew its place: the lobsters in their traps or in a citrus vinaigrette, the other secrets of the deep kept appropriately secret. Fireflies flashed around the porches at night, accompanied by the strumming of hidden crickets, but they'd seemed pretty harmless; her Grandmother Ellis had called their performance "a charming *petit son et lumière*."

Now, on a balmy June day during her second Sagaponack season, Lissy peered anxiously into the patio garden. Everything had to look perfect for that afternoon's meeting of her summer reading club, the Page Turners; she'd already plumped the cushions in the screened gazebo, where they convened. The group was led by Angela Graves, who'd taught English Lit at some tiny women's college in Texas a million years ago. Ardith Templeton had found her through an ad the previous winter in the *East Hampton Star*. "Enhance your summer with the company of great books. Retired professor of literature will lead the way."

The flowers that Pedro and his crew tended were nice enough, fragrant and colorful, except for all the bees they attracted, and the way their brief blooming reminded Lissy of her own mortality. She would turn twenty-eight in October, and although none of her mirrors, not even the cruelly lit and magnified one on her dressing room table, had yet hinted at the ravages of aging or even the slightest dimming of her crisp blondness, she felt that her shelf life had begun to expire. Maybe all that required reading—never her strong suit—was undoing her, or it could just be the forbidding example of Angela herself, who must have faced the sun fearlessly all her life and was now a bas-relief of age spots and wrinkles.

Lissy had felt flattered when Debby and Joy, whom she knew from yoga class in the city, invited her to join the book club. And she was thrilled when they'd accepted her offer of a designated meeting place, along with the name she had come up with for them. The original Page Turners had been the group for slower readers she'd been made to join in the third grade at the Betsy Ross Day School, where the letters of the alphabet had a habit of reversing themselves to her, and she often had to be coaxed into concentration. But she didn't mention any of that to her current book group friends.

Everyone in the Hamptons wanted to get to know beautiful and aloof Ardith better. She was like those savvy, popular girls at school in whose orbit Lissy had dizzily spun without ever coming any closer to them. And Larry Templeton was someone important in Jeffrey's corporate world. Lissy envisioned a brilliant, career-enhancing friendship evolving from this casual connection, and Jeffrey's astonished pride in her.

Every other Tuesday since Memorial Day, Angela Graves drove her blue Chevy Neon from The Springs to Lissy's more desirable neighborhood and sat among the dewy-skinned young members of the grown-up Page Turners, a veritable bulletin from their grim future. Some of the books she extolled were equally grim Victorian novels, in which infants or their new mothers routinely died and, not surprisingly, sexual repression was the rage.

Lissy had been thinking, on and off, about having a baby. Not that she was beset by maternal yearnings, but perhaps it was time. It wasn't as if she had a real career to interrupt; even she knew that being a part-time, freelance party planner wasn't a serious or inspired pursuit. The sprinkling of referrals she'd had so far had been favors from business acquaintances of Jeffrey's: a couple of toddlers' birthday parties, an anniversary dinner for someone's senile in-laws. Balloons and baby lamb chops for every occasion, and all the honorees equally insensible.

Besides, a few of Lissy's friends had started families already, bucking the national trend of waiting until your ovaries dried up and fell off. She might well be in on the beginning of a new trend. It astonished her sometimes that she made so many crucial decisions this way, guided by arbitrary social patterns rather than passion.

But it was how she'd been raised, as if everything depended on some invisible, incontestable clock. Time for dinner, hungry or not. Time for bed (ditto for sleepiness). Time for school, let go of Mummy's hand, Alyssa! Time for deflowering. Time to get married. And why not; how did you ever know if you were really in love, anyway?

Still, starting a family might be inconvenient, or worse, and especially complicated right now. If, as Angela Graves suggested, Mary Shelley's *Frankenstein* was merely an elaborate metaphor for childbirth, what could one expect? Jeffrey and Lissy would have custody of little Miles and Miranda, who would require all of her energy and concentration, during the final weeks of the summer, after their mother brought them back from a European trip. Lissy could play at mothering then, if those beautiful but daunting children allowed it, and make an informed decision for once. Why, it might even be fun.

She was supposed to have finished reading *Can You Forgive Her?* for today's session of the Page Turners, although it was incredibly long and printed in such microscopic type. Angela had given them the title back in January, just after they'd first signed up, instructing them to start reading it then, but Lissy hadn't gotten around to it right away.

And now, flailing to catch up, it seemed more like *winter* reading to her—that endless blizzard of pages flecked with the blown soot of words. She skimmed as quickly as she could through the chapters that dealt with politics and money, in favor of the romantic passages. But even sounding out the characters' names as she flipped through the book—Alice Vavasor, Lady Glencora, Plantagenet—badly fatigued her. Imagine saddling a child with a name like Plantagenet!

The bloated little paperback had been wedged open and propped against the sugar bowl as she ate breakfast that morning, and it was dangling from her hand as she peeked into the flower garden later. In fact, she'd hardly been seen without it for the past few weeks. Jeffrey carefully pried it from her sleeping fingers at night, and he always tucked in one of his business cards to save her place, which never seemed to change. Chapter 14, Alice Vavasor Becomes Troubled. Lissy relied on the chapter headings—she'd read all of those right away. They gave the novel a somewhat predictable shape, something she wouldn't have minded having in her own life. Jeffrey Makes a Killing on Wall Street. Lissy Sparkles in Book Discussion Group. Wherein the Myth of the Evil Stepmother Is Dispelled.

Jeffrey had made more than a few killings on Wall Street, most of them back in the crazy early nineties—the go-go years—long before she even knew him. When she was still a teenager! And then, like everybody, he'd lost a bundle in the downswing. He was still wealthy, though, by most standards, when he and Lissy met and married two years before. There was more than enough for a showy courtship and wedding; this house they'd christened Summerspell; his sailboat, the *Argo;* those outrageous alimony and child support payments; and the extravagant Manhattan life he and his new bride pursued.

But he fretted about the past and about the future. She would often discover him in the middle of the night, a prisoner of his own bad dreams in striped pajamas, his worried pale face eerily illuminated by the glow of his computer screen as he tracked the global markets. Jeffrey was haunted by nonfinancial concerns, too, especially his absentee fatherhood and his survival of the World Trade Center disaster, when so many of his colleagues had perished. To complicate matters even further, he believed that his life had been saved by his then four-year-old son, Miles, whose preschool orientation meeting Jeffrey had attended that fateful morning, instead of going to work on the ninety-sixth floor of the first tower to be hit.

And then there were the letters from Danielle, his ex-wife, so full of vitriol they seemed to burn his fingers when he opened them. Lissy sometimes read them in the privacy of her bathroom later, and felt just as stung by their tone and content. How could she accuse him of abandoning her and the children when he was so generous, and still seemed to have one foot firmly in their lives?

Danielle and Jeffrey had already been estranged when Lissy met him, but Danielle referred to her as "that woman" or "your stupid, blond slut" in her letters as if Lissy were some kind of home-wrecking whore and not his legal, loving wife. And she *wasn't* stupid, even if she felt that way sometimes. Worst of all, Danielle always addressed him as Jeffie, a nickname from his past that looked disturbingly like an endearment on the page, despite the nasty context.

On Jeffrey's troubled nights, Lissy would cluck at him and urge him back to bed, where she'd assume his insomnia and a condensed version of some of his fears—the less personal ones—while he snored peacefully beside her. What if they became poor, or at least not as rich anymore? That was where the chapter headings might have come in handy. Would she have stuck things out? Did she love Jeffrey for himself? Who was he, exactly? How hard it was to separate and sort out the many facets of identity and affection and commitment.

And then he made his comeback, a spectacular and unique killing on some combination of investments and strategies—something to do with offshore drilling in the Gulf of Mexico—that made him the envy of the financial community and the uneasy focus of the SEC for a while. His business card, placed so inconspicuously in her Trollope that it seemed to be a part of the text, soothed her with its tone of authority: JEFFREY J. SNYDER, ESQ. PRESIDENT AND CFO WORLD TRADE CONSULTANTS. But like so many Victorian housewives, real and fictional, she didn't know precisely what her husband did for a living.

Left to her own choice of reading material, Lissy would have purchased a pile of easy, glossy beach books gleaned from the bestseller lists and thumbed her way through the thick, perfumed summer issues of *Vanity Fair* and *Hamptons.* Her membership in the Page Turners forced her into an attitude of self-improvement, although she had yet to sparkle or even overcome her shyness at the meetings any more than she ever had in the classroom. If she'd been able to finish *Can You Forgive Her?* or any of the shorter assigned novels in time for the appointed discussions, she might have fared better.

Unfortunately, she had never moved up to the Whiz Kids, the highest-level reading group at Betsy Ross, and her difficulty with the printed word served as a soporific—more efficiently now than even sex or Ambien—as it had most of her life. She would begin to doze off soon after she began reading, her eyes losing focus first, then the page she'd intended to turn becoming impossibly heavy, even when she was curious about the story's outcome.

In college her roommate, a scholarship grind named Cynthia Ann Pope, had shared voluminous class notes with Lissy and even wrote some of her papers in exchange for clothing and cash. These days, without Cynthia Ann's assistance, Lissy browsed through or just read part of the way into most books, and then hastily checked out plot summaries and criticism on the Internet. She'd Googled her research for *Can You Forgive Her?* even before she'd begun reading the first page. So she knew, if the title hadn't been a big enough hint, that a moral decision was begged of the reader by Trollope, and that most academics, just like Trollope's heroine, had voted in favor of decency and true love. She could probably safely take that stance herself during the discussion.

But right now she had to focus on the refreshments required of her as the Page Turners' hostess, the one job at which she felt proficient. In the kitchen, that sullen new dayworker—Jo Ann Cutty's daughter, what was her name again?—skulked at the sink. The girl needed to tweeze her eyebrows and do something about her posture. Lissy said, "Hi!" and smiled at her with forced friendliness. Without waiting for the usual scowling response, she opened the refrigerator to check on the pile of creamy little sandwiches under their sheltering dome, and the pitcher of mango mint iced tea working up an appealing cold sweat on the shelf just above.

Then she went to the powder room, where the rose petals of soap she'd brought from Paris, when the beach house was still only a post-coital tease, lay nestled in a Lucite shell. She patted the impeccable, monogrammed linen guest towels and gazed critically at herself in the mirror. But instead of touching up her lipstick or adjusting an errant strand of hair, she found herself looking into her own eyes and wondering if she would have forgiven Alice Vavasor for whatever it was she'd done. Well, she didn't have to decide that very second; she could just wait and see what the others said. But then she was ambushed by another stray thought—would *she* ever do anything that would require the forgiveness of strangers?—and felt a shivery thrill of pre-science.

2.

Truth and Beauty

Angela Graves was half in love with the young women she guided through the halls of literature, and half incensed by their laziness or ineptitude. It was the destiny of a dedicated teacher to be conflicted this way, and her calling itself the consequence of being simultaneously homely and intelligent. Would she have traded for ephemeral beauty and everlasting mediocrity, the genetic coding of so many of her students past and present? Probably not, especially now, when any beauty she might have had would be long spent.

But it was a rhetorical dilemma anyway, never a choice that was hers to make. Angela was the heroine of her own life—who else?—but it certainly wasn't the most compelling narrative. As the only child of strict, older, middle-class parents on Staten Island, both accountants, she'd been imaginative and dreamy. *Bookish* was the way her mother accurately described her to people, but with more alarm and disapproval than pride.

Angela *had* to resort to books, though; there was so little to be learned at home, where she'd witnessed only the daily return of disappointment and resignation. And she felt alternately superior and uncertain among her peers, so it wasn't easy for her to make friends. At first, she identified with the deceptively plain, devoted governesses in her favorite novels, who were gloriously redeemed in the end: she had only to let down her hair, literally and metaphorically, and display her good heart and ironic wit. Much later, she saw herself simply as one who served, like the graceless baby nurse Horsie in the Dorothy Parker short story, a permanent extra in the drama of love.

On her first day of teaching at Macon Women's College, in Wellspring, Texas, that little wasteland midway between Dallas and Odessa, she'd asked her freshman Expository Writing class which authors they liked best. There was some restless shuffling, a jangling of charm bracelets, and a few of the students muttered and exchanged glances as if it she'd just sprung a surprise quiz on them.

Angela persevered. "Well, how many of you have read *Jane Eyre*?" This time the room went completely still until, finally, a small white hand slowly rose, a lonely periscope in that sea of ignorance. "Yes?" Angela said, smiling encouragement, and the owner of the hand asked, "What has she written?"

Someone else might have dined out on that anecdote for years. It did earn Angela a rare chuckle once in the faculty lounge, but she was shocked into silence and despair when she heard herself. It was her own life she was mocking. Occasionally, there was a truly bright, displaced student she could lead onto the path of literary enlightenment, and they would gossip like girlfriends about dead writers and their immortal characters. Oh, brains *and* beauty!

There were a few romantic interludes, too. For a long time, Angela's sexual direction was up for grabs. She'd had crushes on various students, and on various male and female colleagues. Sex took place a few times on both sides of the aisle, though never with a student, thank God, and rarely more than once or twice with the same partner.

That was her own doing, for the most part. She'd wanted to be grandly moved or to at least feel dangerously erotic, and she hardly ever fell into either of those states, and never into both at the same time. Had she been ruined by books, by her all-too-willing suspension of disbelief in Mellors and Heathcliff and Moll Flanders?

In her forty-third year, when her figure was still good and her bold features somewhat softened by the luster of character, she lopped off most of her silver-threaded dark hair, like a postulant without an order, preparing to accept a solitary, loveless life. But soon afterward, she embarked on an extraordinary and treacherous affair with a married friend, with disastrous consequences. That such a thing could happen! Almost twenty years later, she could still stir up the embers of those dueling sensations, desire and disgrace, low in her belly.

Stephen and Valerie Keller were both her friends; they'd taken her on because they believed that beneath the armor of her reserve she was a person of value. Stephen taught painting and drawing at Macon, and Valerie was a reference librarian there. She was the beauty in the family, with her wild auburn hair, those unfashionable hips, and that wonderful pale skin—the complete opposite of anyone's idea of a librarian. Stephen's bony face and serious gaze behind wire-rimmed glasses reminded Angela of daguerreotypes she'd seen of nineteenth-century scholars.

They had married right after graduate school and had a precocious and pretty little girl, Charlotte. Angela got to know Valerie first, in the stacks at the library, where they'd conspired to track down a line of verse a student had likely plagiarized, and she met Stephen later at a faculty meeting. It was Valerie's gift to see the best in people. She found Angela wryly funny rather than bitter, shy instead of standoffish, and her opinions were contagious.

The Kellers began inviting Angela to dinner, never seeming to mind having an odd number (in any sense of those words) at their table, the way other couples did. And because they'd accepted her, she became acceptable, socialized, like one of those wild children raised by wolves and then brought into civilization.

All those blissful evenings of food and wine and earnest or hilarious talk at the gray saltbox on Dogwood Drive—the mismatched place mats, the sweet, corny ceremony of candles and toasts. Angela felt at *home* there, an experience she'd never quite had anywhere else in the world, and eventually Valerie and Stephen became as inseparable in her mind as they appeared to be to each other.

Then, one night, she filled in for their regular babysitter, a sophomore art major, who had come down with the flu. It was Stephen's birthday, his thirty-eighth, and he and Valerie planned to go out to dinner—not to one of the steak houses or rathskellers around the campus, but the one nice place that required reservations and dressing up. Angela had overheard Stephen on the phone in his office, commiserating with Valerie about the defecting art major, and she'd rapped on the open door and volunteered her services.

Stephen insisted on picking her up; perhaps Valerie had urged him to. It was late January and there had been a minor snowfall the previous night, followed by dropping temperatures that iced the roads. He waited outside her apartment in the purring Ford wagon without honking the horn. She was already at the window, shielded by the curtains, watching for him.

They'd known each other for a little more than three years; both of them had been hired the same semester. Angela—who'd published several papers in obscure journals—had just been given tenure. Except for a pro forma one-man show at the college, Stephen's paintings had only been hung in a couple of local group exhibitions, and he was still under the tenure committee's scrutiny. They'd deferred making a decision about him until he'd built up a larger body of work. So there was envy and empathy between him and Angela, a new, nervous dimension to their friendship.

She had never been in the station wagon before—no, actually, she had, once in the fall, on a short ride to a Spanish mission—but she'd sat in the back then, next to Charlotte in her car seat, like an au pair or a maiden aunt. Valerie, of course, sat up front next to Stephen, in the death seat, as the students gaily called it, forgoing their own seat belts. *The wife's seat,* Angela thought as she opened the front passenger door the night of Stephen's birthday and slid inside.

It was cozy in the car, with the heater blowing and the inflated sleeves of their down jackets touching. Stephen smiled handsomely at her, kissed her forehead. He was growing a beard, only a few weeks' dark fuzzy growth then, like a boy impersonating a man in a school play.

The car smelled yeasty but not unpleasant, something like the smell of one's own slept-in bed. They were surrounded by family artifacts: Charlotte's empty car seat still strapped in place behind them, a handful of Valerie's books sliding around the backseat; she liked suspense novels. Gravel or cookie crumbs crunched under Angela's boots, and in the pocket of the door next to her there was a collapsed pink plastic pacifier, both touching and slightly obscene, and a few audiotapes, including *The Little Engine That Could* and Bach's toccatas and fugues.

Angela wasn't given to frivolous musings about other people's lives, except in novels, or about her own roads not taken. She was still bookish, but far less imaginative than she'd been as a child. Even at their house, a little later, when Valerie came downstairs, wobbling on her high heels and looking particularly lovely in a short black crêpe dress that contrasted sharply with Angela's corduroy pants and flannel shirt, she'd felt a brief frisson but didn't indulge in any fantasies, domestic or otherwise.

She actually liked her own uncluttered life, a life of reading without the threat of interruption, except for the hours of teaching, about which she'd grown less hopeful but more tolerant. She disseminated ideas in the classroom as if she were blowing the downy seeds of a thought dandelion around. Maybe a few of the students would be pollinated; in any event, she did her best.

Charlotte was still awake, warm and pink-cheeked from her bath, in red, footed pajamas. She was four years old now, a little chatterbox, as her mother had warned. As soon as her parents left, Charlotte became imprinted on Angela, following her from room to room, interrogating her. "Do you want to see my toys?" "Why do you look like a man?" "Do you have a little girl?" She had an established routine for delaying bedtime—water, a story, the checking of monsters' hiding places, a cookie, more water, a retelling of her day, another story. Finally, Angela had to lie down beside her and wait for Charlotte to fall asleep.

It was in that narrow, innocent bed that the worst thoughts began to occur to her. What if the child became ill and died? She'd been exposed to the infectious babysitter a few days before, and it wasn't unheard of for children to die. It was the fear that haunted all Victorian households, where every new baby became another hostage to fortune. But the little girl lying next to Angela—the benefactor of modern medicine and Dickens's veneration of childhood—was gleaming with good health, pulsing with determined life.

What if there was an accident and both parents were killed? God, what was *wrong* with her that she could have such dire notions about her dear friends, without provocation and without the thudding of dread or even a mild flush of shame? What if only Stephen died? "Water," Charlotte slurred piteously from the first layer of sleep, and Angela smoothed the covers around her and crept like a criminal from the bed.

Of course nobody died that night. The Kellers came home from dinner a little buzzed by chocolate and brandy and their few golden hours of freedom. Valerie kept hugging Angela, who was so, so good to do this for them. "We owe you *big*-time," she said, sounding disconcertingly like a Macon sorority sister. She looked a little mussed and vulgarly pleased, as if they'd parked somewhere and made out in the car.

"Not at all. My pleasure," Angela coolly replied, extricating herself from Valerie's white arms, that profusion of flyaway hair, her lilac scent.

In the car once more, Angela had the insane urge to climb over the seat and squeeze herself into Charlotte's car seat, to give up all responsibility for the evil machinations of an uncensored adult mind, the burden of a grown body that could still surprise you with its longings. Instead, she made small talk with Stephen about Charlotte's intelligence and outspoken charm, about the school's curriculum, about colleagues and students.

And then, out of the blue, she said, "Stephen, if they don't give you tenure, they're absolute fools. You're a very good teacher and a wonderful painter." When she said it, it seemed true. She had an approving image in her mind of a group of paintings called Imaginary Portraits in his show the year before at the college gallery. They were realistic and slightly grotesque at once, like Diane Arbus photographs, in which every subject is appallingly human and freakish.

In fact, Angela had wondered then if Arbus had been an influence, but she'd hesitated to ask, for fear he would think she'd really meant to say that he was derivative. And what if he was? Good artists borrow, great artists steal. Who said that, or something like it? Maybe it referred to writers. It didn't matter, though—he *was* a good teacher— the students adored him—and his paintings were striking. She'd even bought two of the portraits after the show. And he was still young enough to grow into his own vision of things. Maybe, armed now with her own recent tenure, she could offer an opinion about him to the committee.

They were only halfway to her apartment—the local streets were truly perilous, and they'd traveled slowly—but he pulled over against a curb near someone else's house, and he let the motor idle as the heater chugged away and the windows fogged up.

"I appreciate that, Angie," he said. He was the only one who'd ever called her that. His voice was husky, as if that was the first thing he'd said all day. "I mean, your opinion really matters to me, and I'm shaky now because we need a little extra security. I just want to paint, and Val wants to have another kid . . ." He took off his glasses and looked at her with his naked eyes in the haloed light thrown by a streetlamp, clearly surprised by his own candor.

Angela was surprised, too. If she'd expected either of them to ever reveal such an intimate married detail, it would have been Valerie. That was the way of close women friends, because a certain daring and a certain trust were always in play between them. It was what men really envied or couldn't get the hang of in their own friendships—that you take a chance and plunge in, the way lovers do.

She began thinking of things to say: *That's not really any of my business, Stephen,* or *Poor Valerie,* or *Don't worry, things will work out.* But all she could manage was a faint "Oh," probably the most ambiguous response of all.

And then, without warning, she pictured them in bed, an image she had only allowed to dart through her mind a couple of times before this—Valerie's loose, milky breasts almost flattened as she lay on her back with her legs flung open, her heavy-lidded eyes varnished with lust. Stephen's dark shadow looming over her, and then his weight descending as he moved his paint-stained hands and his sweetly curling mouth there and there and there.

"Oh," Angela said again, swamped by shock and arousal. The nipples of her own small breasts coiled beneath the flannel shirt, and her heart stampeded. She didn't touch him, but she might as well have, because she felt the quake of connection even before his face bent to hers, his lips smothering whatever cries of protest they were both about to make.

3.

Them

Every year they came down Montauk Highway in a slow caravan of SUVs and Jeeps and Land Rovers, like an army of tanks about to occupy an enemy village. They called themselves the summer people—*proudly,* Michelle Cutty noted, as if they owned the season as well as all that beachfront. She had first heard, or overheard, the term at a party she was working in Water Mill. "We summer people bankroll the whole shebang," a woman in a huge picture hat said as she helped herself to one of the bluepoints Michelle was serving from a bed of washed pebbles, "and they just love to hate us."

"Them" was what they were called behind their backs by the bonackers, especially when a matter of service was involved. "I'm catering for them again on Hither Lane on Saturday." Or "I'm clearing out an acre for them next week; want to pick up a couple hours?" It was similar to the way Michelle and her girl-friends used to refer to one of their mothers as "her" when they were teenagers and still in the stranglehold of supervision.

Her mother, Jo Ann, had gotten her this new job through one of her own regulars in Sagaponack. Michelle had filled in there on occasion, and had obviously passed muster. It would have been hard not to, under Jo Ann's direction. She was about one rung above a slave herself, and she expected everybody else to kiss up and knuckle under, too. Michelle wasn't allowed to take a break, hide somewhere for a quick smoke, or even lapse into a daydream. "They don't pay you good money just to stand around posing," Jo Ann would remind her.

Now here she was on her own, at another house where the occu-pants couldn't take a dump for themselves. But the money really was good: thirty bucks an hour, and all the hours she could spare. It sure beat clerking at Kmart for peanuts or—except for the company—doing small-animal care at the county shelter. This was her third day in a row.

As soon as she'd come in that morning, she made the sandwiches and the tea for some club meeting. Jo Ann had taught her how to do little sandwiches for them—rolled and sliced into pinwheels, or using cookie cutters shaped like diamonds and hearts. No crusts, of course, smears of this and that from gourmet shop plastic containers, sprigs of fresh herbs, and all of it arranged in a tiered, starburst pattern.

After she'd made the bed and vacuumed and straightened the bathrooms, Michelle had walked around with a big yellow sponge in her hand, looking for something else to do, another surface from which she could erase any visible signs of life. But the place was as spotless as a model home. She found herself looking up again and again at the kitchen clock, willing the hands to move.

Michelle's brother, Eddie, and her boyfriend, Hank, were making extra money off some of them, too, most of it in cold cash and off the books, for odd jobs like putting up deer fencing or cleaning out rain gutters. The two men also ran a small party boat, the *Kayla Joy*—named for Hank's fourteen-year-old daughter—on weekends. Six to a fishing party and ninety bucks a head for four hours (double that for eight), and their passengers all went home happy, with bad sunburns and a couple of fillets they could have picked up at Citarella for a lot less.

Once upon a time, before the invasion of the summer people, it had been primarily a fishing and farming community. There were still some commercial boats going out each morning for blues and striped bass, and enough fields of corn and cauliflower to keep the farm stands going.

But there were more party boats now—most of them bigger than the *Kayla Joy*—and more nurseries, growing white pines for privacy, and hibiscus for decorative gardens. A fifty-year-old hardware store had been replaced by a jewelry store called Bling! and a diner once favored by the fishermen, who used to get breakfast there at 4 AM before setting out, now sold souvenirs. Why did they need T-shirts and golf caps to remind them where they were?

Michelle was positive that Lissy Snyder had forgotten her name and felt too embarrassed now to ask her to repeat it. That's why she kept saying "Hi!" in her chirpy chipmunk voice and wore that goofy smile whenever they ran into each other in the house. Michelle could almost hear the wheels turning in that dopey blond head. Marie? Margaret? She was thinking of writing her name in lipstick or soap across the fun-house mirror in Lissy's dressing room, the one that made Michelle look as bad as she had in her yearbook photo before it was touched up.

Michelle's mother, a dedicated Beatles fan, had named her for their most romantic song, but Hank had always called her Mishy, which changed to Mushy soon after they started going out, and eventually to Mush. It was the only thing Jo Ann had against him. "I gave you the most beautiful name in the world," she'd grumble to Michelle, "and he turns it into a bowl of *cornmeal*." But Michelle privately cherished the nickname: it was as if Hank had discovered the soft core beneath her tough exterior.

She liked her real name, too, and when she was eleven or twelve she'd harbored a fantasy that she was either Ringo's or Paul's secret daughter. John was out of the running because of his devotion to Yoko (and because he was killed about a year before Michelle was conceived), and George was simply too boring. Jo Ann had gone to that huge Beatles concert at Shea stadium—she still had the program and a Fab Four button she claimed were worth a small fortune. "Your inheritance," she'd say to Michelle, holding them up in a ziplock plastic bag.

She'd never said a word about actually meeting any of the Beatles then, though, much less starting an affair with one of them that culminated more than a decade later in a love child. But she'd once remarked that "those bad boys" had made her do some crazy things, and another time Michelle caught her dancing with the broom to one of their albums—"She loves you, yeah, yeah, yeah!"—her eyes shut in what could only be interpreted as rapture. That was really all a susceptible little kid needed to hang a daydream on.

Skinny Jack Cutty, freckled as a trout from the sun and smelling of the sea, would be sitting right across the table from Michelle, quietly eating his dinner, and she'd glare at him through slitted eyes, willing him to disappear, so that her real father could come from Liverpool or wherever to claim her. When Jack actually did disappear off his fishing boat later that year, she gave up the fantasy, keeping only a ghost of her guilt about it, and the aching sense that she'd never really gotten to know him.

Lissy's guests started arriving just after one o'clock, the first three driving up together in a bullet-like silver convertible. Michelle heard the spin of tires on the circular driveway, and then the high-pitched, chattering voices, as if they'd all just been sucking up helium.

She watched from the cover of a living room blind as Lissy ran out to greet them, everybody screeching some more and air-kissing, and then walking arm in arm around the back of the house toward the gazebo. The four of them were remarkably alike: tall, willowy, sun-streaked blondes who moved as if they suspected they were being videotaped. They could have been quadruplet models in a Clairol commercial.

A few minutes later, a little blue heap pulled up behind the convertible and a stringy old lady in denim shorts got out and just stood there for a few seconds with her hands on her hips, looking around like she wasn't sure she was in the right place, or even on the right planet. Then she reached back into her car for some books and papers and made her way slowly around the side of the house.

Michelle ran into the kitchen, arranged a rainbow of tall Lucite glasses with stirrers and sprigs of fresh mint in them around the edges of a tray, and plunked the pitcher of iced tea down in the center. She stepped outside through the back door, balancing the tray on the flat of one hand. It was unusually cool and dry, even for early summer, with a nice breeze. The grass had been cut that morning and gave off its familiar green fragrance, mingled with a hint of the bug spray Lissy had ordered the garden guys to use.

The women sat in a semicircle on the cushioned rattan chairs inside the gazebo, each with a book opened on her lap. Michelle heard one of them say "But surely Alice Vavasor must have known—" before stopping in midsentence at her approach, as if she were the one being talked about.

"Hi!" Lissy said brightly as Michelle came in and set down the tray. "Hi!" the other young women echoed in a cheery chorus. The older woman stared intently at Michelle and said, "You know, you look just like Frida Kahlo."

"Who?" Michelle said, surprised to be spoken to in anything but the usual perfunctory manner. She wasn't even noticed on the job most of the time, unless she spilled or broke something.

"A famous Mexican painter," the woman said. "She was very exotic, very beautiful."

Mexican. Just what Michelle needed to hear. The Hamptons were crawling with Mexicans. Eddie complained that they took all the jobs, that they raised chickens in their yards for satanic rituals, that they refused to speak English. But Hank said they just took the jobs nobody else wanted.

"Yes, yes, the eyebrow!" Lissy exclaimed. "Did everyone see the movie?"

"So, do you want the sandwiches now?" Michelle asked, burning with self-consciousness.

"Not yet, thanks," Lissy said. She held up her cell phone and wiggled it. "I'll give you a call when we're ready."

Back in the house, Michelle went straight upstairs to look at herself in the monster mirror. The nose she'd once believed was the image of Paul McCartney's seemed more like Ringo Starr's, distorted like this. Faded acne scars jumped back to adolescent life, and when she opened her mouth her tongue was a large, textured pink slug. The stud on its tip glistened with a rope of saliva.

But the old lady had said *beautiful,* a word never applied to Michelle by anyone before, not even Hank, not even in the final, frenzied moments of their lovemaking, when he mostly said (or yelled, if Kayla wasn't staying over) things like, "Oh, baby!" and "I love fucking you so much!" His way, maybe, of saying she was beautiful. Now she ran her fingers across the silky thicket of her eyebrows and touched the black wings of her hair. Did she look Mexican? Well, anyone would, probably, next to those vanilla beans.

There were cosmetic brushes laid out in size place across the mirrored top of the dressing table, next to rows of little pots and tubes. She flicked the largest brush across her cheek—a butterfly's kiss—and opened one of the pots and sniffed the swirl of pale pink cream inside. It smelled like that soap shop in the Bridgehampton Mall. She glanced through the window as she unscrewed the top of another little pot. The gazebo was visible from her perch on the white leather ottoman; she could easily see if anyone started heading back toward the house.

Michelle had a long-standing habit of snooping in the houses where she worked, although she'd never lifted anything and always scrupulously covered her own tracks. It began when she was about thirteen and babysat for a few of the neighbors. Back then, as soon as the kids were asleep she'd scrounge around in the closets and drawers, looking mostly for sexual information—Polaroid pictures, dirty books, evidence of contraception—and she was rewarded with images that were burned into her brain forever.

Fat Peggy Waller, posing in just a black bra and stockings on her zebra-print bedspread. The packet of tickler condoms in Don Jackson's night table drawer. That wrinkled, yellowed pamphlet showing a woman with a pony. There was a different set of "them" in those days that included just about anyone who'd outlived the tortures of high school and had been initiated into the mysteries of adulthood.

The otherness of the rich invaders was far more extreme, though. Michelle knew that she would never grow into the worldly experience of wealth—except as a bystander—as she had once grown into sexual experience.

In the drawer of the dressing table, there were little silver instruments of grooming: a nail file, cuticle scissors, tweezers. She picked up the tweezers and addressed her eyebrows again in the mirror. Why hadn't she ever noticed before that they seemed to grow together into one dark mink caterpillar? She plucked at several of the hairs where her brows met and was startled by the results, as radical as the surgical separation of Siamese twins.

She cleaned the tweezers, using a Kleenex that she flushed down the toilet off the dressing room, and, after glancing through the window once more, went to Lissy's wall of closets and slid one of the doors open. It looked like a Newtown Lane boutique in there: skirts, sundresses, blouses, sweaters, everything arranged in a subtly changing palette of colors. Long ago, Michelle had draped herself in one of Peggy Waller's tent-like caftans—it went around her narrow hips twice—and, looking in the wavy mirror behind the bedroom door, wondered dreamily what had become of that perverted woman in the pamphlet and, already an impassioned animal lover, what might have happened to the poor pony.

Now she chose a shimmering white halter top from Lissy's collection and slung it over her head and across her chest. Michelle didn't even have to see her reflection to know how great the top looked on her; she could feel its sensuous cling, the way it submitted to the curves of her breasts. Exotic, she thought. Beautiful. *Famous.*

Thirty dollars an hour didn't seem all that much at that moment; it would take her a lifetime of shitwork to buy even a few items like this one. But she felt a new discontent that went beyond mere covetousness and the usual resentment. Was housecleaning what she was going to do forever? Was she ever going to be the lady of the house? She shook the halter top back to its original languid drape, and reluctantly but carefully rehung it in the closet. Just as she slid the door shut, the telephone behind her began to ring.

4.

Faking It

"What is the function of literature?" Angela Graves had posed that question at the beginning of the meeting, before they'd even mentioned Trollope. Someone, either Deb or Joy, said, "Storytelling?" And Angela nodded, a little wearily, before she allowed that stories were certainly important because they inform and console us.

Lissy was reminded of how much she had loved being read to as a child—fairy tales mostly, from a favorite, worn blue volume—by her grandmother or by her nanny, Eveline, as much as she'd always loved having her hair combed or washed by somebody else. She could feel her whole body go languorously lax at the memory.

"But what else?" Angela prompted, jarring Lissy upright

from her reverie, before she led the group into considering the representation of society in novels, and seeing oneself in the fictional other. Henry James, she told them, said a novel's purpose is to help the heart of man to know itself. And she said that the reader's shock of recognition was the litmus test for any novelist.

A literal person by nature, Lissy imagined putting a fork into an outlet and being jolted by a powerful electrical impulse, one that would fill her nerve endings with a sense of a reflected self. Had she ever experienced such a thing when she was reading? She didn't think so. At best, she'd felt a kind of tingling—some existential anxiety, probably—long ago, at Sleeping Beauty's waking words, "Where am I?" She couldn't help thinking that her failure to be stricken by any literary insights since then might not be the fault of the writers whose books she'd struggled to read, but that *she* was the one who'd failed some important test.

But when Angela pronounced toward the end of the meeting that literature teaches us how to live, Lissy looked around her at her pretty friends slouched against the plump polished chintz cushions, at the rings sparkling on her own slender fingers, at the lush greenery and its parasitic denizens kept at bay by the fine mesh screening of the gazebo. She thought of the matched sets of leather-bound volumes in the library of her summer house and decided, defensively, that she didn't need anything else from literature; she already knew how to live.

Not that she'd misunderstood the reference. She knew that Angela wasn't alluding to material objects, but to human qualities like empathy, charity, forgiveness, and hope. And she'd even pointed out a certain "moral ambiguity" in the best fiction that lets the reader make decisions for herself. Yet Lissy raised her hand and said, "If novels are all, like, about morality, why are there so many descriptions of rooms and gardens and gowns?"

And Angela said, "But that's only the wallpaper of the story's soul."

The session was a definite success, even if Ardith had stood them

up again. She was the one who'd started the group; why did she seem
to be abandoning it now? Maybe she wasn't such a great reader, either.
Brenda and Debby and Joy all said they'd had a great time, though,
maybe once too often. But the conversation *had* flowed. Lissy had
made a reasonable contribution herself, although she'd kept quiet or
vamped her way through the discussion of those parts of the book she
hadn't read or couldn't recall. As in any discourse, there were always
perfectly acceptable nonspecific remarks to make.

And the sandwiches were delicious; the new girl was going to
work out. She had an attitude problem, but she seemed to take the ini-
tiative about doing things, and she was fast on her feet. The last one,
Pedro's cousin Coco, was more cheerful and willing enough, but she
kept waiting to be given instructions she couldn't understand. It was
nice to have someone who spoke English for a change, even if she
didn't say very much.

Once again, Angela Graves had been the first to leave when the
session was over—as if she couldn't wait to get away—which gave the
rest of them a chance to talk about her, to speculate, which they had
been doing right from the beginning. Brenda had a running bet with
Debby that Angela was gay.

Lissy noted to herself that a lot of straight older women were just
as plain- and unfeminine-looking as Angela, while so many old men
resembled fading drag queens, as if they'd all decided to trade genders
at the last minute. When she suggested that Angela might have some
other, even more interesting, dark secret, Brenda said, "Really? What?
I mean, *look* at her."

But Lissy hesitated to offer any further conjectures about their
teacher's private life. A few weeks before, Angela's car had been in the
shop for repairs, and Lissy had offered to pick her up for a meeting of
the Page Turners. Angela's house, off Springs Fireplace Road, was as
tiny and quaint as something in one of the fairy tales Lissy had
loved—a woodsman's cottage, perhaps, or where Red Riding Hood's
grandmother might have lived. It was a flash of curiosity that made

Lissy go up to the front door and knock, and then ask if she could use the restroom, rather than simply honk the horn.

She went directly into a small version of a great room that was sparsely furnished, but contained bookshelves that lined the walls from floor to ceiling. There was only one bedroom, right next door—a kind of monk's cell—with a single iron bed covered by one of those cheap Indian throws Cynthia Ann had used to cover the battered sofa in their dorm suite. Anybody living with Angela would have had to sleep on the floor. And even that space was largely taken up by stacks of books.

Lissy was only able to make a quick survey of the place in passing, but there was a conspicuous absence of screens—television and computer—a connection to the larger world she couldn't live without. Even when she wasn't watching TV, she liked to leave it on, for company of sorts, for the squeal and hum and the flashes of color and light, and she and her friends exchanged IMs the way they used to pass notes in school. Lissy didn't notice any photographs in Angela's house, either, or other indications of family ties or personal history. There were just a couple of strange-looking paintings on the bedroom wall, of people you wouldn't want to know.

Jeffrey and Lissy's bedroom in Sagaponack, like its counterpart in the city, had a long shelf crowded with framed photos. Formal wedding portraits, of course, and a collage of honeymoon shots. There was a picture of Jeffrey grinning next to an enormous fish he'd apparently just landed in Montauk; another taken with his fish-white, unsmiling children; and several of Lissy herself in various stages from infancy to the present.

In Angela's bathroom, Lissy ran the water and peeked into the medicine cabinet, where the find was disappointing. The usual basics: Band-Aids, aspirin, Vaseline, cotton swabs. There was only one vial of prescription medicine, recently filled. About thirty tiny pink scored tablets, with the instruction to take one every four hours when needed for pain.

She spilled some of the tablets out onto her palm to examine them and to try to discern their purpose, but they kept their confidence. Maybe they were for headaches—all that reading!—or arthritis. *Heartache*. Where had that come from?

Without thinking about it, she slipped a few of the pink tablets into a zippered pocket of her handbag before she returned the rest of them to the vial, and the vial to the medicine cabinet. Then she flushed the toilet—God, it sounded like Niagara Falls—and ran the water in the sink one more time before she left the bathroom.

In the gazebo, Lissy finally broke the contemplative silence that befell the group after Brenda said, "I mean, *look* at her," about Angela. "She probably didn't always look that way," Lissy ventured.

Joy snorted. "Yeah, well."

"No, I mean she was young once, wasn't she?"

They all considered that, and there was a sense of grudging, unspoken agreement—everyone was young once, although some much longer than others.

Then Lissy said, tentatively, "I think she's in pain."

"Do you mean she's sick?" Deb asked, leaning forward with sudden, avid interest. She was a bit of a hypochondriac, someone who took her own pulse when she thought no one was looking.

Lissy had another flash memory of Angela's modest little cottage, the sense of seclusion and of quiet mystery. Her visit there would make a good anecdote, with certain embellishments, and she already had an engaged audience. Those pilfered little pink pills had to still be in the handbag at her feet, like corroborative evidence. But they were evidence against her, too, as a sneak and a petty thief. Why in the world had she taken them? The urge to gossip died before it could reach her throat. All she said was, "No. I don't know. I mean, she doesn't seem happy, does she?"

"Oh, who is?" Joy said.

Lissy found that she was eager to change the subject. "Do you think they were actually *lovers*?" she said. "I mean Alice Vavasor and her cousin George. Or she and that other guy? That's how everyone in the novel refers to them, isn't it, as lovers?"

"It's just a euphemism, sweetie," Brenda told her, glancing at her watch, seeming to admire it more than noting the time. "That little tease didn't take off her bustle for anybody." And everyone, even Lissy, laughed.

But like Alice in chapter 14, she was troubled. Someone else's possible virginity seemed to engender only scorn or pity—it certainly didn't invite anybody's forgiveness—and Lissy still wasn't sure, despite all the babble that day about the novel, what the reader was really being asked to judge. Maybe she'd never know. And that thing Angela had said, about the wallpaper of a story's soul, kept rippling through her head, like the catchy but meaningless lyrics to some song. Like that oldie, "Windmills of My Mind."

After they'd all left and the girl had tidied up and gone home, too, Lissy stayed out in the gazebo by herself for a while, thinking about Angela and Alice (that fictional other) and, finally, about herself, in terms of love and happiness. Brenda was right: Alice *had* seemed cold and sort of annoyingly self-righteous, a little like Angela, when you thought about it. Passionless.

Which wasn't true of Lissy, who hadn't been a virgin for ages. And she really enjoyed sex. Although she faked it sometimes lately in bed with Jeffrey, as she had skillfully faked some of her comments that day during the discussion, by simply murmuring agreement and echoing the others. "Yes, yes!" she'd cried more than once beneath Jeffrey's thrusting hulk, aware of the slow tick of her heart against the frantic thump of his, and of the digital clock beyond his shoulder flipping away yet another minute of her life.

Well, was that such a crime? All she'd really done was save Jeffrey's feelings by keeping her own to herself. And his flushed, prideful pleasure gave her pleasure, too, just of a different sort, while Alice Vavasor's dogged, pointless honesty seemed to cause more harm than good. Both of her so-called lovers suffered from it, anyway, and so did she.

There were other things, though, for which Lissy pretended to have enthusiastic interest: Jeffrey's work that appeared to have no product other than money. And his children, who were, frankly, far more frightening than they were endearing; in truth, she *dreaded* their summer visit. Maybe Danielle, that wicked witch of Jeffrey's past, would keep them away, just to thwart his paternal longings, as she'd thwarted most of his other needs and desires.

It was a startling unbidden notion, and so was the one snarling at its heels—that Lissy had thwarted desires of her own that demanded attention. She wondered if these atypical ruminations were simply the result of reading, if the function of literature had shown itself to her, like a religious vision in this grotto-like recess of the garden. And was it such a good thing, after all?

Then she noticed that the sun was sinking and the breeze that had kept the afternoon so tolerable had slackened, as if her aggressive thoughts had punctured the day and let all of its quick, fragile beauty run out. Jeffrey's firm's helicopter would be landing in Wainscott in a couple of hours. Where would they go for dinner? What should she wear? She stood and headed toward the house, using her fat, curling paperback to swat at the mosquitoes that, despite all that spraying, swarmed and hummed relentlessly around her.

5.

Personal History

Angela was relieved to be back at her own little house, in the familiar, easy company of her books and the shadows of the sheltering oaks. The greatest blessing of all was not to have to say anything to anyone. Sometimes her throat rasped and ached after she'd met with one of her reading groups, as it used to after a day of classes at Macon. Not that she ever spoke too loudly or too long, but those same words, said again and again with such hopeless, pointless urgency, seemed to scrape like splinters of glass against her vocal cords.

And the idea, the fad, of "summer reading"—as if books were seasonal commodities like sun-ripened tomatoes or root vegetables—slightly offended her. But she was as responsible as anyone for advertising and encouraging it. The whole thing, this leading of groups, was a bit of an act by now, she knew, not much more than a literary shtick. Teachers and writers were always spouting their favorite clichés about art and life as if they were undeniably true and had just been inspired by a fresh insight. What idiot couldn't figure out for herself that life was short and art was long?

Angela remembered a visiting novelist at Macon telling a classroom of bored, silly girls that he wrote in order to imagine being them. That caught their attention for a moment or two the way a glittering mirror attracts birds, but he didn't mean it—he was one of those solipsistic writers whose characters were all only poorly disguised versions of himself—and her students probably sensed his deception before they turned away.

If literature really teaches one how to live, as Angela kept insisting over the years, why did so many ardent, well-educated readers like herself fuck up their own lives? A thoroughly rhetorical, unanswerable question. She made a pot of tea and sat down at the kitchen table with her notes from that afternoon's session.

She kept a separate file on each member of her three groups, including a statement about personal goals that she'd solicited at the first meeting, an old habit from when she had to grade undergraduates who, like these women, had all seemed so much alike. Occasionally she still considered their sameness a result of her own failure to differentiate among them, to evoke proof of each one's unique and complex interior self.

But the Page Turners! Which one of them had come up with that pathetic, peppy little title? They were all into naming, not the natural world, of course, but merely their own possessions: their book clubs, their houses, their boats; she could just imagine what else. Of that whole platinum crew, only Lissy Snyder interested her a little more than the others, because she seemed somewhat less self-confident and more questing. Or maybe she just stood out because she was nervous about discussing a book she clearly hadn't read.

At least she had the grace to duck her head and blush once in a while, and she did seem to possess a modicum of curiosity; she was the one who'd asked that question about morality and materiality. For her personal statement, Lissy had simply written, in an open, childish hand, "I want to change," itself a refreshing change from more common responses, like "I hope to improve my vocabulary through reading" or "It's my goal to get through all the great books." The main thing, though, was that she reminded Angela, physically anyway, of Charlotte Keller. That sheer blondness, the pointed little cat's chin, the delicate shape of her head.

Charlotte would be in her midtwenties now, not that much younger than Lissy. As she had done so often before, Angela wondered where she was at that very moment and what she was doing. She hadn't seen the girl for more than five years, and that last encounter had been accidental and brief and disturbing, like an episode in a dream. It happened in New York City, where the seamless, moving throng gives you the illusion of anonymity, even invisibility, and it's always surprising to run across somebody you know.

Angela had recently retired and bought the house in The Springs, settling into what promised to be a comfortable, semi-rural, semi-suburban existence. She'd chosen this area because it was attractive and affordable—at least on a year-round basis—and because she liked its history of farming and fishing. There was enough self-generated culture in the Hamptons, too—concerts, poetry readings, theater, and art shows—that she could graze for something good.

Her financial situation was modest but stable. She received Social Security checks in addition to her pension from Macon. And she was able to garner a small supplementary income from the reading groups she led. She was aware that she didn't exactly belong, that she wasn't one of those proprietary summer visitors who buys their way in, or a local with deep family roots in the community. She was more like a privileged guest, the way she was when she entered those fictional counties of Barset and Wessex, and was grateful to be here. But sometimes she felt herself aching toward Manhattan, which she'd discovered in her teens, and then had to give up during all those years in Texas.

It was one of those stunning, burnished autumn days. She'd taken the train into the city, with plans to visit the Met—there was a traveling exhibition from the Hermitage—and to walk in Central Park afterward. Climbing the stairs out of Penn Station, she'd seen a lanky young woman walking a few yards ahead on the street, and was struck by how familiar she seemed. Angela raised her hand, as if to hail her, but she couldn't come up with a name to call out.

The girl was no more than eighteen or nineteen, too young to have been one of Angela's former Macon students. It occurred to her that she didn't really know anyone that age anymore. At Macon, the median age of the student population had remained constant while she grew older as rapidly and dramatically as the portrait of Dorian Gray. In retrospect, it seemed completely unnatural.

When she gave up teaching, she decided never to live in any community that excluded children or any other representatives of the normal human life cycle. If there came a time when she couldn't be on her own anymore, she would give it all up rather than give in to a loss of autonomy and privacy, to the application of that sly modern catchphrase: assisted living.

Still, Angela hadn't made any close friends of any age in The Springs. She liked the generous and well-read volunteers at the little library, and the people at the farm stands, where she honored the protocol of not husking the corn or squeezing the tomatoes before purchase. Her neighbors waved from their porches and gardens when she walked or drove by, and she chatted with other browsers at yard sales as she went through the cartons of books for a buck.

Once in a while she had lunch or walked to the beach at Maidstone Park in the early morning with one of the librarians. Or she'd visit with Irene Rush, a divorced, retired social worker who owned a tiny antiques shop called Things—on North Main Street, off the beaten track—with a shelf devoted to used books. Irene lived by herself, too, in an apartment above the shop, which had a modest fenced backyard. Both women were Trollope fans and gardeners, and although Irene wasn't exactly reserved, she appeared to share Angela's preference for the sanctity of private thoughts.

But Angela kept mostly to her own company, eating simple meals at home—usually some freshly caught broiled fish and local vegetables. She realized, with startled amusement, that, except for her book groups and those few acquaintances, she'd carried out her earliest inclinations and become a loner, even a recluse of sorts, the weird old lady who lives by herself in the woods. Occasionally, she would think, but not fully feel, Why, I'm going to die alone, followed immediately by that defensive response: But then, who won't?

And at other times she remembered with sudden, painful clarity those dinner parties at the Kellers. The delicious, ethnic potluck dishes they'd devoured: Moroccan chicken stew, lamb curry, pad Thai. When had she lost her taste for all that? The animated faces in candlelight, the voices overriding one another. Angela could still hear herself, warmed by wine one ancient evening, declaiming Wordsworth's dependence on his sister's diaries, and the way the other women began to name all the female literary muses—in shrill, synchronized glee, like sixties backup singers—until one of the men thumped the table, making the glasses tremble and spill over.

There was always music—Chet Baker and Charlie Parker, who might have been surprised to find themselves wailing away on an off-brand stereo in a Texas hamlet—and poetry, especially Philip Larkin's, recited from memory to show off and to illustrate some shared dark vision. In retrospect, Angela was astounded by that abundance and variety of talk and noise and food, and how great her own appetite had been then for all of it.

That day in New York City, she'd followed the tall blonde for several yards, connecting her somehow to Macon, but struggling vainly to identify her—a student's younger sister? A faculty niece? And then it came to her, with what felt like a seismic tremor, that this might be little Charlotte Keller, grown overnight out of her red, footed pajamas into this long-legged, jeans-clad, almost graceful woman. Angela's hand immediately lowered to her side, and she even stopped walking for a moment or two, causing a near pileup of pedestrians whose stride she had broken.

Then she hurried to catch up, coming right alongside that familiar stranger, averting her own profile slightly without losing sight of the girl's. You're deluded, she told herself; there must be a million similar-looking blondes in the city, and she had no way of knowing how Charlotte might have turned out.

But there was something compelling about this girl, about her carriage and her expression, as if she owned the world. And she was physically like Valerie—with lots of silky, static-charged hair, and that translucent skin—toned down, though, and not quite so blatantly sexual. She wore glasses, Angela noticed now, like Stephen, and her jeans and sneakers were splattered with paint. It *was* her, it was!

Angela wondered then, with a flutter of fear, if Charlotte could possibly recognize her, too, after all this time, and what, if anything, she might know or remember of their shared past. The Kellers had left Macon, had left Texas, soon after Stephen failed to get tenure, dragging the ruins of their marriage along with the furnishings of the house on Dogwood Drive. They moved to a town in central Pennsylvania, where Stephen started all over again as a visiting art instructor at an even smaller, less distinguished college, and Valerie had to settle for a secretarial job at a local elementary school, news that reached Angela belatedly and thirdhand. But she had experienced an enormous, conflicted sense of loss and relief as soon as she knew they were gone.

The sad irony was that under other circumstances she might have helped to save Stephen's position at Macon. Right before they'd become involved, she had thought about speaking on his behalf to the tenure committee. Angela may not have been in Stephen's department, but she was regarded by most of the art faculty as someone serious, with a genuine knowledge of and interest in painting. She had taken a minor in art history at Sarah Lawrence, and she'd even published a paper once about Pre-Raphaelite paintings in Victorian novels. It was called, of course, "The Soul's Wallpaper."

But she'd never offered a recommendation to the committee. She and Stephen couldn't afford any unnecessary attention paid to their friendship once it had turned so suddenly and radically into something else. Every previous innocent gesture between them—a peck on the cheek in hello or goodbye, the passing of a book or a wineglass from one of their hands to the other's—was newly charged with eroticism and a sense of risk. Even making ordinary eye contact became a daring act in the theater of deception. That was part of what made it all so exhilarating and so terrible.

Macon was a conservative, isolated place, both god-fearing and godforsaken, as Stephen once described it, but Angela had been able to live with that dichotomy because, ever since she'd been taken up by the Kellers, she had her own open-minded, culture-driven cell of friends, most of them from the English and Art departments, the very people who used to gather for those famous dinner parties. They were a sophisticated lot and fairly used to dalliances, in life and in literature.

Two of Angela's former lovers, Jenna Barker, who managed the Paradise Art Gallery in Jackson City, about thirty miles from the college, and Roger Day, a sculptor for whom Angela had given up Jenna, could both sit with her at the Kellers' table without any apparent hard feelings. Jenna had done some stupid things right after Angela's defection—a pair of shredded underpants sent in the mail, a few middle-of-the-night silent phone calls, but she got over it quickly, and went on to someone else. Roger did, too. They'd all only been flings, anyway.

Sometimes a seriously involved couple they knew split up because of an infidelity, but others managed to get through the trauma and reconcile. Everyone knew everything, though, as surely as they knew about Anna and the count, and about Emma and Rodolphe riding horseback under sun-dappled trees—that was the nature of such a tight and insulated society—yet there was an underlying sense of discretion, and of collective forgiveness. The community neatly closed itself over the wound.

Of course, some weeping and shouting usually took place first behind closed doors at the Health Service, but no one committed suicide. The only real taboo at Macon was anything sexual between a professor and a student. That had happened just once during Angela's time there, resulting in a firestorm of gossip and a lost job, just as her affair with Stephen had, but the latter occurred because of the manner in which it became public, and the reverberating wake of humiliation and pain.

Trotting up Seventh Avenue alongside the miraculously transformed Charlotte, Angela was shocked anew by the details of her own personal history, by how she had once allowed passion to overcome conscience and ordinary common sense, the way rock succumbs to paper in the children's game.

They had played that game one afternoon on Dogwood Drive, at a Christmas party attended by several faculty families. It was before the affair began, Angela was certain of that, because her memory of the day's events wasn't complicated by the thrill of secret happiness or by guilt. That afternoon, she was merely enjoying the benign roles she usually played at the Kellers: good friend and colleague, sister-of-sorts, courtesy aunt. At other times, when she was at a psychic low, she'd even taken a turn or two as their overgrown surrogate child.

Charlotte, their actual child, the heart of the household, was too young then to understand the rules of Rock, Paper, Scissors, but she had sat on her father's lap and then on Angela's when he got up to help Valerie in the kitchen, imitating the gestures the adults and older children made, in the aggressive manner of a small child competing vainly with people much older and bigger than herself.

She was such a fierce, determined little girl. Angela could still recall her impatient, bouncing weight, the rising color of her hot skin, and the piping squawk of her voice whenever she lost a round, protesting over and over again that it wasn't fair. And Angela remembered in equally sharp detail how Charlotte had shadowed and interrogated her when she'd babysat on the night of Stephen's birthday—"Do you have a little girl? Why do you look like a man?" and so on—only hours before it all began.

Did that artless little inquisition have anything to do with what happened later that night? Had she been goaded by a pushy child—an infant, really—into sexual action? Angela had never considered such an absurd possibility before. But as she walked abreast of Charlotte on Seventh Avenue that fine October morning, purposely keeping in step now, it didn't seem all that fanciful.

And then the girl abruptly turned and fixed her gaze on Angela, as if she'd overheard her thoughts, and Angela's heart seemed to scale her ribs before it plummeted. But there was no discernible flash of recognition behind the rimless glasses, not even a flicker of casual interest. Angela obviously didn't look at all familiar, and she was old, years and years beyond the circumscribed curiosity of someone that young. She slowed her own gait, so that Charlotte could plunge ahead of her and be absorbed by the crowd, but it took minutes before her pulse slowed down, too.

Sipping tea at her kitchen table five years later, she marveled at the seemingly random, hit-and-miss trajectory of memory, like a driverless car in reckless motion: how innocuous Lissy had somehow reminded her of fervent Charlotte, how everything was so quickly dredged up again and heightened, and how Charlotte had failed to register Angela's face or connect it to what must have been the most telling episode of her own childhood. The end of Eden, the beginning of ordinary, imperfect, mortal life.

What did Charlotte remember of that day in the gallery, or even understand? What had she been told?—those were the questions Angela had allowed to pass quickly through her consciousness on several occasions over the years, but that somehow began to persistently plague her on an ordinary summer afternoon and evening in The Springs, as the trees around her cozy little house went from green to black, and the Greek chorus of crickets overcame the peaceful silence.

6.

Savants

The boys were off chasing a car again, the only activity that interested them, besides eating, since they'd been fixed. Michelle could never figure out what animal instinct roused them from their sleepy sentry at the side of the road, or how they knew which cars and trucks belonged to neighbors and which ones to people just passing through on their way to somewhere better.

She'd once seen a TV program about retarded people with one singular skill—savants, they were called. They were all spastic and drooly, and they didn't know how to dress themselves or make normal conversation, but one of them played the piano like a master and another could reel off the day and date of every event in recorded history. Pete and Bill

were like that, two savant golden Labs whose sole talent involved spot-
ting and chasing the invaders' vehicles.

She whistled for them a few times, and they came running back
home, panting from their exertions and pure canine joy. Nobody else
was ever this wildly glad to see Michelle, and she was just as glad to see
them. "Where've you guys been, huh?" she asked, picking brambles
and leaves from their coats as they writhed around her in ecstasy. "You
catch any of them yet? Were they delicious?"

Jo Ann wasn't in the house; she was probably still at work at
Poseidon Point, the Frenches' mansion on Indian Wells Highway,
where they always found one more thing for her to do—hand-
washing some delicates, straightening a couple of closets or drawers,
alphabetizing the spice rack or something—just as she was about to
leave. And, of course, she never said no to them.

That meant that Michelle had to start supper again, and she went
about it briskly, pulling out the package of ground beef, the bags of
corn and green beans, while Bill and Pete circled her, letting out little
grunts and yelps, casting their own affirmative vote for whatever food
she was assembling. Hank had once referred to them as the meat in-
spectors. With Hank in mind, she added the bottle of hot sauce to the
other ingredients on the counter, and a jar of chili peppers.

Michelle liked to cook—not the fancy, insubstantial items she'd
learned to put together at places like Lissy Snyder's, but solid, belly-
filling stuff that gave off a hearty, oniony aroma, along with its own
good brown gravy, and didn't need any decoration, like ribbons and
blobs of pastel color squirted from a pastry tube around the edge of
the plate. But she was distracted that afternoon by her own distorted
reflection in the chrome frame of the toaster oven, and in the black
glass oven door. She wondered for a moment or two about that Mexican artist she was supposed to resemble. Maybe she could look her up
somewhere, online at Hank's or at the library, and even get to see her
photograph, but the name was lost as she kneaded the meat and added
the salt and garlic powder and ketchup and bread crumbs.

Hank came in, yelled "Hey, baby!" in her general direction, and put some wrapped fillets from that day's catch into the refrigerator. Then he took a long shower, singing pop songs from the eighties— "The Heat Is On," "Make Me Say It Again, Girl"—so loudly and with such abandon, he might have been shouting for help. "Get outta my dreams and into my car," he wailed while Michelle husked the corn and set a pot of water on to boil.

But later a faint hint of fresh flounder still mingled with the scent of her lavender soap as he tossed a damp, deflated red ball across the room for the dogs to catch and return, catch and return. Finally, Michelle snatched the ball and threw it out into the yard, and the dogs whizzed past her after it.

She yanked off the baseball cap Hank had pulled over his wet hair, and combed the tangles with her fingers until his curls stood up in an electrified halo around his face. He looked like one of those angels in the stained-glass window at The Springs Presbyterian Church. That is, if angels had deep suntans and premature wrinkles around their eyes from squinting at the brilliant, rippling tinfoil of the ocean all day.

There was no music, but Hank grabbed Michelle and danced her around the room as if a live band were playing, and the dogs, who he'd let right back inside with the saliva-slick, grass-coated ball, put on a phony display of concern, barking and play-nipping at their legs. She knew that she'd have to put them out of his bedroom later that night when she and Hank made love. "So do you see anything different about me?" she asked suddenly.

"What?"

She tried wriggling her eyebrows at him, and he said, "Do you mean besides that tic?"

"Don't be funny. *Look* at me, will you? Who do I look like that's famous?"

"That's a trick question, isn't it?" Hank said.

"Come on," she said, bumping him hard with her hip.

"Okay, okay," he said, pretending to look thoughtful. "Lindsay

Lohan? Monica Lewinsky, I hope, I hope? Minnie Mouse?" He nuz-
zled her neck, ran his tongue along her hairline.

"You stink," she told him, pushing him away, "and I have to check
the meat loaf."

By the time Jo Ann came home, supper was ready, and Hank and
the dogs had calmed themselves enough to be sprawled in front of the
TV, where he kept switching channels as if he hoped he'd find one
with better news. And he talked back to the newscasters. "Tell me
something I don't know," he told them, "Yeah, right," and "Boy, I
don't believe this."

Hank had been high on the war in Iraq when it started, but now
he'd grown leery of its lack of conclusion, the continuing pileup of ca-
sualties. He kept changing the bumper stickers on his pickup.
BUSH/CHENEY went up before the election in 2000. Then he stuck on
GOD BLESS AMERICA right after September 11, adding a yellow ribbon
saying SUPPORT OUR TROOPS once they were over there. But recently
he'd scraped everything else off in favor of one that said WEAPONS OF
WHAT? That had gotten him into some squabbles down at the marina,
especially with Michelle's brother, Eddie, his best buddy, who was
gung-ho about the war and claimed that he would have enlisted right
away if he wasn't almost deaf in his left ear.

When they were all sitting at the kitchen table, Jo Ann asked
Michelle how things were going for her at the Snyders'. Michelle made
a face before she shrugged and said, "Okay, I guess."

"Miz Scarlett working you too hard?" Hank asked.

Michelle remembered watching the clock, plucking her eyebrows,
casing the closets, and trying on the halter top in front of the mirror.
Jo Ann would freak out if she knew; she had such a strict work code.
"No," Michelle reluctantly admitted. "There's hardly anything left to
do after a couple of hours."

"Oh, boo hoo for you," Hank said. "Well, we could always use another hand on the boat."

"You have to be creative," Jo Ann said, a familiar refrain. She was into putting special finishing touches on the houses where she worked: tucking the ends of the toilet paper rolls into neat points, like a man's pocket handkerchief; making sachets and potpourri from dropped flower petals and dried orange rinds; ironing everything in sight, including socks and dish towels; and tying pink and lavender silk ribbons around stacks of freshly washed underpants before she returned them to the dresser drawers.

Her ladies loved her for these innovative extras as much as for her cheerful disposition, earning her cash bonuses, some barely worn designer hand-me-downs, and lots of leftovers. Today she'd brought home a huge slab of coconut cream cake, which she'd refrigerated as far from Hank's fish fillets as possible. The crazy thing was the way she loved her ladies back.

"I do my job," Michelle muttered, stabbing another slice of meat loaf she didn't really want and plunking it down onto her plate.

"Not with that attitude, I hope," Jo Ann said.

"They don't pay me for my *attitude*," Michelle snapped.

"Thank God for that," Hank said. He put several bits of meat and corn onto his broad, callused palm and lowered it to the floor. Pete beat Bill to the handout, as usual, so Hank had to do it all over again, shoving one snout out of the way in favor of the other.

"Don't feed them at the table, Hank," Jo Ann said in a weary monotone, although she knew how completely useless it was to scold; the Labs were as hooked on begging by now as circus dogs were on jumping through hoops, and Hank was just as incapable of unlearning old tricks. Still, he said "Yes, ma'am," with feigned obedience, and waited for his lion's share of the coconut cake.

Michelle declined dessert on principle, because it came from them, and because she hated coconut, but she watched Hank eat his with secret pleasure until he laid his fork down, sighed, and leaned back contentedly in his seat. Then he began to watch her as she cleared the dishes, with that heavy-lidded gaze she could feel on her skin even when her back was turned.

Still, after she'd shooed her tired-looking mother out of the kitchen and upstairs to bed, she took her own sweet time cleaning up the place just the way Jo Ann liked it done. This was a far cry from the way Michelle had been as a teenager, when she'd give everything a couple of fast swipes, and did even that under duress, while her friends waited for her outside so they could ride their bikes to Louse Point and meet up with some boys from school and smoke pot and make out. If Jo Ann said one critical word to her about the kitchen or anything else in those days, Michelle would explode. "Lincoln freed the slaves!" she'd shout, the only lesson from history that ever seemed to serve her in life.

Hank was patient or pretended to be while Michelle carefully wiped down the counters and cabinet doors, and dried the pots and put them away. At his place later, she undressed slowly, too, aware of putting on a girlie show for him but thinking about other things at the same time. Maybe she was a savant, like the Labs, and this was *her* one trick, a kind of juggling act of the mind.

She thought, for the first time, that you seemed to be young forever, and then you weren't. Look at her mother, with her swollen feet and her leftover coconut cake. She had once loved the Beatles, had screamed with the other girls at a concert; she had probably loved Michelle's father.

Michelle and Hank had been seriously involved for almost two years. People thought it was strange that they weren't married by now—that they didn't even live together. Eddie's wife, Kathleen, had hinted broadly about it a couple of times. It *was* strange, Michelle supposed as she peeled off her T-shirt and unzipped her jeans.

But there were financial considerations: Michelle contributed to Jo Ann's household, and Hank couldn't afford more than the small add-on apartment he rented in the village from an elderly couple named Smith. And he was wary of commitment because he'd been burned in his short marriage, and because he had a child, born when he was still a kid himself, to care about for the rest of his life.

Michelle was reminded of that joke she'd once overheard at a party she was working, about the couple who stayed together for seventy miserable years before they divorced, because they had to wait for the children to die. She was shocked by the brutal shouts of laughter from the older crowd at that party.

For a long while, Michelle had been in the fuzzy background of Hank's life—Eddie's baby sister, eager to grow up, to catch up to them. And somehow she had. Hank never exactly said "I love you" to Michelle, although he came up with approximations that were both affectionate and sexual, like the lyrics to the songs he liked. *Make me say it again, girl. You're all I nee-ee-eed . . .*

She thought about that ball field of a bed in Lissy Snyder's room, piled with enough plush pillows to accommodate a whole harem of women. What went on in there? What was it like to be rich and married, to have another woman working in your kitchen while you looked at yourself in the mirror? Michelle's mother sometimes said, "They're just like us, you know, only . . ." And Michelle would finish the thought for her, "Only luckier? Prettier? Only . . . better?" *Shut up,* she told herself, *stop thinking,* when she was down to just her white panties that caught the shaft of moonlight in the room with fluorescent clarity.

Once she was in bed, at last, Hank was on her in seconds. She could hear the dogs whining and pacing outside the door. She'd have to trim their nails again. And then everything was swept from her head, as if she'd suffered a blow and been stricken with amnesia, except for the galvanic sensation of Hank's kisses, everywhere, as he pinned her down, and the way her legs lifted and went around him as swiftly and urgently as her arms.

7.

Vanishing Acts

When the clown-caricaturist that Lissy had hired failed to
show at a birthday celebration for seven-year-old twins back
in May, she'd resolved to become an on-site party planner, just
to make sure that everything went smoothly on her clients'
big day. That time, after several frantic, fruitless phone calls to
find a replacement clown, she'd had to settle for some ruthless
mime who demanded three times his regular fee and ended
up screaming at the bored and restless kids just to get their attention to his silent performance.

This party was proving to be another challenge. Samantha
Woodcock, the birthday girl, was only four, and she and her
fifteen guests, ranging in age from eighteen months to six

years, seemed to embody all the symptoms of ADHD. Lissy had hoped to see Samantha's parents, heavy investors with Jeffrey's firm, or rather to have them see *her,* the perfect corporate helpmeet, going beyond the call of duty on their daughter's behalf. But they'd arranged to be elsewhere during the festivities, at some horse thing in Bridgehampton.

Well, at least the weather was good, so the party could be held outdoors on the Woodcocks' generous, sloping back lawn, and the kids appeared to like the food Lissy had ordered—the mini pizzas and bite-sized burgers—for eating and throwing. And the decorative theme, based on the *Shrek* movies, looked really good. But Dr. Delirium, the magician Lissy had selected for the afternoon's entertainment, turned out to be another poor choice.

He wasn't all that dexterous—he kept dropping things—and his routine was geared to a much older audience: in their fifties, maybe, who could have been seated without physical force and who might have gotten some of his jokey references to Jimmy Hoffa and Judge Crater. She'd have to start auditioning people instead of depending on their ads in the *Star* or the Yellow Pages.

Dr. Delirium, she remembered, had billed himself as "A Tough Act to Follow." As it was, Samantha's smallest guests chased one another noisily around the lawn all during his presentation while a couple of the older kids repeatedly yelled that they could see the missing playing card hidden up the sleeve of his shiny tuxedo. His paste-on mustache had slipped a little down his lip, giving him a comical sneer, and he kept glancing over at Lissy in a disconcertingly knowing way, as if they shared some special secret.

One little redhead named Cassandra was terrified of anything disappearing, especially the twitchy white rabbit swallowed by the tall black hat. Even after the rabbit had been retrieved, she continued to be upset, unconvinced that it was the same one. "Where's the *real* bunny?" she kept crying, while her babysitter said, "*¡Mira, mira, chi-*

quita! Look! *¡El Conejo regreso!*" But she had to cart the disconsolate girl off, finally, grabbing the requisite balloons and goody bags on their way out.

Lissy felt pangs of sympathy along with her dismay at the disruption. When she was Cassandra's age, and even older, the whole world seemed scarily ephemeral, especially after her parents' divorce. It was no wonder she'd stubbornly clung to everything, from her outgrown, mangy, stuffed Sheepie to the paper cup in which she was given her last sip of water at bedtime. She'd had a whole collection of collapsed and shredded cups in her toy chest until someone discovered them and threw them out. Her father may well have gone down through the bottomless tunnel of some other magician's top hat for all she saw of him once he'd moved out. Clearly, nothing was safe.

Twenty-odd years later, he still lived at a great geographic and emotional remove from her—in Tahiti, of all places, along with his second family, including three replacement children she'd never met. And Lissy's mother hadn't ever fully gotten over his desertion, becoming another kind of vanishing act as she sank into regular periods of depression and rage, even when she was in plain sight. "You!" she sometimes cried when she noticed Lissy standing tentatively in a doorway, as if her own child was the last person she wanted to see.

And then, so soon after her father left, Lissy's nanny, Evie, the mainstay of her existence, the benevolent shadow over her sleeping and waking self, was gone, too. A burst appendix, Lissy was told, and she searched Evie's bed in the alcove next to her own room for the horrific evidence of a human explosion, for tatters of flesh and bone and even the popped pink balloon of the appendix itself. There was nothing there, though, but the cold rubbery weight of Evie's abandoned hot-water bottle. Any decent shrink or serious book on child psychology could have explained the dynamics of separation anxiety to Lissy. In fact, a couple of them already had, but that didn't completely stop the flashbacks or her sense of permanent loss.

How had she carelessly contemplated having a child of her own, when, even now, she could so easily and keenly revive the anguish of having been one? And how was she going to deal with Jeffrey's two during their extended August visit, when they'd already exhibited so many dire effects of a broken home?

Miles was still bed-wetting at nine, and he was given to acting on his every impulse; he constantly talked out of turn at school, and he'd broken his arm in two places a couple of years ago, leaping from the top bunk bed at a friend's house. Six-year-old Miranda never made eye contact with Lissy, looking just past her, instead, like some social-climbing matron working the room at a cocktail party. And both children had atrocious table manners; they might have been raised in the wild. *Their* father was far from a vanishing act, though; he was about as overindulgent and hands-on as his ex would allow.

In Lissy's crowd, every first wife was deemed criminally insane by the husband's subsequent wives and their friends—it was a kind of ritualistic judgment—but Danielle often seemed genuinely certifiable. Those crazy "Dear Jeffie, you bastard" letters she sent, and all of her impossible demands. Fencing and method-acting lessons for Miles, a medical plan for Miranda's Angora cats. She used the children to get to him, canceling his scheduled time with them at the last minute for the most absurd reasons—did kids actually get migraines?—while telling them awful and untrue things about their daddy and Lissy, and demanding enough child support to sustain a small African village.

Still, Jeffrey pounced on every visit with the children that Danielle and the courts granted him, and he spoke to Miranda and Miles on the phone almost as often as he spoke to Lissy. How many times had she overheard him murmur things like "Of course I will, honey" and "We'll have lots of fun, you'll see"? Even when she couldn't quite hear what he was saying, she could tell by the mournful, pleading tone of his voice that one of his little blackmailers was at the other end of the line.

Sometimes she succumbed to shameful little spasms of jealousy, to the dark notion that Jeffrey's love for Miranda and Miles was *too* profound, and took up too much of his emotional energy. What if he ever had to choose between them and her? Jeffrey's first marriage had been a religious mix, like his and Lissy's. He was a nonobservant Jew, and an agnostic at heart. Lissy had lapsed, too, from her Episcopal faith, but when they decided to marry, she'd wanted the solemnity and pomp of the church, and maybe even to give God another chance.

Jeffrey had given in to her wishes on everything else—the lavish reception at The Temple of Dendur, the formal wedding wardrobe, all those pink tulips flown in from Rotterdam—but he was adamant about having just a civil ceremony first, performed by a court of appeals judge he knew. Yet he seemed to observe every damn holiday with his hybrid kids, from Ash Wednesday to something called Tisha B'Av. His parental devotion was boundless—why couldn't Danielle appreciate that?

The only other adults, besides Lissy and the family's housekeeper, on hand at the Woodcock kiddie party were the children's sitters and a few grandmothers, reminding her of the patron angels of her own childhood: her beloved Eveline, who'd come all the way from a farm in mythical Scotland to rescue and take care of her in her parents' emotional absence; and Grandmother Ellis, with her oddly comforting queenly reserve and beautiful, aging face.

These Hamptons nannies alternately cuddled and scolded their charges in broken English, and whispered in Spanish among themselves. The grandmothers lounged on the sidelines under an arbor of huge sun umbrellas, sipping what Lissy suspected, from their escalating voices and piercing bursts of laughter, was spiked lemonade. They could have been mistaken for young mothers until you got close to them, as Lissy did, offering slices of Fiona cake, and saw how tightly their faces had been pulled upward, as if by some spooky reversal of gravity, so that every expression of human emotion except for perpetual surprise had been expunged.

It was the signature look of the decade's most popular plastic surgeon, a man at Lenox Hill with two first names—Simon Spencer or

Spencer Simon; everybody kept inverting them until Lissy couldn't remember their proper order. Her own mother had been done by him a few months before, and all the physical proof of her psychic pain—those lines and shadows of bitterness and regret—if not the pain itself, had completely vanished. And she was scheduled for even more work. When the time came for Lissy to do something about her face, she hoped there'd be another hot surgeon around, one with more variables to his work.

The phalanx of grandmothers seemed a little unsettled by her presence at Samantha's party. They knew that she was part of Grace and Lester Woodcock's social set, but now here she was, apparently in some position of domestic service. Grace's mother had greeted Lissy cordially enough on her arrival, and she said, "Doesn't that look nice?" about her slice of buttercream birthday cake, which she quickly set aside in favor of her drink.

The other women murmured their polite acknowledgments of her, too—"Lissy Snyder, isn't it? Oh, how nice to see you again, dear." Of course they *had* seen Lissy before, at the Maidstone Club and around town at the restaurants and shops, sometimes in the company of their own children. But it was as if they'd just pulled her name out of an invisible directory rather than from any personal memory.

They didn't seem the least bit persuaded when Lissy said, "Just stopping by to check on things, you know. Aren't the children *precious*? So sorry to have missed Grace." Their responses were muffled by insincerity and a surfeit of collagen and vodka; they were like bad ventriloquists with their plumped-up, barely mobile lips, and they didn't invite her to join them in the restricted shade of their umbrellas.

Lissy looked back somewhat wistfully at the knot of babysitters, whose circle seemed just as closed, and at the rampaging children to whom she was as obviously invisible as the blades of grass they were trampling. It was like field day at the asylum. Well, her responsibilities here were over with, anyway; she had to go home and start reading—belatedly again—the novel Angela Graves had assigned for the next meeting of the Page Turners. She paid Dr. Delirium, avoiding his impudent eyes and mentally crossing him off her employment list, before she said her goodbyes and left.

. . .

Villette, Angela had told the Page Turners, was inspired by Charlotte Brontë's own experiences at a school in Brussels. On a literary website, Lissy learned that the novel's heroine and narrator, Lucy Snowe, was poor and plain and, like Brontë's Jane Eyre, had to make her own way in the world. One becomes a schoolteacher, the other a governess. Angela said that they would discuss the employment of Victorian women without wealth, and other matters affected by their gender and socioeconomic class. She advised the group to keep those issues in mind when they were reading *Villette,* and to think comparatively about the lives of contemporary women, like themselves.

At home, Lissy went upstairs with the novel in hand and a determination to read without skipping any passages this time, or falling asleep in the middle of a sentence. It was only four o'clock; she'd have about three hours before Jeffrey came in from the city. At least *Villette* wasn't quite as oppressively long as the Trollope, and although her vision was excellent, Lissy had bought the large-print version of the novel, because it had the inviting aspect of a children's book. Maybe someday, after they became friends, she would pass her copy on to Miranda. Maybe they could even talk about the topics Angela had raised with the group.

Lissy sighed; she really *did* want to change, as she'd written in her statement about personal goals for the reading club, only she still wasn't exactly certain of what she'd meant by that, besides some hazy notion of self-improvement. She could make a real attempt to become closer to her stepchildren, starting by being less competitive with them. Or maybe it would be sufficient to just develop better habits, to be less careless—as Jeffrey always gently suggested whenever she left the bathwater running until the tub overflowed, or the keys in the ignition of her parked car—and to see things through to the end once she'd begun them.

The cleaning girl was just coming out of the master bedroom as Lissy was about to enter it. She was as startled as if she'd encountered a burglar, although the girl had been in the house when Lissy left for the Woodcocks'. But she managed to smile through her tachycardia and say "Hi, there! How are you?" The girl only nodded and hurried past her down the stairs. Why did she always look so sullen and furtive? Lissy made an instinctive, hasty inventory of the room, but everything seemed to be in perfect order.

She took off her shoes and lay down against the deliciously cool mound of bed pillows and opened her book, with Angela's instructions and her own new resolve in mind. "My godmother lived in a handsome house in the clean and ancient town of Bretton. Her husband's family had been residents there for generations, and bore, indeed, the name of their birthplace . . ."

Lissy had never thought very actively or deeply about social class; almost everyone she'd ever known well had moved within her own privileged sphere. There were those others she'd come into more casual contact with during her life: teachers, salesclerks, dentists, waiters, trainers, plumbers, hairdressers, domestic help—a whole army of people offering their various services—of whom she was less sharply aware, especially when they were out of her immediate view.

The exception, of course, was Eveline MacLeod, with her soft burr and chapped hands, who couldn't be categorized that simply. If anything, she was in a class by herself, the way religious heroines are. You didn't primarily think of Joan of Arc or Saint Bernadette, for instance, as poor or middle class, well educated or self-taught. It was their sacrifices you remembered, and their peculiar glamour. *Oh, my Evie,* she thought.

Lissy could feel the book leave her boneless hands, and when she opened her eyes Jeffrey was tucking in one of his business cards to save her place. How tall and boyish he looked, with his unruly shock of dark golden hair and a day's growth of stubble, as if his chin had been lightly breaded. "Honey," she said. "I didn't even hear you come in."

He sat down beside her on the bed and kissed her brow, her nose, her lips, taking care not to chafe her sensitive skin. He smelled pleasantly masculine, what she thought of fondly as his city scent: a mix of fading aftershave, somebody else's cigar smoke, his lunchtime gin-and-tonic, and a mechanical fragrance—the motor oil or exhaust of the helicopter he'd flown in on to be here next to her. "Hello, sleepyhead," he said, and he lay down, too, taking her into his expansive embrace.

Where am I? she almost said, but didn't. She knew perfectly well where she was. She was home, safely, in a handsome house in Sagaponack, in the clean and ancient town of Southampton, and she was in the arms of her prince.

8.

In Search of Heroines

Angela was in the East Hampton library, waiting for the reference librarian to get off the telephone and help her to research something on the computer. She wasn't on a literary mission, though. Angela prided herself—foolishly, maybe—on being a Luddite, a mere hitchhiker on the information highway. Most of her knowledge of the world and the interior lives of its inhabitants had been gleaned, over the years, from reading and from simple observation, and she had no intention of changing her habits.

Occasionally, at the Macon library, with Valerie Keller's assistance, she'd looked something up on one of the computers, a bibliographical list for a class she was teaching or some esoteric cross-reference to a couple of authors of the same period, but it was books in hand she usually sought there, and that she feared would disappear en masse someday with the proliferation of the Internet. She hoped it wouldn't happen in her own lifetime.

Even now, she noticed that there were about as many people in the room devoted to DVDs and videotapes as there were browsing in the stacks. And then she saw someone vaguely familiar—a dark-haired young woman with a shoplifter's shifty glance, running her hand across the spines of a row of books as if she were checking them for dust. Where had Angela seen her before?

Then she remembered: it was in Lissy Snyder's gazebo, the day they'd done the Trollope. She was the one who'd served the refreshments, and had been so amusingly surly. There was something different about her, though.

The librarian was still on the phone, so Angela walked over to the stacks and said, "Hello. I'm Angela Graves. I met you at Lissy Snyder's, but I don't think we were introduced."

"She doesn't know my name."

"What?"

"Not that she'd introduce me, even if she did know it." After a beat, she added, "Anyway, I'm Michelle."

She said that resignedly, as if she wished she were someone else, or at least some*where* else. She had weeded her eyebrows a bit—that was the difference, Angela realized—but she still bore a strong resemblance to Frida Kahlo. There was character in this Michelle's face, too, and dramatic intensity. A line from Eliot came into Angela's head. "I am aware of the damp souls of housemaids."

"Excuse me for a moment," Angela said, and scanned some shelves nearby until she saw the book she wanted. "This is the artist I mentioned to you that day." She handed Michelle the Herrera biography of Kahlo, the edition with that compelling self-portrait with the monkey on the cover. How many times had she done just this, placed a book into the hands of a young woman who just might be transformed by it, but hardly ever was?

Michelle clutched the book, staring at the portrait. It was difficult to read her expression. Then she said, almost accusingly, "She has a mustache."

"Yes. I guess she was self-confident enough not to hide it."

Michelle's fingers fluttered to her own smooth upper lip and then to her slightly altered brow.

"You might enjoy reading that," Angela said. "She had a really interesting life."

"Hmm," Michelle said, still gazing at the portrait. Then she tucked the book under her arm and said, "Maybe I'll take this out," as if it had been her own idea. She'll probably just look at the pictures, Angela thought, and then decided that both she and Eliot were condescending.

By the time Michelle left, the librarian was available. "I've been trying to locate someone I've lost contact with," Angela told her. "I understand that you can do that on the computer."

"Yes," the librarian said, "especially if the person you're looking for doesn't mind being located. You just access your search engine—Yahoo! is the one I generally use—and then go to People Search—"

Angela held up her hand. "That's the thing. I don't have a computer, and I don't know how to use one. I'm not even sure what a search engine is." She was conscious of sounding prideful and ignorant at the same time. "I was hoping you could help me." Now she was being ingratiating as well.

"I'm afraid that's not the kind of research we usually do here," the librarian said. But then something in Angela's face or bearing must have persuaded her to make an exception.

After the barest hesitation, she beckoned for Angela to follow her into a little office cubicle, where the cursor on a large computer screen was blinking. The librarian sat down and began clicking the keyboard, and the screen flashed with changing images. "Here we go," she said a few moments later. "What city?"

"New York," Angela said.

"Name?"

"Keller. Charlotte Victoria Graham Keller." Valerie's maiden name and grandmothers on both sides honored. The girl had finally grown into that mouthful of a moniker. As a toddler, Angela remembered, she'd referred to herself in the third person as Sharly, mostly to make her needs known, or to establish her rights. *Sharly wants. Sharly's toy.*

Angela had looked in the Manhattan telephone directory and then called information, but there was no listing for a Charlotte Keller, or the less gender-specific C. Keller, in any of the five boroughs. She could have just been visiting the city that day, like Angela.

But her long-legged stride in those paint-spattered jeans had seemed comfortable, even proprietary—*Sharly's city*—as if she belonged there. And so many young people, young artists especially, lived in shared apartments and lofts, with the telephone listed only in the leaseholder's name.

"I think I've got it," the librarian said. "Do you have a pencil?"

It was that easy. No telephone number, but there was an address in the East Village, on St. Mark's Place, that seemed to bear out Angela's speculations. Stephen and Valerie had started out in that neighborhood, too. Charlotte may have even been born down there.

"Thank you. Thanks very much," Angela said. Her heart was beating in her ears, and her hands shook as she rummaged in her purse for a pencil and a scrap of paper.

She could feel the librarian watching her as she scribbled down the information, and when she looked up, she saw an expression of avid interest and sympathy on the other woman's face. *Why, she thinks I'm looking for a child I gave up for adoption,* Angela realized with a horrified rush, and tried to seem more casual in her own manner. "My long-lost cousin," she said. "A few times removed," she added, but even that didn't dim that intolerably compassionate gaze. Well, it had sounded like a lie to her, too.

At home, Angela still felt disturbed by the encounter. The librarian was wrong in her assumptions, of course, and why should she care what that woman thought? They were strangers to each other; they hadn't even exchanged names. Angela used the smaller branch library in The Springs most of the time, anyway. It had far fewer books but a more appealing, rustic atmosphere. And it was convenient; she could even walk there and often did.

But all of her reasonable arguments weren't much of a consolation. She had violated her own sacred privacy by leaking that little bit of information from her past. And she had once entertained the fantasy of Charlotte being her own child.

The affair with Stephen had been going on for months, and Angela's period was late. She decided not to tell Stephen; whatever the outcome, it might mortally affect their relationship—that fragile thing for which she had such unabated greed. Even as she lay locked with him in her bed or in his car, or in some sad little motel room miles from campus, she kept thinking *More, more.* Who was it, again, who'd referred to female genitalia as "the wound that wouldn't heal"? Some male writer, probably, but he'd gotten it right.

Angela had taken great satisfaction in her own ability to separate the various parts of her newly complicated life. How else could she have managed to teach, to read, to eat and drink at Valerie and Stephen's table? Maybe it was true that even subtle hormonal changes could have radical emotional effects. For the first time since it all began, she became weepy and had trouble falling asleep. *What will I do? What will I do?* kept running through her head in an endless loop.

She would have an abortion, although she'd probably have to go all the way to Austin to find a clinic. The affair would resume, the affair would end. Or she would leave Macon and go back East to have the baby, which she'd either keep or give up for adoption.

Her mind changed by the hour, by the minute! She would just have to risk telling Stephen, so he could help her make a decision. No, she would confide in Valerie, instead, and beg her forgiveness. The two of them would go off together and raise the child as Charlotte's sibling. That was the solution she finally fixed on and kept imagining even as she recognized its lack of logic, the utter madness at its heart.

As it turned out, she wasn't pregnant after all, merely peri-menopausal, the beginning of the beginning of the end. And with that knowledge, she turned her attention back to Stephen with even greater fervor while giving up her foolish reveries of ever being any-one's mother, especially Charlotte's. But she had never completely stopped thinking about her, just as she was doing right then with such disquieting force.

Angela took her copy of *Villette* and lay outside in the string ham-mock under the trees. Only reading, she knew, could distract her from her obsessive thoughts and restore her sense of peace. She had read this particular volume so many times, the pages were softened from han-dling and slightly loosened from their binding. There were whole pas-sages, especially toward the end, that she could recite from memory. Yet she began from the beginning, the only way the novel's pleasures could be fully renewed.

She read with care, but quickly, as if she couldn't wait to see how things turned out. It was the darkest of Charlotte Brontë's novels and the one she related to the most, with a heroine who appears passive, even cold, to the outside world and who anticipates a solitary future, yet is aroused by unidentified longings and feels "obliged to live." At other times in her life, Angela had experienced that famous shock of recognition reading passages in other books, and was fickle in her love for Isabel and Dorothea, for Jane and Emma and Tess.

When she was an adolescent, and metamorphosis still seemed possible, she'd found the marriageable Elizabeth Bennet a reasonable role model. Angela's parents expected her to marry, too, when she took her nose out of those books long enough, although their own example offered so little inspiration.

Pragmatic Lucy Snowe has no such romantic expectations—"Suitor or admirer my very thoughts had not conceived"—but is brimming with self, anyway. She's closely observant, opinionated, and outspoken. When her student, the vapidly beautiful and vain Ginevra Fanshawe, drags Lucy in front of a mirror for a "who is fairest of them all" comparison, the teacher concedes the beauty contest, but claims that she wouldn't ever choose to exchange places. Yet she retains a kind of wry affection for the younger woman, and seems to give her the benefit of every sensible doubt, as if she were capable of real change.

There was always at least one student under Angela's tutelage who could play Ginevra to her Lucy. Lissy Snyder was this season's ingénue—she was certainly shallow and pretty enough, though less self-assured. Angela envisioned the girl's folded brow and the way her finger moved slowly across a line of text when she was asked to read a passage aloud, and she wondered if Lissy was dyslexic, if she'd ever even finish reading *Villette* and find her own reflection in its pages.

The sun had dropped behind the high branches of the trees, and Angela knew that she would need her glasses to continue reading as the light faded. If she had to get up to get them, she might as well go inside and start dinner. It would be dark soon enough, and she was getting hungry. *Chapter 16, Auld Lang Syne,* she mentally noted—she'd never needed a bookmark or dog-eared a page—and shut the book and went into the house.

There, as she sliced a bloody and beautiful summer tomato and made a fragrant chiffonade of basil, she thought again about Charlotte, walking away from her on Seventh Avenue until she was out of sight, her blond head disappearing like the sun. Tomorrow Angela would meet with the Bridgehampton Bookettes, another of her reading groups, but she would be free the following day.

She went into the bedroom and looked in her purse for that scrap of paper she'd scribbled on in the library, but she knew before she could find it that she had committed Charlotte's address to memory, just as she had done with the place she'd left off reading in *Villette*.

9.

Mermaids

Kayla was still in Hank's bathroom with the shower running full force. Michelle figured the ceiling had to be peeling off by now, and that the girl was probably either smoking in there or puking up her brains. Either way, she'd yank the window open afterward to air out the place, gargle with Listerine, and spritz around some of that powerful room deodorizer she carried in her backpack. The stink would cling to the shower curtain and towels for days. Even though Michelle was the only other person at home, she rapped sharply on the door and yelled, "Hey, there's a line forming out here!"

When Kayla finally stepped out in her tiny shorts and cropped top, surrounded by a mist of pine-scented steam, her dark hair was plastered to her head. Michelle was reminded of the little barefoot braves in a picture book she once had. *Where you go to school today, Indian children used to play.* "So," she said, "didn't you want a cup of coffee with that Marlboro?"

She'd guessed correctly; she could tell by the guilty flicker of Kayla's eyes, but the girl recovered quickly. "What?" she said, as if there was too much noise for her to hear properly. In fact, it was quiet, except for the muted roar of somebody's distant lawn mower.

Michelle remembered that trick of convenient deafness from her own girlhood. "You heard me," she said. And she grabbed Kayla by one of her sunburned Olive Oyl arms and pulled her so close, she might have been about to kiss her on the mouth. But Michelle was just smelling Kayla's breath. "Yuk!" she cried, stepping back, holding her nose. "You'd better quit that, you little moron, or you're going to die!"

This was not the subtle approach Kayla's parents advocated. They were more into government health pamphlets and earnest, cozy chats. *Honey, we have to talk.* It didn't really matter; Kayla had the same re-action to both the good-cop and bad-cop routines: a willful indiffer-ence that occasionally morphed into defensive outrage, as it did now. "Just lay off," she told Michelle with the contemptuous little sneer she'd perfected. "You're not the boss of me!"

That familiar, mechanical plaint was technically true. Nobody ever was the boss of a teenage girl, except maybe some horny little teenage boy, and definitely not someone with the dubious status of her dad's girlfriend. But Michelle believed that her own tough-love method was more valid and effective than Hank's and April's careful diplomacy. At least she could still remember what it felt like to be that young, while they'd sacrificed their own youth to playing house. "Oh, no?" she said, on automatic pilot now, too. "We'll just see about that."

Kayla Joy was conceived when Henry Keifer and April Dreschen were seniors in high school, but it was several months before anyone, including them, knew that April was pregnant. It was one of those cases of a slightly overweight girl with erratic periods who didn't really show, and who managed to be in complete denial. By the time Hank caught on and April finally admitted, to herself and to him, the way things were, it was too late to do anything about it. And it was close to graduation, so they went to the prom as if they were going hand in hand to the gas chamber, and got married a few days later.

They stayed together, more or less, for about three years, while their passion, even for quarreling, faded and April got heavier and heavier. Hank once told Michelle that she seemed to be hiding out in her own body. He hid from her, too, spending long hours on his father's fishing boat wondering how his life had taken this weird turn and what was going to happen next. In the meantime, their baby became a toddler, a little miracle of locomotion and speech, who would bind them, in some ways, forever.

Hank and April were only another object lesson in the dangers of unprotected sex when Michelle entered East Hampton High. She had seen April around, wheeling Kayla in her stroller, and she'd known Hank for years as her older brother's friend, one of a rowdy bunch of boys who were always laughing harshly and shoving one another. They'd made her feel acutely conspicuous and invisible at the same time.

Years later, soon after she and Hank began going out, he confessed that he'd thought she was a cute and funny kid back then. "You were always giving us one of your famous *looks,*" he said, and he did an uncanny imitation of her quick, piercing glance, which was so much like Kayla's. His mimicry made Michelle feel awkward again, almost mortified, as if he had just caught her hanging around the closed door of Eddie's room, sending frantic mind signals to Hank, which she'd so often done.

Kayla swept past Michelle into the living room, where the dogs were lying on a cool patch of wood floor at the edge of the sisal rug. They struggled to their feet, two gallant older gentlemen, as Kayla knelt between them and raked their coats with her chewed-up fingers.

Feathers of golden fur flew upward like dandelion puffs in a wind-storm. "Who are my best babies?" she crooned, and they collapsed at her touch and rolled over helplessly onto their backs. "Who wants a yummy yummy?"

Not *you*, I'll bet, Michelle thought. But, as usual, she softened at the sight of Kayla and the Labs. There had to be goodness at the heart of anyone who loved animals the way Kayla clearly did. And Pete and Bill, far less discriminating in their affections, loved her right back, and served as inadvertent peacemakers in the household. They could work for the United Nations, if they could only learn to stop chasing cars.

"Do you want some breakfast before we go?" Michelle was able to ask in a calm voice, and Kayla looked up at her benignly, as if they hadn't just exchanged angry words outside the bathroom. "No, thanks," she said.

It hadn't been the worst weekend in their short history as a pickup family. Kayla, who was smart but lazy, and had to repeat social studies in summer school, had done that week's required reading without a hassle. And the day before, she and Michelle had gone for an early swim in the ocean while Hank was out on the boat. Kayla rode the waves with suicidal glee. When she emerged, blue-lipped and shiver-ing, she allowed herself to be clenched between Michelle's knees, wrapped in towels, and massaged back to life. While the girl was trapped in her swaddling, Michelle took the biography of Frida Kahlo from her tote bag and held it up. "Look at this," she said.

Kayla glanced suspiciously at the book, as if it were some novelty item that might suddenly spill its ink or explode. "What about it?" she said. And then, "Ooh, what a cute monkey!"

"Yes," Michelle impatiently agreed. "But what else?"

"I don't know," Kayla said, struggling against her bonds. When she'd finally broken free, she said, "Hey, what if my name was Kayla Kahlo?" And then she jumped up and ran back into the surf.

Michelle opened the book and began to read. "The story of Frida Kahlo begins and ends in the same place." But she kept one eye on the dark head bobbing in the roiling water.

In the afternoon, Kayla greased herself and courted skin cancer on a blanket in the backyard, and Michelle stayed inside, listening to the Beatles' *White Album*. "Ob-La-Di, Ob-La-Da" and "While My Guitar Gently Weeps."

She remembered that December day in 2001 when George Harrison died. Michelle was working at Kmart then, and she'd come home in the evening to find her mother curled up on her bed. She must have just come in, too, from one of her houses, because her coat was still on and she hadn't even refrigerated the leftover chicken marbella she'd brought back from the job. It was sitting on the dresser in a Calypso St. Barths shopping bag. "Are you okay?" Michelle asked.

"Uh-huh," Jo Ann said, but in such a tremulous voice, Michelle flopped down beside her and began giving her a backrub. And then Pete and Bill scrambled into the room and added their throbbing animal heat to the human huddle on the bed. Michelle knew what was wrong with her mother; she'd heard the news on her car radio. It was only a few months after the attack on the World Trade Center. Flags still hung at half-mast everywhere, alongside the festive Christmas trees, a mixed public message of despair and hope.

When Michelle heard the bulletin about George Harrison, she'd had a pang of guilt for not having liked him more, for never even considering him as a contender as her biological father. It was really strange the way you carried stuff around from your childhood all of your life, long after you understood what was real and what you'd invented to make yourself feel better.

She might have said something about that to Kayla when she came back inside, but the girl headed straight for the bathroom and the moment passed. That night, they'd all gone out for burgers and a movie, some PG-13 horror-fantasy in which teenage robots ruled the world. Kayla had begged to see it. Then she sat between them in the

theater like a forbidding chaperone, hogging the armrests, and wolf-
ing popcorn and guzzling Coke. It was probably all in the plumbing
by now.

A sexual charge had gone back and forth between Hank and
Michelle that whole evening, despite Kayla's dividing presence, but
she'd stayed up so late on the foldout sofa in the living room, watching television, they'd just given up and fallen asleep. Hank had left the
house before dawn; Michelle sensed his absence the moment she
awoke, although she didn't remember his leaving. They'd finally made
love around midnight, forced out of their separate dreams by habit
and stubborn impulse, but with only a Sheetrock wall between them
and Kayla, Michelle had kept her own boisterous inclinations down.
She might as well have been gagged and bound—though not in a
kinky way.

It was Sunday, the biggest party-boat day of the week. Eddie must
have come by silently for Hank on the dark street while Michelle was
still fast asleep. She was going to work, later, too, just about when the
Kayla Joy pulled into the harbor in Montauk after its first run. Lissy
and Jeffrey Snyder were hosting a brunch at noon that Michelle and
her mother would help to serve and then clean up after. But first
Michelle had to drive to Hampton Bays and drop Kayla off at April's,
and then she'd swing by and pick up Jo Ann.

She swigged some coffee and ate a buttered bagel, standing up at
the counter and watching through the window as Kayla and the dogs
climbed into the car and sat waiting for her.

Hank and April shared custody of Kayla, so she was built right
into his relationship with Michelle. She was surprised by how little she
minded having a kid around in the middle of their romance, and how
reasonable and friendly April always seemed about everything. If
Michelle and Hank ever split up, it would probably kill her to see him,
or even imagine him, in the company of another woman. But April
waved affably from her cashier's station at CVS whenever they
shopped there. She even offered to buy stuff for them—vitamins and

shampoo—at her employees' discount, and she didn't give Hank a hard time about money or the custody arrangements.

In the car, Kayla resolved the everlasting question of conversation between them by tuning the radio to a Connecticut rock station and turning the volume way up. She put the air on at full blast, too. Michelle immediately turned them both down, but not too much. That was the way she circumvented unnecessary battles, by giving in a little, but never conceding the whole war.

When Hank and Michelle first began going out, Kayla seemed to have a kind of crush on her. They played endless rounds of Go Fish and Stealing the Old Man's Bundle—Michelle didn't throw the games to Kayla the way Hank did—and Kayla seemed to appreciate that show of respect, no matter how much she hated to lose. They sang in harmony with songs on the car radio and they hung out at the beach together like a couple of mermaids, collecting shells and combing the sand out of each other's hair.

But things changed as Kayla herself did, growing out of her girl-ish sweetness into a tangle of adolescent nerves, as if she'd swallowed some awful magic potion to which there was no antidote but time. She had always bitten her nails, and she'd started fasting, or gorging and sticking her finger down her throat, about six months before. Right about the time she'd gotten her braces. Then the smoking began. Michelle hoped that was all she was doing with her busy, metal-filled little mouth. And only God knew what went on inside her head as she was shuttled back and forth between her parents. Maybe she'd decided that being civil to her father's girlfriend was an act of dis-loyalty to her own mother.

Well, good riddance then, Michelle told herself as she pulled up to April's place and Kayla pushed the door open as if the car were on fire. April was waiting at the curb, and Michelle was sideswiped by a rush of tenderness for them both—for Hank's unpredictable daughter and his obese and worried ex-wife. She even attempted to embrace Kayla as she left the car, only to be shaken off with a shuddering shrug, like a blackfly on a horse's flank. The girl had reached into the back-seat, though, to pet the dogs, to let them slather her bony arm before she slammed the door behind her.

April knocked on the passenger window as Kayla made her way up the path to their house with her backpack, and Michelle rolled it down. "Did she eat all right?" April asked.

It was the same anxious question she asked every time Kayla was returned to her, and Michelle had to assure her once again that her daughter had been properly fed outside her own vigilant surveillance. What a bad joke it was, that the mother was so big and the girl so skinny. It's safe, you can come out of there now, Michelle wanted to tell April. And she might have run past her into their bungalow and told Kayla that she should stop trying to hurt herself, that nothing was her fault; despite all their superstitious thinking, children are power-less against the stupid choices their parents, and all the other adults in their lives, make. But instead she just gunned the motor and stuck to the script, saying, "I've got to go. I'm working a party for them today."

"Well, thanks for having Kayla," April said.

No, thank *you* for having her, Michelle thought. Then she said, "No problem," as she always did, before she drove away.

10.

Bad Boys

In *Can You Forgive Her?* Lissy recalled, friends and relatives were constantly sticking their noses into one another's love lives. And it wasn't anything like the comfortably chatty relationship of the four women on *Sex and the City*. When one of Trollope's characters decides to break off her engagement, a distant cousin—someone she's never even met!—is compelled to write a letter and offer her opinion and advice. Everybody still had opinions, of course—it was a free country—but except for Dr. Phil and a host of bloggers, most people kept theirs to themselves, or merely indulged in a little harmless gossip.

At Lissy and Jeffrey's brunch, there was a current of gossip running just beneath the regular party chatter about

Ardith and Larry Templeton, who were late as usual. But it wasn't their lateness that was particularly noted; they were the sort of couple, exceptionally rich, prominent and, who always made a dramatic entrance, and who were always being talked about with a nervous mixture of worship, envy, and malice.

Ardith seemed to have dropped completely out of the Page Turners, which she'd started in the first place. Lissy remembered with a wistful sigh how foolishly happy she had been to join the club, and the high hopes she'd once held about becoming a special friend of Ardith's.

Recently, in a recurrence of that old adolescent fear of exclusion, Lissy had imagined an intricate plot in which the other women dropped out of the reading club, too, one at a time, just to rid themselves of her. When she'd confided that disturbing fantasy to Jeffrey, he said, "That's crazy, you know, everybody likes you. They *love* you. You just have to have a little more self-confidence."

And Jeffrey was right, on one point, anyway: there was no evil plot. Ardith was the only defector, and she didn't just come right out and quit. Instead, she called shortly before every meeting with another excuse: some indisposition, like a migraine or an allergy attack; or unexpected out-of-town guests; or the sudden obligation to host a business acquaintance of Larry's.

Once, only a few hours after Ardith claimed to be laid low by a stomach virus, Lissy saw her strolling down Job's Lane in Southampton, looking perfectly healthy. She was wearing impeccable tennis whites, showing off her tanned and athletic legs to great advantage, and her long auburn hair was tucked into that calculatedly careless knot. Her skin had a moist and almost incandescent glow; maybe she'd just come from having a facial or a massage. Ardith hadn't noticed Lissy, who ducked into a shopping alley with her heart lurching, as if *she* were the one who'd barely missed being caught in an outright lie.

Only a little later, in the funereal cool of Saks, did she allow her-

self to wonder why Ardith bothered going through that elaborate deception, when she might have simply said that she was bored by the
reading group. That would have at least won Lissy's understanding
and sympathy—despite Angela's claims about literature, it wasn't exactly transforming her life, either. She and Ardith might have even
commiserated about that, sparking a kind of renegade friendship.

The weather was glorious on the day of the brunch—had there
ever been a better summer? The caterer, someone new in town who
was introducing a northern-southern fusion, had laid out the buffet
on the long pine trestle table under the Palladian windows in the library, but most of the guests wandered outdoors with their filled
plates to the little clusters of folding chairs and tables set up under the
trees.

The waiters moved among them, pouring from pitchers of Belli-
nis and mint juleps, while Lissy flitted from group to group, sipping
club soda and gathering compliments for the food she hadn't prepared
and the weather she had only wished for. Jeffrey was doing the same
thing at other tables—the brunch was important to both of them, and
they were a solid team. It seemed to be a good party, so far, if not a
great one. Every once in a while, Lissy glanced expectantly toward the
trellised arch of clematis at the entrance to the lawn, but no one but
the serving staff passed through it.

Debby and Joy were sitting together with their husbands near the
rose garden, and as Lissy approached, Ardith's name wafted toward her
on the soft, fragrant air. "So what did I miss?" Lissy asked.

"We were just speculating about Lord and Lady Templeton," Joy
said. She patted the empty chair beside her, and Lissy obediently sat
down. "Something big is going on there, and we're trying to figure it
out."

Lissy looked at her watch and frowned. "Well, they're always late,
aren't they?" she said.

Joy didn't even bother acknowledging that disingenuous observation. "Deb thinks there's trouble in River City," she said.

Deb laughed and took a long swallow of her drink before she spoke. "Do you know Guido Masconi?" she asked Lissy.

"Well, not personally," Lissy said. She knew who he was, though; everyone did. He was a restaurateur with purported connections to the mob, and he and his wife, a former soap opera actress, were in the process of building an outrageously large estate on the ocean in Water Mill.

There was something in the local papers every week about emergency town board meetings involving protests and variances, but the construction was still going forward, and Masconi's famous seafood place in Montauk was still perpetually overbooked. She and Jeffrey had gone there once. The noise level had been intolerable, and they hadn't run into Masconi. "What about him?"

Deb looked at her husband, who seemed to be totally focused on his poached salmon and truffled grits. "Stanley saw Ardith and Masconi having lunch together at the American Hotel," she said. Stanley kept on eating, neither affirming nor denying his wife's assertion.

"That could have been perfectly innocent," Lissy said, "couldn't it?" She held the cold glass of soda against her burning cheek.

"Sure," Joy said. "She was planning a surprise birthday party for Larry at The Battered Clam."

"No," Deb said. "She was planning to have him *bumped off* at The Battered Clam." Everyone burst into laughter, and Joy's husband, Dick, said, "Don't laugh, Larry wrote up the formal complaint for the Concerned Citizens group."

Stanley put down his fork and blotted his lips. "He cited wetlands protection and the desecration of the dunes," he said with a smirk.

And Deb said, "Oh, please. All anybody cares about is the view."

Lissy knew that this was true; an unobstructed view was essential in the Hamptons, practically sacred; ancient trees were often felled in its cause. Even at the movies, people went nuts if someone overly tall or broad sat directly in front of them; she once heard one man threaten another with decapitation. And several Water Mill home owners' views of the ocean were going to be compromised or completely obscured by Masconi's mansion and all its proposed outbuildings.

"Guido is like one of Angela's bad boys," Joy said. And when Lissy looked blankly at her, she said, "You know, like in the Trollope? Alice Vavasor's cousin, George, and that other no-goodnik, Lady what's-her name's boyfriend, Burgo."

She was referring to Angela Graves's comment, during the discussion of *Can You Forgive Her?* that women had been attracted throughout history to men of dubious character. Lissy hadn't gotten far enough into the novel to respond in substance, then or now, but she immediately thought of a correlation to *Sex and the City.* Carrie Bradshaw's on-again, off-again boyfriend, Big, certainly fell into that category of bad boys, with his devilish style and resistance to commitment. The thing was, she knew, they tended to be sexier than good men—on television, in Trollope, and in life. *Big, Burgo, Guido:* even their names had a similar blunt, aggressive energy.

She was about to say something about that when Jeffrey came up behind her and put his hand on her arm. Her drink sloshed a little. Then he squeezed in next to her on the little folding chair. There really wasn't enough room, and his thigh was warm and heavy against hers. "Is everyone having fun?" he asked.

He was a good man, despite a few lingering questions about his business practices. You could tell by his open face, his clearly affectionate regard for his wife, and the almost morbid concern he had for his children. Did that make him any less sexy? Certainly not!

But Lissy couldn't help thinking of Ardith and Guido Masconi clinking glasses in the American Hotel, of his deadpan face in a newspaper photo, with its five o'clock shadow like a bandit's mask, and of the way Ardith's complexion seemed to give off its own light that afternoon in Southampton.

Lissy stood and planted a kiss on Jeffrey's head, close to his burgeoning bald spot. He started to rise, too. *"Stay,"* she said, as if she were giving a command to a dog, and then, more softly, "Don't get up, honey, I'm just going to circulate a little."

Back at the house, the caterer was crimping tinfoil around a tray on one of the kitchen counters while Jo Ann and her daughter pulled clean wineglasses from the dishwasher. "Watch it, Michelle!" Jo Ann warned, as the girl grabbed three stems at once and the bowls of the glasses chimed an alarm. Michelle!—*that* was her name. Lissy filed it firmly away in her memory and said, "Great job!" to the caterer, and "Jo Ann, Michelle, hi. Is everything all right?"

It wasn't a genuine question—Lissy had come inside to escape her own heated thoughts, not to chitchat with the help—and it didn't evoke a genuine response. The mother only smiled and nodded at her, and the daughter turned away and reached for more wineglasses.

Lissy continued to look at them, though, as if they were actors on a stage. Consider the lives of others while you read, Angela had instructed the Page Turners, and try to relate them to your own. But just the act of reading took so much concentration and energy, and nothing in fiction seemed that relevant. On top of everything else, there was all that *French* to translate in *Villette*.

Standing in her gleaming modern kitchen trying to picture the lives of working-class Victorian women, Lissy saw that the caterer's bushy red hair was caught up in a black mesh snood, like a fishnet. A hygienic precaution probably. Evie had worn a spiderweb version of the same thing whenever she'd prepared Lissy's lunch or afternoon snack; she'd called it an invisible hairnet. "But I can *see* it," little Lissy once said, making Evie laugh that deep satisfying rumble of approval.

Michelle could never have been transported here from another century; her earlobes were pierced by lots of little silver studs, and she had a tiny flower tattoo just below her waist; it popped up whenever she bent over. Jo Ann's broad feet were cushioned by a pair of funky pink, high-end running shoes. Lissy had seen them before on someone else Jo Ann worked for; they were probably hand-me-downs. She should thin out her own closets and give stuff she didn't wear to

Michelle. That white Lurex halter top, for instance, had definitely been a mistake, encouraged by tricky lighting in the dressing room. White didn't really do anything for her, not the way it did for Ardith.

Lissy wondered when the rumors about Ardith and Masconi would reach Larry Templeton's ears. He was a powerful man, and she suspected that he had a short temper. She really had nothing to base that on, except the time she'd seen him use his cell phone to kill a fly at the beach. He kept banging at it long after it had stopped buzzing, until it was reduced to a disgusting little pulp. Guido Masconi wasn't known for being mild-mannered, either, and what about his wife?

Her professional name was Delora Deane, and she'd played a man-hungry, trigger-happy cop on a now defunct nighttime soap called *Original Sin.* Lissy had seen her in person a few times, at the nail salon in Wainscott, and she'd always seemed ordinary and a little shopworn. But Lissy couldn't shake the onscreen image of an innocent, blue-eyed blonde turning on a dime into a murderous sexpot. She was either a pretty good actress or had an unstable psyche.

Lissy became aware of the three women in her kitchen watching her, as if she were the one on stage, an actor who'd forgotten her lines. "Well," she said, with a self-deprecating little laugh, "I can't remember what I came in for."

Then she opened the refrigerator and pretended to check on something in there. She just wanted to play for a little time and cool her face, but she pulled out an orange and tossed it back and forth between her hands, as if it were too hot to handle.

Finally, she dropped it and it rolled across the room and under the big worktable. She was as clumsy as that magician, Dr. Delirium. "Whoops," she said, "I'll get that," but Michelle ducked under the table at the same time and they bumped heads. "Ouch," Michelle complained, and then she made eye contact with Lissy for a long moment as she handed her the orange.

Lissy had the oddest sensation, as if she were being compelled to return Michelle's gaze in that confined space, and think: Who *are* you? before she backed out and stood up, a little dizzily.

Michelle stood, too, and grabbed a platter of pecan tartlets that she hurried outside with. When Lissy followed her through the trellised arch, still holding the orange, she saw that the distribution of her guests had changed. Several of them were standing together in the middle of the lawn, and others were moving in that direction, as if they were being drawn there, like iron filings to a magnet.

For a moment she worried that people were preparing to leave, even before dessert was served, which was always a bad sign. But then she saw that no one seemed to be going, and that the Templetons had arrived, at last.

It was so rude of them to show up this late without calling, but Lissy knew that their appearance cemented the success of her party. The hum of conversation had grown louder and more urgent, and the men were glad-handing Larry, as if he'd come just in time to save them. But from what?

As she got closer, Lissy saw that Ardith was wearing white again, a backless sundress this time, with a delicate, drooping hem. She looked virtuous and self-disciplined, like one of the dancers in *Swan Lake*. But Lissy imagined the dress in a pale puddle at Ardith's feet, and Guido Masconi burying his mobster's face like a stiletto between her breasts.

11.

In Which Art and Love Collide

Angela had come into the city with the earliest commuters, and now she was sitting in Marty's coffee shop on St. Mark's Place, directly across the street from the tenement where Charlotte lived, waiting for her to show up. Manhattan looked like a drypoint etching in the rain—practically the antithesis of The Springs, which always took on a painterly verdant luster on days like this. The vague ache in Angela's chest as she looked through the coffee shop window felt something like homesickness, only she wasn't sure which place it was that she missed.

The Village had changed. Institutions like the 8th Street Bookstore and the Fillmore East were long gone, and there were lots of tiny new boutiques and ethnic restaurants. Some of the old industrial buildings, where young artists and writers had once lived and worked illegally, had been converted into legally over-priced loft condos. The population had changed, too, accordingly. There seemed to be more older people now, and more people in for-eign dress. A man wearing a red turban went by, and then a woman in a dashiki, as if they were hurrying off to a costume party.

But the essential atmosphere that Angela remembered—laid-back yet electric with possibility—was the same. She was certain that this was still the best place to be when you were young, when poverty had a romantic temporality, and you might turn out, with a little luck, to be anybody at all. Maybe what she was feeling was only nostalgia for her own youth, when the future was still a tantalizing, unresolved mystery.

But what was Charlotte in the act of becoming? An artist, from the look of her paint-stained jeans that other time. She probably didn't hate or resent her father, then, if she'd chosen the same work as his. Angela wondered if Stephen and Valerie were both still alive, and if so, whether they were together anymore. Valerie had wanted a second child; maybe that had been the crucial bargaining chip in a reconcili-ation between them.

They were a few years younger than Angela was, but they might be retired, too, by now. Maybe they lived in Florida or Arizona, with all the other retirees, although she couldn't really picture them in the cliché of that migration. Had they grown to despise her? She became aware of her own reflection in the coffee shop window, a ghostly image of some withered crone, superimposed on the façade of Char-lotte's building.

It was definitely Charlotte's building. Angela had gone up the steps earlier and read the names alongside the doorbells, most of them in pairings or groups of three or four. And there was a C. Keller, shar-ing space with a J. Schwartz in 6D.

She had pushed their doorbell, tentatively at first, then hard and long—Charlotte had been such a heavy sleeper as a child—but there was no answering buzz, no crackling query through the intercom. She'd peered through the glass pane of the outer door into the dimly lit entrance, but all she could see, beyond a second paned door, was the bottom of a stairwell, littered with takeout menus. It was a fool's errand. Charlotte could be anywhere—in Europe, staying overnight with a friend, or visiting her parents, wherever they were.

Angela had taken her copy of *Villette* along, in preparation for the next day's meeting with the Page Turners. On the train, she'd flipped through the book, reviewing her notes and making new ones. She took it out again now, in the coffee shop, opening to one of the pages she had flagged with a Post-it. The sentence she'd underlined read: "There is, in lovers, a certain infatuation of egotism; they will have a witness of their happiness, cost that witness what it may."

She knew that passage by heart, and every time she read it or just thought the words—they would appear in her head in a little frame, like a sampler—she remembered what had happened in Texas, the notorious way her affair with Stephen was exposed, bringing it to an abrupt and ugly end.

They had been lovers for more than a year, and Angela had perfected the art of putting her conflicted feelings into separate little compartments she could open or close at will. Here was her craving for Stephen, here was her friendship with Valerie. They were both necessary and they could coexist; she didn't have to sacrifice one for the other.

If that reasoning seemed unreasonable in retrospect, it made a kind of complicated sense then. She and Stephen were discreet enough. They never made love in the Kellers' house or in any campus building, where they might have been discovered. There were additional rules, too. She wasn't permitted to ask about his sexual relationship with Valerie. And Charlotte was never used as a foil or an unwitting accomplice to the affair; Stephen was particularly adamant about that. In the presence of his family, Angela simply assumed one of her usual roles among them.

All the other aspects of their individual lives continued, amazingly, on a parallel plane. Stephen painted his canvases, they taught their respective classes, bought groceries, went to the dentist and to the movies. The furtiveness of their conspiracy and its self-imposed restrictions, she knew, served as a further aphrodisiac. And there wasn't enough dead time, as there is in a sanctioned relationship, like marriage, to become bored and irritable, to fall into the stifling predictability of routine.

They were always in a hurry, she marveled now—that was the thing—although back then they kept lamenting the lack of leisure to slowly peel away their clothing, rather than tear it from their bodies like emergency medical workers homing in on a bleeding wound. The clothing itself was worn as a shabby disguise of their essential nakedness.

"Let me look at you," Stephen would say fiercely as soon as they were alone somewhere, as if she'd been hiding herself, deliberately depriving him. Nothing gave her more pleasure than his excitement at seeing her body, which was so insignificant compared with Valerie's.

She couldn't discuss that with him, of course, but she thought about it with wonder. Why did he desire her teacup breasts and boyish hips, her sallow coloring, when he had all that radiant abundance at home? In fact, she and Stephen were like fraternal twins in their slenderness and their dark, cropped hair, a trick that seemed to be done with mirrors when he entered her, when they entered each other and disappeared.

His painting was going well, he said, and Jenna Barker was talking about giving him a one-man show at her gallery in the spring. One day, Angela met him at the studio to look at his work in progress. The smell in there, that acrid mix of linseed oil and turpentine that was only a faint perfume on his hands in bed, gave her an instant, heady rush, and she had to touch the wall for balance.

He'd almost finished a cycle of paintings based on some of the lesser-known Grimms' fairy tales, like "Fundevogel" and "The Salad," oversized portraits that incorporated elements of nature he hadn't painted before—birds and trees and fish—woven into his subjects' hair or garments. He had constructed the frames himself, the way he always did, using a simple, sanded pine that didn't distract from their contents. These paintings were wittier than any of his previous ones, and freer in their execution, with bolder strokes and a more vivid palette. So much red, and all those raw and fleshy pinks.

His tenure would be secured by this new work, Angela was sure, and she felt what might have been described as a collaborator's pride in him. Wasn't all art predicated on desire? And she had introduced him to those obscure stories in the first place. She'd even read them with theatrical verve to Charlotte, who loved all the graphic, grisly details—the threatened boiling of children, human heads in a sack—and shrieked with nervous laughter. *He cut the heart out of the bird and swallowed it whole.* Some of the text should be in the catalog; Angela would speak to Jenna about that.

It wasn't that she didn't ever think it would end between them, but the little flashes of foresight she had were like thoughts of one's own death, another irrefutable truth that could be shunned or at least sidestepped in the intoxication of current happiness. Still, it occurred to her that their lust could cool back into friendship, or that he would find someone else, now that she'd given him license to be unfaithful. *Then I will die,* she told herself, immediately aware of the narcissism and melodrama in such a pronouncement. You didn't die of sorrow any more than you lived for joy.

He called the show Children of Fortune, at Angela's suggestion, after another one of the Grimms' tales he'd referred to in the paintings. The opening at the Paradise Gallery was set for a Friday evening in late March, just before the Easter break. There would be a buffet supper afterward at another colleague's house.

Whenever Angela saw a notice for the show posted on campus— she had helped Valerie hang them everywhere—she felt a surge of exhilaration, like someone receiving unexpected good news. It had been a dreary, unusually cold and long winter, and things were finally thawing out, even greening up a little, which added to her sense of anticipation.

Angela had three classes to teach on the day of the opening. Oddly enough, the thing with Stephen had rendered her more focused than ever in the classroom, another psychological feat—this one a kind of transference—as if the rapture she experienced with him fed the rapture she found in books.

Did the students register any change that year in her, their maiden-lady professor whose life must have seemed so pathetic, with its narrow perimeters and academic concerns? Her sophomores, in the final class of the day, were reading *Villette.* She sat on the edge of her desk and read aloud to them: "I had feelings: passive as I lived, little as I spoke, cold as I looked, when I thought of past days, I *could* feel." Then she closed the book and asked, "Does Lucy's behavior ever betray her passionate inner life?"

They were clueless, as usual. One girl in the back row was seeking herself in her compact's mirror; another seemed to be nodding in sleep. To be fair, it was a Friday afternoon before a long holiday, the room was overheated, and Brontë's Lucy Snowe was only referring to her childhood, while Angela was thinking of the day before, of Stephen's deep, drinking kisses, of her head banging senselessly against the headboard in the Jiffy Motel outside Mineral Wells.

Then school was out at last and she was on her way to Jackson City. Valerie had asked her to pick up a platter of cheese and fruit at their house; it was sliding around on the backseat of Angela's Volkswagen Bug. She had to get to the gallery a little early to deliver these hors d'oeuvres, but not so early as to seem inappropriately involved. It was all part of that intricate dance of danger and safety to which the steps always seemed to be changing.

As she parked the car in the first available spot down the street from the gallery, she could see some colleagues getting out of their cars up ahead, and a little gathering of people in the road. It would be a success; it would be Stephen's moment and, vicariously, also her own.

She could still recall the cold, brittle weight of Valerie's Saran-wrapped glass platter, and how she had to balance it against her hip to open the door of the gallery. Jenna was seated right inside at a high reception desk, where the catalogs and price lists were neatly stacked.

Was it only in hindsight that she saw the peculiar way Jenna looked at her when she came in, with that wide-eyed smile, as if Angela were the guest of honor, the one she'd been eagerly awaiting? But the true guest of honor and his family were already there, just putting their coats on the rolling rack near the desk. Angela was relieved of the tray, and there were greetings and embraces all around. Then she and the Kellers walked, *en famille,* into the main room of the gallery, a sizable space for a smallish western town not noted for its devotion to culture.

Some friends and a few strangers were already there, clutching their plastic glasses of white wine, and there was a hum of conversation that put Angela in mind of swarming bees. The larger-than-life portraits gazed back at their viewers with the insolence she knew made the work so arresting.

Charlotte was hanging on to Stephen, clutching his hand and then plucking at his sleeve and his belt, as if to slow him down and to draw on his newfound power. Her high-pitched voice pierced the swarming noise. "*I* want to see, Daddy," she said. You'd think someone was trying to stop her.

"Look, Sharly," Valerie said. "There's Fundevogel and Lina." Then somebody came in behind them, and Stephen was pulled away to receive more embraces and congratulations.

What happened next? It was a question Angela had considered many times over the years, as if she might be asked to give court testimony one day about an ancient accident or a crime. But she could never be certain of the exact sequence of events.

She knew this much: there was a smaller room adjacent to the main gallery, and a few people had wandered in there. It was where Jenna usually displayed the lesser or less showy works in a show, the artist's drawings or prints.

Angela didn't go in there right away. Maybe she lingered to look at the paintings, or to speak to someone near the threshold between the rooms, to a student or to Roger Day. She could vaguely recall an exchange of civilities, inanities. And there was laughter. Someone else—Jenna?—must have put a glass of wine into her hand, although she still couldn't remember receiving or drinking it, only that it spilled onto her shoes later.

At some point, Charlotte, who had temporarily lost contact with her father, attached herself to Valerie and Angela, pulling them by their hands into the anteroom. The others in there turned to look at them as they entered, and then stepped back, as if in fear or respect. Charlotte freed her hand and pointed. "Angela!" she said, and Angela turned and asked, "What is it, dear?" But Charlotte wasn't looking back at her.

The pen-and-ink drawing, behind glass in an elaborate gilded frame that might have suited a vintage valentine, was on the facing wall, by itself. Charlotte, a commanding little docent whose only instruction was that one uttered name, was still pointing at it. Not that the drawing needed to be identified; it was that good a likeness.

What Angela saw first were the two shocks of dark hair and the blind eyes of her own nipples. The figure—herself—was lying back against pillows in a languorous pose, and with a glazed expression any fool would recognize as postcoital. Her legs were splayed and one of them was bent at the knee. "Let me look at you," Stephen always said, and now everyone was invited to do the same.

Time didn't stop, as it's supposed to; the room didn't fall into a hush. She didn't vomit or faint, although she'd felt she might do both, and of course she didn't die. Valerie ran past her, dragging Charlotte, who looked back, like Lot's wife; maybe that's when the wine spilled.

Or maybe it was when Angela charged past Stephen, who'd come into the room moments after his wife and daughter had left it. "Oh fuck!" Angela heard him say, just enough to establish that he was as surprised to see the drawing there as she was.

Except that she hadn't even known it existed. She hadn't posed for him, except perhaps in his memory. *They will have a witness of their happiness, cost that witness what it may.* Everything else clicked into place as she drove like a maniac back to Wellspring. The way Jenna had looked at her when she came in. The petty acts of jealous spite she'd been capable of right after Angela broke things off with her.

Jenna had gone to his studio to crate the paintings. God knows where she had found the drawing hidden, and where and when she'd had it framed. Stephen had helped her hang the show. The drawing must have gone up later, probably just before they had all arrived that evening.

Angela sat in Marty's coffee shop, staggered by memory. And she'd had enough cups of strong black coffee to make her heart quicken and skip. All the time she had been there, only a few people had gone in or out of Charlotte's building. A woman with a baby and bags of groceries worked her way up the stoop and disappeared through the front door, and about half an hour later two men emerged and went arm in arm down the street under the sudden bloom of a big black umbrella. But there was no sign of Charlotte.

Other diners were coming in to Marty's; they would probably need her table soon. She'd have to give up this convenient post and find another place to wait and watch. She signaled for the waitress to bring the check, and began to gather her books and purse and umbrella.

When she was standing and putting on her slicker, she glanced through the window again, in time to see a leggy young blond woman without any rain gear stride down the street and hurry up the steps of the tenement across the street. Angela rushed to the door of the coffee shop and out into the street. "Charlotte!" she called. "Sharly! Wait!"

12.

Letting Sleeping Dogs Lie

Pete and Bill were guide-dog school dropouts; that's why they'd been put up for adoption. The woman at the agency had said that they were intelligent enough for the job, just not very motivated. "They might have had a brilliant career," she told Michelle, wistfully, "if they weren't so darn distractible."

Michelle was already familiar with the dogs, and may have contributed to their distractibility. She had volunteered to take them, newly weaned, along with a female littermate, for several consecutive weekends of "socialization," in preparation for their training to accompany and assist the blind.

"Just what we needed," Jo Ann said when Michelle first brought home the carton of squirming, mewling puppies. But beneath her sarcastic tone she seemed to genuinely mean it, to acknowledge that the family needed *something* to provide comfort and amusement.

This was several years after Jack Cutty had been washed overboard in a sudden storm during his regular three-day tuna run, but his absence still hung over the household like a pall. Maybe that was because his body had never been recovered. "Just what we needed," Jo Ann said again, sticking her fingers into the carton and allowing them to be nibbled on and suckled.

Eddie wasn't living there anymore by then—he'd moved in with Kathleen, a couple of years before he was able to convince her to marry him. But he came by his mother's place regularly to visit and help out with the heavy chores. Bear-like Eddie was a self-proclaimed animal lover, although he hunted, and he tended to tease and play roughly with the dogs, pretty much the way he'd always treated Michelle.

"Well, looky here, it's the pee patrol," he said when he first saw Pete and Bill and their sister, Gidget, skidding around on newspapers in a penned-off section of the kitchen. Then he grabbed a dish towel and began waving it at them like a bullfighter's cape, and they scrambled all over one another to get to it. By the time Eddie left, the dish towel was in shreds and the puppies lay in an exhausted heap.

At night, Michelle took them upstairs and into bed with her. She wasn't supposed to; that was more socialization than was required, or recommended. But they were going to yelp all night down in the kitchen, anyway, keeping her awake. This would just save her a few trips, not to mention the loss of sleep.

As the woman at the training place later said, the pups were intelligent enough; at least they knew that the big ticking alarm clock, even wrapped in a heated towel, wasn't their mother's drumming heart, and that the stuffed Lassie left over from Michelle's childhood was merely a toy, something to be exposed as an imposter and destroyed by tiny, needle-sharp teeth. Maybe they'd also figured out that Michelle wasn't their mother, after roaming the bed in a vain search for golden fur and milky teats, and just settled, finally, for her second best, but available, human presence.

She played with them all the time. As they got older, and she was supposed to start allowing them more independence and solitude, she initiated games, like Find the Ball or Catch the Windup Car, with rewards of forbidden people food. "You're getting them all revved up," Jo Ann would complain. "And stop feeding them that hamburger. That's our supper."

But Michelle couldn't control herself. She even woke the dogs for company when she was unable to sleep, because of lovesickness over some boy, or for imagining her father growing old on a distant desert island—the fantasy she'd long outgrown but couldn't quite throw off—or, worse, lying in his lapping grave.

Maybe Gidget had a better sense of duty or of her destiny than her brothers. After all those weekends of nonstop fun, she turned out to be focused and trainable, and went on to become some unknown, unsighted person's guide and companion. But the boys were declared hopeless—they'd already begun chasing cars and squirrels, even deer in season, sometimes deserting their "blind" charges in the middle of the road—and eventually Michelle got to keep them.

As they grew up, their separate personalities emerged—Pete the adventurer, the gang leader, who even dreamed about the chase, his legs twitching and churning in his sleep, and sweet, shy Bill, who was given to bouts of sighing, and seemed to go along with Pete just for the ride.

They were almost nine years old now, not young anymore, certainly, but with a youthful spirit, like those wiry, gray-muzzled old members of the Polar Bear Club, who ran around the Main Beach parking lot in their Speedos every February to warm up before plunging into the icy ocean.

Hank was fond of the dogs and accepted them as part of the bargain, pretty much the way Michelle cared about and accepted Kayla. And Kayla, in turn, was attached to Pete and Bill; Michelle once overheard her referring to them as her stepbrothers. When you really thought about it, there was nothing preventing Hank and Michelle's relationship from ripening into something serious and final, except perhaps for his history of failure with April, and his fear of something—but of *what?*

Michelle wasn't exactly sure. But she was getting tired of it, of her own patience with him, the growing list of excuses she made to herself and everybody else on his behalf. Even Frida Kahlo and Diego Rivera had a permanent commitment—in a letter he called her "child of my eyes, life of my life"—although they sometimes lived in separate houses, and they both screwed around an awful lot. It was all in the book.

Michelle would never stand for that, she knew; she was too jealous, too possessive. Kathleen felt the same way about Eddie. "If I ever caught him with someone else," she told Michelle one afternoon as they were driving to Riverhead, "he'd be singing soprano in a heartbeat." And she honked long and hard at someone who'd dared to try passing her.

They were on their way to the Tanger Mall to buy birthday presents for Eddie, who would turn thirty the following day, a milestone that Kathleen worried might make him restless in his fidelity, or even reckless.

"Come on, Kath," Michelle said, "you know he's crazy about you." That fact was undeniable—Eddie openly adored his fiery, redheaded wife. He'd pursued her relentlessly after they met in the emergency room at Southampton hospital, where Kathleen was the nurse who'd assisted in the removal of a fishhook from Eddie's thumb. He had fainted when it was over, which she'd never let him forget.

"And he's probably scared shitless of you, too," Michelle added. They laughed. And then she said, "I just wish I could be as sure about Hank. He never even *says* it."

"What? That he's scared of you?"

"That he loves me." She hadn't ever told anyone that before, and she'd surprised herself with her sudden confession to Kathleen. Maybe it had something to do with being in the car together, speeding away from the familiar ground of their daily lives—the way you might tell secrets to a total stranger on a bus or a train. But earlier that morning, when Michelle was letting the dogs out, she'd begun to acknowledge her dissatisfaction with the way things stood with Hank.

It was a really stupid comparison, but she'd thought about how she could always *count* on Pete's and Bill's return, on their devotion, that a dog's love for a person was complete and without any ulterior motives. They had sworn themselves to her, and if they could speak, they would say so. Why shouldn't she expect the same assurance from her boyfriend?

"You're kidding, right?" Kathleen said.

"No. It's like he's not *allowed* to say it."

"You mean because of April? But they've been over for ages."

"No, no, that's not it. I don't know what it is."

"Do you want Eddie to talk to him?" Kathleen asked.

"God, no!" Michelle said. The last thing she wanted was her crazy brother strong-arming Hank into submission, or into just cutting out, and then torturing her about it for the rest of her life. "Don't even tell him, okay?" She was beginning to be sorry she'd said anything—not because she didn't trust her sister-in-law's discretion or sympathy, but because saying it aloud made it all the more true. And now she couldn't stop thinking about it.

Kathleen bought Eddie a cashmere sweater. Michelle got him a few CDs—that achy-breaky cowboy music he liked—and she picked out a couple of sport shirts for her mother to give him. The shirts were on sale, and there was a soft blue plaid one she could imagine Hank wearing, how it would pick up the blue of his eyes, and the way his hair would curl against the back edge of the collar. Right there in the middle of the Ralph Lauren outlet, she felt her knees buckle a little and her heart contract.

The party was supposed to be a surprise. Jo Ann had asked Eddie to stop by on his way home from the dock to replace the pump in her washing machine. And they'd all gone into hiding on the back deck as the zero hour approached. But Kayla stuck party hats on the dogs at the last minute, and they came running out to greet Eddie as soon as his pickup pulled into the driveway. Hank, who'd been in on the secret, doubled over laughing in the passenger seat.

"Yo, buttheads," Eddie said as Pete and Bill slobbered all over him. He was the real butthead, though, still feebly attempting to act surprised when everybody converged in the house, even starting to go down to the basement to look at the washer.

They ate grilled steaks and home fries, Eddie's favorite artery-clogging foods, and then Kathleen brought out the lopsided carrot cake she'd baked in Jo Ann's kitchen. He made a fuss over his presents: the cashmere sweater he threw right on, even though the night was muggy; the country-western music he accompanied with a falsetto twang and an air guitar; the shirts he shrugged into, one over the other on top of the sweater; and the yellow rubber Lance Armstrong bracelet Kayla had slipped off her own wrist and pushed onto his.

Michelle gathered the wrapping paper and ribbon and began to clear the cake plates. She felt nervous, almost chilled, beneath the easy pleasure of the occasion, as if she alone knew some really bad news, which she was about to reveal, spoiling everything. "Go away," she told Hank when he came into the kitchen to help her, and he was strangely obedient. She wondered if he knew intuitively that something was up.

Kayla wasn't staying over at Hank's; Hank and Michelle were supposed to take her home before spending the rest of the night together at his place. But she begged off accompanying him on the drive to Hampton Bays, so that she could finish cleaning up. She told him to come back for her later. By the time he did, her mother would be asleep and Michelle would confront him with her feelings.

After everyone was gone, Jo Ann went upstairs to bed and Michelle made short work of the kitchen. Without Jo Ann around, the dogs got to lick the plates in the dishwasher—the pre-rinse cycle, Hank called it—and then Michelle let them out and went upstairs, too, to take a shower, shunning her scented soap in favor of her mother's industrial-strength bar of Dial. She even shampooed with it.

When she stood in front of the mirror in her bedroom, toweling her hair dry, she noticed that a few dark hairs, like spiders' legs, had sprung up again between her brows, threatening to reunite them. She rummaged in the dresser drawer for a pair of tweezers, but changed her mind before she could find them.

Then she shimmied into a pair of oversized carpenter's pants and a faded T-shirt, and looked in the mirror again. Her face was scrubbed free of makeup, including the candy-flavored lip gloss Hank loved. Even the seven little silver studs were gone from her earlobes, like stars from a morning sky. This wasn't going to be a seduction scene. If Hank ended up saying the right thing, it would be because of something a lot deeper than just sexual attraction.

Michelle went downstairs, barefoot, and opened the screen door for the Labs. They should have been there by now, waiting for her, ready to nose their way back into the house; the lower screen was full of puckers to prove it. She'd left the porch light on for them, but there was only the usual cluster of moths and gnats in its beam. She gave two short whistles, their signal, and listened for the clinking of the dogs' collars, the sound of their paws padding across the grass.

She hoped they hadn't caught something, that Pete wouldn't come trotting up with some small, dying creature in his jaws, Bill right behind him, a cheerful accessory to the crime. That had already happened a couple of times. On her birthday in May, they'd brought a screaming rabbit, and dropped it, like a gift, at her feet. "Come on, guys, let's go," she whispered into the darkness past the porch.

When they still didn't come, she went back inside for the flashlight and her shoes and then went looking for them. Hank came by a few minutes later, and she got into the car beside him. They drove slowly around the neighborhood—up and down Lincoln Avenue, where that mean, territorial rottweiler lived, but he appeared to be in for the night; that house was dark. And so was the one on Eau Claire, with the loony old woman who was said to set out pellets of cheese laced with rat poison under the trees in her yard. The boys would eat anything that wasn't nailed down.

Michelle didn't give voice to any of the terrible thoughts in her head, that might have given them credence. She'd learned her lesson all those hours ago, in another lifetime, it seemed, when she'd spoken up to Kathleen about Hank. But maybe he'd read her mind, because he said, "Don't worry, okay?" And he took one hand from the wheel and put it on her thigh—his hand, his hand!—and under the dumb camouflage of the carpenter's pants she felt her blood leap up in response. As they were about to go by her own house for the second or third time, she saw that the dogs were waiting on the porch. They seemed to be laughing.

13.

The Specials of the Day

Angela's mind seemed to be elsewhere. She kept gazing out past the screen of the gazebo, as if she expected someone else to show up. But the Page Turners were all there, for once— even Ardith Templeton—with their books open on their laps and their eyes turned to the dark, speckled sun of Angela's face as they waited for her to begin.

Lissy sneaked a glance at Ardith, whose appearance at the meeting, her first in weeks, had been such a nice surprise. She was as coolly lovely and stubbornly inscrutable as ever, in what looked like a pair of men's white silk pajamas. But what had Lissy expected—that she would give off some spark or scent to betray her secret life? The rumors about Ardith had escalated since the brunch, but no one was absolutely sure of anything.

The novel they were about to discuss was *Madame Bovary*, which seemed eerily appropriate, and gave Lissy an advantage of sorts, since she had read most of it in college. She'd even written the bones of a term paper about the text's symbols and prefigurations that Cynthia Ann Pope had fleshed out for a small fee. Lissy especially remembered Charles Bovary's dead first wife's dried wedding flowers, and newlywed Emma wondering what would happen to her own flowers after her death.

At Lissy and Jeffrey's wedding, she'd tossed a mock-up of her bouquet of calla lilies and folded aspidistra to her squealing circle of single friends, and then had the real thing preserved by a freeze-drying vacuum process. Those flowers, which she kept on her dressing table in the Manhattan apartment, still looked perfect in their little glass-topped shadow box. They certainly wouldn't bring morbid thoughts to anyone's mind.

"So," Angela said at last, "what do you think of Emma?"

It was funny, really, the way everyone looked directly at Ardith, as if they were all in a play, and her cue to speak had just been delivered.

"Not much," Ardith said. "She's boring and self-centered. And she has lousy taste in men."

That was pretty much what people in Lissy's Lit 101 class had said years ago, and although her own take on Emma Bovary was more sympathetic—after all, she ends up dying for *pages and pages*—Lissy couldn't comfortably say so because her paper, with Cynthia Ann's substantial contribution, didn't reflect that opinion. But somebody else finally came to poor Emma's defense, saying that she was the product of narrow provincial life and thought, and that Flaubert had punished her much too severely for her unoriginal sins.

Yet here was Ardith, the probable proverbial pot calling the kettle black. And the others agreed with her immediately, like a church choir seconding a critical point in a sermon.

"So what did they see in *her*?" Brenda wanted to know.

"She was hot, apparently, and an easy lay, for a narcissist," Joy declared, fondling a strand of her own hair.

"Right," Deb said, "but what a lamebrain. I mean, listen to this." And she read a line of Emma's dialogue from the novel in simpering tones. " 'I find nothing as inspiring as sunsets,' she said, 'but especially at the seashore.' "

Lissy blushed; she'd often thought that the sunsets at Main Beach were really awesome. It was one of the few things in nature she actually liked. "Well, her husband is pretty boring, too," she heard herself say, which is what she might have said in that lit class if she'd felt confident enough, and she thought that Ardith looked at her with more than passing interest for the first time.

Angela perked up, too. "Ah, but he saves her from herself, doesn't he?" she said. "He romanticizes her, the way Emma romanticizes her own shoddy little affairs. And he endows her with more than surface beauty from the moment he meets her." And she read aloud the passage near the beginning of the novel in which Charles Bovary admires both the deep color and the "bold candor" of Emma's eyes.

Everyone in the gazebo seemed to go into a little reverie then. It was like those moments of silence in assembly at Betsy Ross, when you were supposed to think about a classmate who had died, or children starving in faraway places. That was probably the headmistress's way of dealing with the controversy over school prayer. Lissy had never been able to concentrate on the designated victims. She had thought about herself, mostly, in the dreary silence, about how hungry she was for lunch, and that she, too, might possibly die someday. Maybe all of her schoolmates had similar selfish thoughts, despite their bowed heads and fixed expressions of sorrow.

She could swear that the other women in the gazebo were also turned inward, rather than toward Emma Bovary and her shallow life and terrible death. Deb closed her book and her eyes, holding two fingers to her wrist, while Joy worried a hangnail with her teeth. Brenda surreptitiously checked her cell phone for messages. Ardith might have been thinking about Guido, and a torrid moment in the recent past or the near future, or of Larry and the treacherous terrain of their marriage; it was hard to tell. Even Angela had that glassy-eyed look of introspection, of a retreat into memory.

As for Lissy, she felt a quiver of apprehension. She flipped through the pages of her book, the way Evie used to search for a comforting passage in the Bible, and her finger came to rest on the part where Emma and Rodolphe are about to ride their horses into the forest. Slowly and methodically, she traced the words, careful not to move her lips as she read. *She kept turning her head away in order to avoid his gaze, and then she would see nothing but the evenly spaced trunks of the pine trees, the unbroken succession of which made her slightly dizzy.*

There were pine trees all around the gazebo, and Lissy was so easily suggestible, she had her own long moment of vertigo when she looked out at them. Her heart was a flurry of hoofbeats. *Think of the starving children,* she told herself sternly, over and over, until the feeling passed.

• • •

That night, Lissy picked Jeffrey up at the jitney stop in Bridgehampton and drove them out to Montauk, where she'd made a nine thirty reservation at The Battered Clam. A little late for them, but she was lucky to get anything there at practically the last minute. The restaurant's name was redolent of the local cuisine and of mob culture at once, but maybe that was because she knew the reputation of its owner, Guido Masconi, who was supposed to be an evident and amiable host in The Clam's dining room.

It was still one of the area's most popular eateries, and even the midweek off-hour didn't diminish the crowd and its celebratory roar. "Jesus, Liss," Jeffrey said in the din, "what are we doing here?" and Lissy cupped her ear and smiled at him, shaking her head. What could she say? She knew very well that he preferred smaller, quieter places closer to home, like the 1770 House or The Maidstone Arms, especially after a long and difficult day at the office. And he wouldn't be happy to hear that it was mere, albeit burning, curiosity that had drawn her to this madhouse.

Lissy had told him the whole story about Ardith and her alleged lover when they were in bed the night after their brunch, and he was skeptical and disapproving then. He couldn't see big, powerful Larry Templeton as a cuckold, and he said that rumors of that sort flew around the Hamptons every summer like flies. "Don't you and your girlfriends have anything better to do?" he'd asked.

Now she watched nervously as he made a survey of the hectic room, looking vainly for someone he knew. The hostess apparently didn't know Lissy and Jeffrey, either; despite their confirmed reservation, they had to wait in the crush at the bar for about twenty minutes.

They were jostled a few times, and people screamed and laughed right in their faces. Jeffrey groaned. "C'mon," he insisted, "why'd you pick this joint?"

"Oh, just for a change," Lissy said, evasively. "Why don't you have a nice stiff drink, honey? I'm the designated driver tonight."

By the time they were seated, he was starting on his second vodka tonic and his mood had lifted a little. There was a basket of warm, crusty bread on the table, and a dish of tiny fried olives. Soon a busboy brought a bottle of chilled mineral water. "See," Lissy said, patting Jeffrey's hand. "This isn't so bad, is it?"

And she went through her purse in search of the picture postcards, both bearing the same slick image of the Eiffel Tower, that had come that morning from Paris, from Miranda and Miles. Nothing made him feel better than any sort of contact with his children. An adult, their mother probably, had addressed the cards, with some sadistic motive in mind—like, *see how far away they are!*—just to Jeffrey. Lissy didn't even get a mention.

The handwriting in both messages was awful, as usual, as if they were written by someone blindfolded on a bumpy bus ride, but this time it was awful in French. *"Papa, ici le Tour Eiffel,"* Miles had written, and Miranda had conjugated a list of verbs for her father's delectation. *"Je suis, tu es, il est, nous sommes . . ."* Not a single *"Je t'aime,"* in the lot. Still, Jeffrey wiped happy tears from his eyes.

Then the waiter came and boomed out the specials of the day. There were several offerings for each course, and all of them seemed to require a complex explanation. Basically, it was a lot of seafood, none of it simple battered clams.

There was a she-crab velouté, prepared with aged Solera sherry; a brandade, in appetizer and entrée portions; the chef's signature Catalan Suquet; and a whole dorado or pompano, to be filleted tableside and dressed with a choice of innovative glazes and reductions Lissy had trouble remembering or even imagining.

And after that dazzling recital, they were handed menus as large and glossy as annual reports. Lissy used hers to shield her face as she scoured the room for Guido Masconi. She could probably ask for him, but under what pretext?

In a little while, he appeared, unsummoned, at their table, and he was shorter than she'd expected, and not terribly handsome, except in a thuggish, simian way. He definitely had a manly presence, but he also had a bull neck and a pinkie ring. God knew he wasn't Lissy's type; *Jeffrey* was her type. And Guido Masconi was spoken for—she was suddenly positive of that. It was as if Ardith herself had just told her so in a fevered whisper. As if they were chummy enough to exchange such confidences in the first place.

Masconi put one broad hand on Jeffrey's back and flashed his considerable smile at Lissy. "Good evening, my friends," he said, his baritone pouring over them like a dark liqueur. "Are we treating you well? Have you heard the specials yet?" *Hot tongue on the half shell. Cock au vin.*

Lissy saw Jeffrey shrink slightly in his seat. He didn't like to be touched by strangers. "Yes, thanks," he said, curtly, so Lissy spoke up before Masconi could back away. "But what exactly is a brandade?" she asked.

It was probably Flaubert's fault. Didn't Angela once say that literature teaches you how to live? And there was Emma, a romance reader, besotted by the atmosphere at the ball—the mirrors and the candles—

and the smells of the meat and truffles and her lover's pomade. Maybe the life lesson came at the end of the novel, in her long agony. But you didn't have to read it all the way through if you didn't want to.

"What was that all about?" Jeffrey asked when Guido Masconi finally left their side.

"What do you mean?" Lissy said. But she couldn't hold it in any longer. *"He's the one,"* she hissed, and she sat back in her chair and hugged herself, waiting for his reaction.

"What one?"

"That I told you about." She looked quickly around her for possible eavesdroppers, and then she leaned forward and said, "You know, with *Ardith.*"

Jeffrey sighed and shook his head. "Don't tell me *that's* why we came all the way out here," he said.

"Well . . . ," she said. But she couldn't pretend that it was for the ambience or even for the food, which began to arrive soon after, with great ceremony, on oversized, overheated plates.

"Lissy, darling," Jeffrey said, "get your head out of the clouds. The Templetons have a prenup that would put your little friend back in Astoria before she could blink."

"Everything isn't about money," Lissy mumbled, looking down glumly at her diver scallops.

But everything *was* about money, of course. You could never completely forget that out here. It made all the difference between one side of the highway and the other, between Kmart and London Jewelers, between labor and leisure, between being herself and what's-her-name—Michelle—with whom she'd bumped heads under the kitchen table the day of the brunch. "Imagine the other," Angela had instructed the Page Turners when they were about to start reading *Villette,* and Lissy finally had, if only for one dazed, head-pounding instant.

She picked up her fork and then put it back down, carefully aligning it with the edge of her plate. "Excuse me," she told Jeffrey, "I'll be right back." And before he could say anything, she stood and headed toward the rear of the dining room. She almost collided with a waiter who had just come through the swinging kitchen door and was balancing a tray of desserts on his shoulder. "Excuse me," she said again. "Are the restrooms this way?"

"It's you," the waiter said, and the tray tilted precariously toward Lissy until he righted it.

"Pardon?" she said, looking blankly at him.

He was young and nice-looking in his Battered Clam server's uniform—a black turtleneck and black jeans. His dark hair was caught up in a ponytail. "Abracadabra?" he said. "Presto change-o?"

"Oh," she said, "you've lost your mustache." The naked space above his lip—what was that called again?—was charmingly indented. She was aware of the muscles in his arms, the slope of his jaw. He looked so different now; maybe he really was a sorcerer.

"Yeah," he said. "Hey, you look beautiful. I'm sorry I made you disappear."

"I haven't booked any more children's parties," Lissy said, apologetically. That was true, but she'd never had the intention of hiring him again, in any case.

"That's all right," he said. "This pays better."

"Well," she said. There was a sign beyond him, pointing to the restrooms.

"I don't suppose you're here alone," he said.

"No, no, I'm not." But she didn't say that she was with her husband. "Well," she said again, aware of someone glaring at them through the porthole window in the kitchen. She indicated his tray. "They must be famished." *Think of the starving children.*

When she was in the restroom, patting her face with a damp paper towel, she heard the inevitable crash of dishes in the dining room.

14.

The King of the Golden Mountain

There was a low cloud cover early on the morning of the Fisherman's Fair, but by ten o'clock the clouds had lifted to reveal saffron sunlight, and all of the vendors were set up under their canopies, ready for business. Angela loved this annual event held on the grounds of Ashawagh Hall, spilling over across the road onto The Springs Library lawn. It was a commercial endeavor, of course, but relatively modest and low-key. She imagined that the men and women and children buried in the little church cemetery in the near distance had once attended similar fairs on similar bright summer mornings, and the sense of history and continuity pleased her.

This year she had a particular mission, to buy a gift for Charlotte, whose birthday—her twenty-fourth!—was coming up in early September, an excuse to contact her again. But none of the jewelry or pottery on the crafts tables seemed to be right. The only piece of jewelry Charlotte had been wearing that rainy day in the city was a dented silver bangle that might have been her mother's. It had looked familiar to Angela, setting off a riffle of nostalgia and anxiety.

She bought a clam pie to take home for her lunch, a jar of home-made blackberry jam, some potted rosemary, and a string of raffle tickets to benefit the Animal Rescue Fund. The prizes were the same as they were in previous years: dinner for two at various local restaurants. She had never won anything, but she couldn't resist those canine and feline poster children gazing beseechingly at her, and the young women behind the raffle table who were so clearly impassioned by their cause.

Angela had given some thought, from time to time, to getting a pet. One winter, she'd fed a little band of feral cats that hung around her yard, stalking the birds. If any of them had made the first move, she might have taken it inside, but they all remained aloof and predatory, and then, before the spring thaw, simply disappeared. A domesticated cat with a quiet demeanor and an independent spirit—even a couple of cats—would have suited her more than a demonstrative dog. But then she would start thinking of how easily she could be seen, in her solitary life, as a crazy cat lady, a poor woman's version of *Grey Gardens*.

The library had purged itself of books that had not been borrowed from their shelves since the previous Fisherman's Fair, and they were up for sale, bargains all, arranged loosely by category on tables around the lawn: fiction, nonfiction, children's, cookbooks. Maybe she would find something among them suitable for Charlotte—the unlikely trophy of a fine first edition, or an especially handsome volume on art.

In any case, this was Angela's favorite part of the fair, although her house was already overrun with books. She should be giving some of them away rather than looking for others. Yet there was a wonderfully eclectic assortment here that reflected the eclectic community. The local writers' own galleys and remainders, with their boastful, futile blurbs; the ancient books on science and economics, many of their theories and postulations long disproved; the detective stories and romances, advertised as easy beach reading by the sand that spilled out when you opened them; the outgrown, scribbled-in children's books; the astrology and psychology and gardening guides; and the cookbooks whose spattered pages gave indelible proof of their best recipes.

Angela browsed through the books on every table. She liked discovering inscriptions and annotations, and the letters or store receipts used as bookmarks. Someone who'd apparently only made it halfway through *The Red and the Black* had paused in the middle of the Napoleonic Wars to buy a lawn sprinkler at the True Value hardware store. Someone else—a high school girl, judging from the handwriting and all the *i*'s dotted with tiny hearts—had scrawled expletives: "Fucking boring! Stupid jerkoff!" throughout *Silas Marner,* which she had probably been forced to read by an unimaginative teacher. Angela had been assigned the same book at Port Richmond High and had felt the same way. Why didn't they start them off with *Middlemarch* instead?

She had gathered an armload of books for herself and, for Charlotte, a few old copies of *ARTnews* addressed to Perle Fine, an abstract expressionist who was dead now, but who'd lived in The Springs. Then, on the children's table, Angela found a copy of the Grimms' fairy tales that closely resembled the one she'd read aloud to Charlotte such a long time ago, about Fundevogel and Snow White.

The dust jacket of this one was missing, but it had a red cloth cover like that earlier edition, with an inset picture from one of the stories, "The King of the Golden Mountain." Under the matching illustration inside, of two men—one young, one elderly—being addressed by an evil-looking dwarfed creature, the caption read, "My business is with your father and not with you." Serendipity, the only religion in which Angela believed.

Heather, one of the library volunteers, checked out Angela's purchases, and her colleague, Mary Ann, gave her a Waldbaum's shopping bag in which to cart them away. Then someone behind Angela said, "Find any treasures?" It was Irene Rush, from the antiques shop on North Main, in her signature skinny, threadbare jeans, and with her graying auburn hair pulled back with a scrunchie. Like Angela, she didn't try to look younger by using makeup or camouflaging scarves, but managed to somehow, anyway. She was carrying her own bulging shopping bags, with the rusty spout of a blue watering can hanging out the top of one of them.

"They seem like treasures, don't they?" Angela said. "At least until we get them home."

"Ah, but I can resell my mistakes," Irene said. "Anyway, I couldn't stop myself from looking for whatever I'm always looking for, even if I wanted to."

"I know," Angela said, as if there were some ultimate consolation prize to be found among the detritus of other people's lives.

"But I'm ready to call it quits for now," Irene said, hefting her bags. "Do you want to unload and get some coffee in town?"

"I'd like to," Angela said, "I really would, but there are so many things I have to do today." That was both true and untrue. She did have to prepare some notes for her reading groups, and the flower beds were in urgent need of weeding, but none of that would take the entire rest of the day, and something else was on her mind.

At home again, she ate the reheated clam pie with the book of Grimms' tales propped in front of her. She had never read "The King of the Golden Mountain" before. Like so many of the other stories in the collection, it was about loss and redemption, but it was particularly dark and convoluted, the way troubled dreams often are, and in a little while Angela grew sleepy and had to go into the bedroom and lie down.

In her dream, she was in Texas—she somehow knew that, although nothing in the landscape was identifiable. Just scraggly fields and a mirage-like snowcapped mountain in the distance. And then her mother appeared, dressed entirely in black, with a heavy black veil almost concealing her face. They were at someone's funeral. Angela knew that it couldn't be her father's; her mother had preceded him in death. Even dreaming like that, a certain sense of logic was still in place.

She felt so oppressively sad, holding her mother's cold, black-gloved hand as they stood at the brink of the grave, and aware of the ironic fact that *they* were the Graveses. I am asleep, she told herself, this is only a dream. But wasn't that what you imagined when you were awake and wished that you weren't? The sun on the mountain gave the snowcap a luminous golden patina. "Stephen!" her mother cried from behind the veil that muffled and disguised her voice. "Stephen!" she said again, in Angela's own voice this time, and she awoke before she could be pitched down into the darkness right on top of him.

It was as easy to decipher as an O'Henry story, right down to the tacky surprise ending. It was not really a surprise, though, except to her unconscious mind, which had mostly closed itself off these past weeks to the fact of Stephen's death. When Charlotte told her, she had felt a convulsive shock, as if she had grabbed hold of a live wire, but she hadn't screamed or done anything else that would have given her away. A lifetime of reserve must have protected her. Their conversation had continued; eventually the subject was changed. God.

"Sharly!" she'd called, and Charlotte had turned around and looked at her without a glimmer of recognition. "It's Angela, Angela Graves," she said. "I knew you in Texas, a long time ago, when you were a child."

"Oh," Charlotte said. She moved a step or two backward, as if she'd been pushed. "I think I remember. You were my mother's friend."

Angela almost let out a cry of relief, of horror. "Yes, I was. I taught at Macon. In the English Department." She waited, but nothing in the girl's aspect indicated antagonism or even thoughtful reflection. The Charlotte that Angela had known would surely have spoken her mind by now. She was too young when it had all happened to remember it, that was all, or she had repressed everything, and no one had ever filled her in.

"Hmm," Charlotte said. Her eyeglasses were fogged; her face was streaming with rain. She glanced behind her at her building. "I live here," she said. And then, "I'd ask you to come up, but my—my roommate is sleeping."

Lover, Angela amended. "That's all right," she said. "Another time, maybe. But would you like to get something to eat?" She indicated Marty's coffee shop across the street, where she'd already put in what had felt like hours and hours of surveillance.

The girl came under her umbrella as easily as she had once slid onto Angela's lap, lured by the promise of a story or a game, and they made their way together to Marty's.

The woman behind the register said "Two?" with no more recognition in her eyes than Charlotte had had moments before. It had to do with the uniformity of old age, Angela knew, a former curse turned suddenly into a blessing.

At least they weren't seated at the same table she'd occupied alone. Instead they were ensconced cozily in a booth, where Charlotte grabbed a handful of napkins from the dispenser and wiped her face and her glasses and blotted the ends of her rain-tamed hair. The damp, crumpled napkins littered the table the way her toys had once littered the living room on Dogwood Drive. While Angela gathered them into a pile, Charlotte ordered something from the vegan side of the menu, with seitan and sprouts. Angela, already drowning internally, asked only for more coffee, iced this time. Her skin was on fire.

"*Caffeine,*" Charlotte observed, disapprovingly. "Do you eat meat?" And without waiting for an answer, she proceeded to deliver a little lecture on the brutal slaughter of innocent animals, with *faces,* and the fatty buildup in people's hearts. People at an adjacent table glared at her as they ate their hamburgers.

After their own orders had arrived, Angela remarked on the coincidence of running into Charlotte like that. She said that she lived all the way out on eastern Long Island now, but sometimes she came into the city she still missed, this neighborhood especially, for a hit of the atmosphere. Manhattan was so beautiful in the rain, wasn't it? *The lady doth protest too much, methinks.*

Charlotte seemed to buy the whole package. But why had she been so agreeable to going off with someone she barely remembered? Maybe she was poor and just wanted a free meal. Or maybe she had outgrown her childish egotism and had her mother's generous heart, a less likely possibility.

"How are your parents?" Angela asked, plunging in, but still afraid to ask about them individually.

"Mom is good," Charlotte said. After a pause she added, "And I guess you've heard about my dad."

Angela wished she had ordered hot coffee, to dissolve the marrow congealing in her bones. "No," she said. "What?"

Charlotte poked her fork at the seitan, as if she were looking for something unpleasant under the pale, gelatinous little cubes. "He passed away. He died," she said, correcting herself.

Angela clutched the edge of the table. "No," she repeated, a hoarse, feeble protest this time. "When?"

"Five years ago. Almost six."

"I'm so sorry," Angela said.

"Yeah," Charlotte murmured.

"What happened?" Angela asked. *Let it be quick,* she silently begged, as if it hadn't yet happened.

"Cancer," Charlotte said, a word she uttered with authority, but that she surely hadn't even known the last time she and Angela had spoken. "Lung," she said. "*Both* lungs," she added, almost proudly, as if to say that Sharly's father would have never done things half-assed.

But he hadn't smoked, at least when Angela knew him. A moronic, knee-jerk thought, but she was trying to be practical, to fight off the urge to become hysterical, and she needed something or someone to blame. "Sorry," she said again, and closed her eyes momentarily against the onslaught of images. Ivan Ilych in his protracted suffering, paintings of the Crucifixion, her own father struggling for breath at Bellevue in the final stages of congestive heart failure. Stephen, alive. *Let me look at you.*

She had steadied herself and asked after Valerie then, the way any concerned, if long-lost, friend would have done under the same circumstances. "How is your mother doing?" was the way she'd put it.

"Okay, like I said. She's still in Indiana, you know." Indiana? Charlotte ate a little of her food, washing it down with a swig of water. "Retired now. But active." That young person's euphemism for doing things that don't really matter with the time you have left. "Hey, you guys should be in touch! Do you do e-mail? Give me your address, and I'll send it to her."

"I don't even have a computer," Angela admitted, and Charlotte eyed her with that old impatient, imperious expression. "You're kidding," she said. But she didn't ask any other questions, and Angela, unnerved by the girl's continued silent inspection of her, said, "Tell me about you. What are you doing with your life?"

That's how she had blithely changed the subject, after allotting only a couple of minutes to Stephen and his death, and even less to Valerie and her survival. She'd found out that Charlotte was studying painting at Parsons, after getting a B.A. from Ball State. Her boyfriend, Jimmy, aka the J-Man, the J. Schwartz on the doorbell nameplate, was an actor. They supported themselves one way or another. Angela hardly listened after that. She'd taken Charlotte's phone number without offering her own. All she could think of was that, somehow, she had gotten off scot-free.

In her bed in The Springs the day of the Fisherman's Fair, Angela felt queasy. The clam pie, probably, and lying down so soon after she'd eaten. Her legs ached, too, as if she'd been running in her sleep. She chewed an antacid tablet and took two of her pain pills. No more shellfish for a while, or standing on her feet too long. A little later, the phone rang. It was someone calling from Ashawagh Hall to tell her that she had won one of the raffle prizes: dinner for two at a restaurant in Montauk called The Battered Clam. She didn't know whether to laugh or to throw up.

The book of fairy tales was still open on the kitchen table where she'd left it, and the issues of *ARTnews* in a little stack nearby. She took the magazines back to bed with her and browsed through the glossy color reproductions of paintings—Turner's burning skies, de Kooning's ferocious, fractured women. How marvelous they were. She stroked a page and then sniffed it. But it only smelled like someone's moldy basement.

Had Charlotte told her mother yet about their "chance" meeting in the Village? She probably had by now, stirring up all that old, surely nearly extinguished, sorrow and rage. But it was still not too late to simply drop out of the picture before any more harm could be done, the way Stephen and Valerie had, so many years before.

Charlotte's life and certainly her ego had not been destroyed. She was studying art and she had a live-in boyfriend. She mourned her father and cared about her mother. Angela felt her own defenses mounting. *My business is with your father and not with you.*

Valerie was another story, of course. But what could Angela hope to accomplish there, anyway: a grand scene of rapprochement? Some miraculous expiation of her own guilt? Maybe just a chance to explain—but explain *what*? That she had never posed for the drawing, that she'd had no intention of hurting anyone with her deranged appetites. And that all she felt now in her ruined, cranky body was useless regret. It had been over for such a long time.

And then she was back with him in another bed, in another room she couldn't really remember except for its tangy fragrance of body oils and paint oils, where he took her into his arms and led her slowly up that slippery ramp of love, of sex, of sexual love, both of them scrambling for purchase, climbing each other with a grunting effort toward some remote peak of what seemed like happiness then, that lost kingdom of the golden mountain.

15.

Wishing Will Make It So

When Jack Cutty was lost off the deck of the *Maureen Claire* in a sudden squall, Michelle was thirteen years old. Eddie was eighteen and had been going out on regular fishing runs with his father for a few months. He was onboard the day of Jack's disappearance, just a little more than an arm's length away when it happened, and he had nightmares about it for months afterward. Michelle would wake in the dark to the overlapping voices of her mother and brother—Jo Ann's steady and calming, and his working its way down gradually from noisy anguish to a quieter grieving, a boy crying for his missing dad.

Michelle was more inclined to keep things to herself. She'd almost grown out of her Beatles fantasy by then, but she was still in a state of disconnectedness from everyone in her given family. How could she belong to them? It wasn't true, it wasn't fair. Her mother with her wide nurse's shoes and red, sympathetic face; her brother who either tormented or ignored Michelle, and shot innocent deer and rabbits in the woods. Her unknowable father. She had tried to break their hold on her; if Eddie had actually seen Jack Cutty vanish, washed away in a moment like some soluble stain, she had willed it.

Never mind that she'd only been a child then; some children have uncanny abilities. She had wished for a kitten once, and a sweet, bedraggled tabby had shown up mewling at the back door the very next day. And what about the time she'd implored God—right in church—to kill Mrs. Blaney, the fifth-grade phys ed teacher who'd made her climb the ropes when she had her period? She was one of the first girls in her grade to get it, when it was still mostly a rumor among them, as unlikely as those other rumors, about disgusting sex and everlasting death.

Michelle didn't wave a magic wand, or wriggle her nose, like Samantha on those reruns of *Bewitched,* to wield her amazing powers. She simply shut her eyes and thought so fiercely about what she wanted that her brain ached. Most of the time, though, it didn't work, which was just as well because she often wished for things in a fit of temper or with the injudiciousness of a child. What would she have done with a billion dollars, anyway? And Mrs. Blaney didn't inhale her gym whistle or die of food poisoning in the school cafeteria. Her car was rammed into one morning by a drunk driver, and it turned out that she had kids herself.

The lack of a resolution in Jack Cutty's disappearance was both Michelle's cross and her redemption. She didn't tell anyone, but she knew that if she had thought the word *die* instead of *disappear* at the supper table, while he unsuspectingly chewed the flounder or bass he'd caught that morning, a fish bone might have lodged in his throat then and there. There would have been a scene of dying, a dead body, a viewing, a burial. What people today called "closure," and was supposed to be comforting, but made her think of the slamming shut of a coffin lid, with the light of the world on one side and suffocating darkness on the other.

As it happened, there was a belated but official finding of death by drowning, followed by a funeral service without a coffin at the overflowing church, where the mourners sang "They Cast Their Nets at Galilee" and "Jesus Is My Anchor." A few months later, Jo Ann was listening to some golden oldies radio station while she prepared dinner, and they played a song called "Wishing," which began *Wish-ing will make it so . . .* Michelle, who was doing her homework at the kitchen table, looked up sharply at her mother. But she was whistling softly along with the music and didn't seem to be thinking of Michelle at all.

What she began to recognize as mere superstitious practice, like the fear of broken mirrors or Friday the thirteenth, continued to have its hold over Michelle. There were lucky pennies and unlucky pennies, heads or tails. She could play solitaire for hours, with the outcome of each game coupled to the outcome of some event in her life.

Magical thinking again, but she was careful not to make the stakes very high. If I win this hand, she'd tell herself, I'll pass the history midterm. If I lose this one, there won't be another snow day all winter. It was the way she caught Hank's attention, finally, after mooning after him for years. *He will really look at me,* she thought, laying out the full deck of cards in a variation of solitaire called Threes, and her heart ascended with every upturned ace.

Michelle's father had taught her how to play in the first place. She was sick with something that had kept her out of school, sick enough for Eddie to have been solicitous, for him, letting the water run before he gave her the drink she'd begged for, and then playing a couple of rounds of War with her, although he cheated, pulling winning cards for himself from the bottom of the deck.

Her father came home from work before her mother. He didn't put his palm to her forehead as soon as he walked in, the way Jo Ann would have done. He just asked her how she felt, and then stood quietly in the doorway, and even from that distance and with her stuffed-up nose, she could detect the salty, fishy leather of his skin, an aroma she'd later recognize in her female self and try to bathe away with scented soaps.

The cards were still on her bed, scattered across the coverlet, the queen of diamonds and two of spades irrevocably bent because she had slept on them. He gathered them all up and sat down on the side of the bed, shuffling the cards between his roughened hands with surprising dexterity. Then he began to lay them out in a row, slowly and deliberately—the first one, a red king, faceup, the next six cards facedown, and so on. And it worked out perfectly that first time, a miracle that gave her lasting false hope for the possibilities of chance.

Michelle was a quick study. She learned that classic version of the game in just a couple of hands. In the next few days, he taught her some of the others: Klondike, Pyramid, Spider, Golf, and Threes. By the time she went back to school, she was an expert of sorts, already beginning to make bets with herself against the outcome of individual games.

There must have been other such easy moments between her father and herself, but she was hard-pressed to recall them, or unsure of what she'd invented and what had actually taken place. She had never seen her parents kiss or dance together, although they must have. What did she really know about him? The few facts that her mother released, gradually, over the years: that his mother used to hit him with a wooden spoon; that he'd grown a mustache when he was seventeen to look older and joined the navy; that he'd once wanted to move to Australia, but Jo Ann didn't want to leave East Hampton, where she was born and had grown up.

Was Michelle's real life, if not her true family, waiting, unused, somewhere Down Under? It was one of those unanswerable questions that still came into her head once in a while, especially when she was doing some mindless chore at Lissy Snyder's. This time she was scooping the seeds out of cucumber wedges and filling them with salmon mousse, in preparation for another meeting of that book club, while

Lissy was upstairs getting dressed. She had been at it for more than an hour.

Lissy's room would look like a disaster scene afterward, the bed and floor strewn with all the clothing she'd decided *not* to wear, and Michelle would have to go up there and put everything away. In Australia, she might have been a sheep rancher. The boys would have loved that, except that she wouldn't ever have known them; they would have had another life, too, maybe as the disciplined and contented companions of a blind couple. And what about Hank, and Kayla? She shook her head, as if to clear it—her crazy thoughts were wearing her out.

Then the women began arriving for the book club meeting, and Lissy came downstairs to greet them, in jeans and a plain cotton shirt after all that time. They strolled out to the gazebo together, yakking away, and Michelle went upstairs to straighten the bedroom. As she'd suspected, there was clothing everywhere, and the usual makeup tubes and jars littering the dressing table.

She had gotten bolder in her exploration of Lissy's things, and now she sat right down on the ottoman in front of the mirror and carefully applied some eye shadow, in a shade called Wood Violet, using her pinkie rather than the little felt-tipped wand. The eye shadow could be removed later with a few swipes of a damp, flushable Kleenex. She checked her watch. There was plenty of time; she was supposed to deliver the snacks in forty minutes, and Lissy would telephone if she needed anything before then.

Michelle wasn't sure why she suddenly became aware of the ottoman beneath her as something more than just a seat. Maybe her old intuitive powers were still at work. But she didn't really know until she stood and tugged at the top that it was cleverly hinged inside the leather tufting and lifted easily to reveal a secret storage place.

At first glance, Lissy's stash was disappointing. No drugs or money. There was a teddy bear, with one golden glass eye missing, and its coat as worn as a heavily trafficked rug; a few faded photos of someone, a large woman holding a golden-haired little girl; and a note-book, the kind Michelle had used in elementary school, with a black-and-white-speckled cover and lined pages.

She figured this last was probably another relic of Lissy's child-hood, and she opened it, expecting to find the kind of homework she dimly remembered from her own past—pages of numbers or letters printed out with pencil in a fat, childish hand that wasn't always able to stay within the lines.

Instead the writing was a cramped longhand that took Michelle several seconds to decipher. There was a recent date at the top of each page, followed by a rundown of that day's activities. A kind of diary, and typical Lissy: what she wore, what she ate, what her friends wore. Michelle flipped impatiently through the pages.

There was lots of stuff about the book club, what everyone said about art and life—blah, blah, blah. Some words were underlined in red ink. *Can you forgive her? Wallpaper of the soul. Alice & George V. & John Grey. Rodolphe & Emma in the woods.* And later, *Ardith & Guido,* encircled by a red heart that bled right through the page. Directly under that, like an afterthought, there was a much smaller, fainter heart with *L & Dr. D.* scribbled in pencil inside it, and then not quite erased. It looked like Lissy had the goods on everybody.

Michelle had never kept a diary, for the most obvious of reasons: if you wanted to keep something private, you didn't write it down. Those little gilt-edged leatherette books, in which some of her high school friends had recorded their sexual activity and drug and alcohol use—like they were the first person to ever feel turned on or spaced out or wasted—were protected by puny locks any moron could crack. As many of the morons in their families eventually did. And maybe Michelle didn't have perfect recall, but who needed a written account of every last thing she'd ever done or thought?

She found herself whistling, her mother's habit, as she went around the room, gathering Lissy's discarded garments and putting them away. There were several new items she noticed when she opened the drawers, especially undergarments—lacy bras and wispy thongs and a couple of garter belts, in black and candy-colored pastels. Maybe she ought to buy a few things like that for herself, except it clearly wasn't a lack of sexual attraction that kept Hank from making a commitment.

That shimmering white halter top was still hanging in the closet, obviously unworn, its tags still attached. Whenever Michelle bought something new, she felt compelled to wear it right away. Sometimes she wore her purchases directly home from the store, carrying her old things in a shopping bag. It was as if she were slipping into a new skin, even an entirely new self.

That's how she felt when she tried on Lissy's clothes. And she didn't just hold them up to her body anymore; she got undressed and put them on as if they belonged to her. She could probably walk out with a couple of things that would never be missed. Like the halter top or the pink push up bra that she dangled from one finger and idly swung in an arc.

All that time she kept whistling, so softly she almost couldn't hear herself. The same tune over and over, she realized, although she didn't recognize it. Dah-dah, da da da da. If that woman hadn't been bare-foot, and as stealthy as a panther, Michelle might have heard her on the stairs before she appeared, just like that, in the doorway.

Michelle was completely decked out by then: the halter top, with those annoying dangling tags, and a pair of cropped, cream-colored satin pants. They didn't even *go* together, and her feet were smaller than Lissy's, so that she was clomping around in the red Jimmy Choo mules like a kid playing dress-up in her mother's closet.

The woman in white—the one Lissy had greeted before, with a squeal, as Ardith—stepped into the room and shut the door behind her. "So is this part of the job description?" she asked.

At that moment, Michelle wished she was one of the Mexican housecleaners, so she could simply shrug and smile to indicate a lack of comprehension before she picked up the feather duster. She also wished, fervently, that Ardith would vanish from the face of the earth. "Wishing"—*that* was the song she had been so gaily whistling when she was caught in the act.

> *Wishing will make it so*
> *Just keep on wishing and care will go . . .*

Michelle's special powers had dwindled over the years, though. She knew perfectly well that she was busted, and that this knowledge was also apparent to Ardith, who clearly wasn't going anywhere. In fact, she'd stretched out on the striped silk chaise on the far side of the room and lay there with her arms folded across her chest. "I think Lissy would want to know about this, don't you?" she said.

Michelle could feel her heart flicker under the forbidden halter top, which she was trying clumsily to unfasten as she teetered on the mules. She'd seen this woman before at parties, usually at the center of things. The one all the other women seemed to love and also hate. She'd shown up late at the Snyders' brunch a couple of weeks before with that big, cigar-smoking husband of hers. He had heavy, freckled eyelids, like a giant frog. "*Look, it's Ardith and Larry,*" someone had said in a stage whisper, as if royalty had just crashed the party.

Michelle kicked off the mules and stepped out of the satin pants. It was beginning to feel like a private strip show, so she stopped struggling with the knot at the neck of the halter. Instead, she placed her fists on her hips and turned to face Ardith where she lounged, and scrambled for something to say in response. *You bitch* came to mind, as did some of those weak, dorky comebacks she used to use when she felt cornered in fights with her girlfriends or her brother, like *Oh, yeah?* and *Shut up* and *Screw you.* Ardith was smiling, a lazy, insolent smile that dared her to be stupid and helpless.

If Michelle were a dog, she would have probably just bitten her. "Yes," she said at last, with as much dignity as her state of undress allowed. "And maybe Larry would like to know about . . . *Guido.*"

16.

Mother Comes to the Rescue

Lissy's mother, Bernadette Ellis, née Borge, wasn't a frequent guest at Summerspell, although she lived just across the water, in Old Lyme, Connecticut, and there was a convenient ferry service connecting the two spits of land. She came up with a multitude of pretexts not to visit, from the weather (too awful for traveling, or too beautiful to go anywhere), to her fragile health (numerous syndromes, including carpal tunnel, chronic fatigue, and irritable bowel), to previous plans (a defrosted chicken she had to prepare immediately and then eat, a game of bridge, a "little medical procedure"). The procedures were all elective and cosmetic. Dr. Spencer Spencer, as Lissy had begun thinking of him, was slowly transforming her mother into someone she might not recognize in a chance meeting on the street.

Jeffrey had to go to London for several days, to attend a conference involving an international merger he was trying to negotiate, and Lissy called her mother and asked her to keep her company while Jeffrey was gone. It took some persuading, with promises of a shopping spree, of mother-and-daughter day-spa treatments, and a menu limited to the few foods Bernadette's holistic nutritionist permitted her to eat.

Lissy hadn't seen her mother for a while, but she didn't actually miss her. They'd never gotten along very well; Bernadette was so hard to please, and her general discontent flowed over into the very atmosphere she occupied. It was more a matter of Lissy wanting to reassure herself that she was still someone's daughter, and with the faint but dogged hope that maybe this time things would be different between them. She also needed a chaperone of sorts, a valid excuse not to have a rendezvous with Dr. Delirium, whose real name she now knew was Patrick Curran.

He had been calling her fairly regularly since they'd run into each other at The Battered Clam. At first he pretended that he was contacting her about work. He said that he'd decided to start accepting party engagements again to augment his income from waiting on tables. So he hoped she'd keep him in mind whenever she needed a magician. Then he admitted that he was on probation at The Clam, due to some broken crockery and a few screwed-up orders, and might be completely out of a job pretty soon.

And finally he changed the subject, abruptly, like a salesman making small talk until he has his foot wedged in the door and can begin pitching his product. In huskier, more urgent tones, Patrick told her that he'd been thinking about her nonstop since he'd seen her in the restaurant, and that his thoughts were probably rendering him too weak-kneed to carry trays. Since it was her fault, could he see her again, for a cup of coffee or a drink, just to regain his equilibrium?

Lissy had been thinking about him, too, in equally inappropriate ways. She said, in a breathless rush, that she was really much too busy to meet him, what with her book group and all the usual social craziness, and now her mother was coming for a visit. She told herself afterward that she'd handled it well, but she was rattled by the exchange.

As if his clumsiness were contagious, *she* became prone to dropping things, even the telephone once when she recognized his number on her caller ID. Yet she continued to take his calls, attempting weakly to defuse them by changing the subject back to the possibility of booking him for another children's party, which she still had no intention of doing.

And she mentioned her "husband," pointedly, as she'd failed to do that night at The Battered Clam. Her husband had liked the food there, but not the ambience, she informed Patrick, as if he'd asked for Jeffrey's review of the place. Her husband said the unemployment rate was going to fall in the next quarter. Her husband was due home any minute; she really had to go. Lissy almost swallowed her tongue in an effort not to mention Jeffrey's upcoming trip.

She didn't want to think about his trip, either, because he'd made tentative plans to catch up with Danielle and the children in the Cotswolds after his business meetings in London. It was ridiculous to worry about that, she knew. He couldn't stand Danielle; Lissy had listened often and sympathetically to his complaints about her disturbed, vindictive behavior. And she'd seen the evidence for herself, in those terrible letters Danielle kept sending. It was really to Jeffrey's *credit* that he'd risk an unpleasant encounter with her in order to spend a little time with his children.

He was a wonderfully engaged, if mostly absent, father. He'd carried those scruffy postcards from Paris around with him ever since Lissy had turned them over. Once, when she saw him take them from his pocket to look at for the millionth time, she found herself welling up with a misery she was reluctant to name.

The therapist Lissy had seen just before she and Jeffrey were married had prompted her to air her feelings about his children, with references to her own childhood, especially to her father and his second family. Of course she could see the parallels, the reasons to feel jealousy and unease. As Dr. Saunders pointed out, Lissy was the villain in one scenario and the victim in the other, or, as she sometimes thought of herself, the "do-er and the do-ee." But you rose above the psychological underpinnings of your life, didn't you? They were only *children,* for heaven's sake, and no one knew better than she did how they must feel.

After much negotiation between Jeffrey and Danielle, Miranda and Miles had been permitted to attend the wedding. During the ceremony, Miranda managed to hurt herself somehow, only a little finger scrape, but she carried on as if she had suffered a mortal wound. Even after her nanny—who'd had to be invited, too, of course—hauled her off someplace, you could still hear her muted wails, like the lamentations of a displaced ghost, and Lissy could sense Jeffrey's divided attention as they made their vows.

At the reception, though, the little girl seemed to have completely recovered. She and her brother danced with their father to "Tonight I Celebrate My Love," a song Lissy had requested, each of them perched on one of his shiny black shoes, determined little ballasts keeping him firmly in their lives. When Lissy gamely tried to join them on the dance floor, Miranda broke away, trampling Lissy's train and dragging Miles with her. In one of the photographs Lissy later rejected for her wedding album, the kids were only a furious blur of motion between the startled bride and groom.

Jeffrey left for London on Wednesday, directly from his office, and Bernadette arrived in Sagaponack the following afternoon. "Mummy!" Lissy cried, running out to meet the car, which Bernadette had parked so that the back tires were resting on the lawn. Lissy would move it later. Now she opened her arms to Bernadette, who received her embrace as if there were a bramble bush between them. Lissy dragged her mother's overnighter from the trunk; it seemed to be filled with rocks. "How was your trip?" she asked.

"Well, you know I don't enjoy that single-lane traffic," Bernadette said, as if other people might. And then, "What have you done to your hair?"

Lissy put one hand up to touch the blond version of Ardith's carefully arranged windblown coif. "Don't you like it?" she said, recognizing that familiar anxious edge to her seemingly casual question.

But Bernadette's attention had already strayed to the house they were approaching. She didn't say anything critical about that, though— how could she? Summerspell, with its weathered shingles and striped awnings, more than lived up to its name in the amber August light. And so did the double rows of butterfly bushes lining the bluestone walkway. In truth, Lissy didn't usually notice, much less appreciate, them, but now they seemed enchantingly alive with mauve blossoms and the fluttering creatures they'd attracted. *Look at all this,* she wanted to say to her mother. *Surely I must be worthy of it, mustn't I?*

Of course she didn't say anything of the kind. Instead she opened the front door and let Bernadette precede her inside. Michelle was in the kitchen, putting the finishing touches on some canapés (without salt, shellfish, celery, or mayonnaise), and Lissy called to her trillingly. "Mummy's here, Michelle! Would you please show her to her room?"

But Lissy shadowed them as they went upstairs to the guest bedroom. In some ways it was the nicest room in the house, because of the cozy, cushioned window seats and the little domed ceiling. Jeffrey called it the Guest Womb. He was only joking, of course, but the name struck Lissy as seriously apt, and strangely inviting. Sometimes she curled up in there in the afternoon to write in her journal or read one of the books for the Page Turners, and if she fell asleep, it seemed natural and not because of the tediousness of the text.

The night before her mother's arrival, she'd had Michelle prepare the sleigh bed with the lace-edged linens from Frette, sprinkled with lavender water. There were new satin-quilted hangers in the closet, and the dresser drawers were lined with William Morris wallpaper. Lissy herself had turned back the covers just before her mother's arrival, and she'd placed a cranberry glass vase filled with gerbera daisies on the nightstand. Then she'd carefully chosen some magazines to lay alongside the vase in a neat little stack. The latest issues of *Vogue* and *W* and *Architectural Digest,* the last with a photograph of a house similar to Summerspell on its cover. At the last minute, she stuck her copy of *Can You Forgive Her?* on top of the magazines.

Bernadette indicated the vase of daisies to Michelle with a dismissive flick of her hand and announced that she was going to take a nap. She was already blindfolded by her sleep mask before Lissy tiptoed out of the room after Michelle—who clutched the flowers like a disgruntled bridesmaid—and shut the door behind them. The telephone rang then, and Lissy hurried down the hall to her own bedroom to answer it. Maybe it was Jeffrey; what time was it in London? But it was *him,* Patrick, calling, as if he'd been watching the house and had seized upon the moment Lissy was alone.

"Just put me out of my misery," he said, by way of a greeting.

"Pardon?" Lissy said, although she had heard him perfectly well. Her hand went directly to her heart.

"Just tell me, what are the magic words?" he begged, and she thought *Please and thank you,* and wondered when those innocent phrases learned from Evie in the nursery had taken on such a sexual connotation.

"I need to see you," Patrick said. So much for small talk. Lissy looked at her own magnified reflection in the dressing table mirror. She was flushed and she could see the pulse beating in her throat, like something from reckless nature trapped just under her skin. "I'm sorry," she said, "I really can't do this," and she hung up before he could say anything else.

In the bathroom, she splashed her face and neck and wrists with icy water, wetting the whole front of her shirt, so that her nipples became darkly visible. She groaned and pulled the shirt off, and then the long, girlish flowered skirt she'd put on to greet her mother. She still felt hot, but she was shivering now, the way you do when you have a fever. *Stop it. Don't be crazy,* she advised herself, but a lot of good that did.

She ended up taking a tepid bath, trying not to linger or to look down at her own long pale body floating there, at her pubic hair rising up in the water like golden seaweed. Her mother's door was still closed when she went downstairs in her terry robe to dismiss Michelle for the day. Lissy had made dinner reservations for Bernadette and herself at Della Femina. They would have some sherry here first, and nibble on the canapés Michelle had prepared. Everything was under control; nothing had really changed. She'd even brought down the Lurex halter top she had been meaning to give to Michelle.

The girl seemed to blanch when she saw it. "What?" she said.

"Oh," Lissy said, "I bought this on one of those mad impulses you get. You know. I mean, I still like it, but it doesn't really suit me." She indicated the store tags. "It's never been worn," she said, beginning to feel like a high-pressure salesclerk. "I wondered if you could use it. It would look nice, I think, with your dark hair."

Michelle still appeared flustered, and more than a little leery. "Well, maybe," she conceded at last. And she reached out and took the top from Lissy.

"Good, then," Lissy said. "Great." She glanced around the sparkling kitchen. "So. Everything looks great around here. I don't think you need to stay any longer, do you?"

Upstairs again, Lissy took off her bathrobe and opened her closets and a few drawers to choose an outfit for the evening. Her underthings were in neat, frothy little color-matched piles. Lissy knew that she tended to be careless, even sloppy sometimes, but Michelle was really very good about restoring order. In fact, she was turning out much better than Lissy had ever expected. But had she been a little offended by the gift of the halter top? It was so hard to read her. The top was brand-new, though, as Lissy had pointed out, and it cost more than the girl's wages for an entire day.

For the first time, Lissy tried to contemplate Michelle's life beyond the perimeters of this house. What did she do in her spare time? Did she have a boyfriend? Would he like seeing her in the halter top? Then she pulled out the black thong and matching garter belt she'd purchased on another mad impulse several days ago. They were scantier and more suggestive than anything she'd ever bought before. What had possessed her?

She put them on, along with the new net stockings and plunge-push up bra, just as she had done for Jeffrey while he was packing his suitcase the night before he left for London. He was shocked with pleasure and arousal, and they'd ended up dumping the suitcase onto the floor, and then falling, almost locked together, in its place on the bed.

Later, she helped him repack his clothes, and he kept kissing her and saying "What a sendoff!"

That was exactly what she'd had in mind, sending him off to another continent and his ex-wife with indelible erotic images of herself, as a preemptive strike against whatever strategy Danielle might have planned. But she hadn't been thinking about Jeffrey when she'd bought all that underwear in the first place.

In *Madame Bovary,* Lissy remembered, Emma dresses carefully, almost craftily, for the ball—even putting a flower in her hair—but when her husband tries to kiss her on the shoulder, she rebuffs him, saying, "You'll wrinkle my dress!" I'm not like that, Lissy thought, defensively.

But she posed before the mirror in her flimsy lingerie with similar self-absorption and a sickening sense of excitement. That was how her mother found her a few minutes later when she opened Lissy's bedroom door without knocking, and said, "Where do you think you're going in that getup?"

17.

The Other Side of the Wall

In a reversal of the usual sexual politics at Macon, Stephen was deemed more culpable than Angela for the unfortunate event at the gallery, and even for the affair itself. The victims in the wake of their misdeeds were his own family, and Valerie was especially well liked by faculty and students. Maybe it was the perversity of his taste that nailed Stephen, his choosing the somewhat androgynous Angela over the feminine ideal of his wife. And, despite its naked subject and Jenna Barker's malicious involvement in the scandal, the drawing was *his*. Whatever the reasons, he was denied tenure and his year-to-year appointment wasn't renewed at the end of the spring semester.

Angela's punishment was having to stay on, the object of

pity, disdain, and, she was certain, an epidemic of nasty jokes. She did have tenure, and if she had decided to forfeit it and leave, the strong references required to land another position would not have been forthcoming. The atmosphere on campus felt poisonous. She wasn't shunned, exactly—most people were too curious or falsely tolerant to do that—but she isolated herself as best she could from all the gossip and speculation. And she was mourning the loss of her best friends.

For weeks after the incident, Angela taught her classes and attended a few mandatory meetings, mostly hiding out in her apartment the rest of the time. She fell into exhausted sleep every night, only to awaken abruptly a couple of hours later with searing pain in both her legs that she had to try to walk off. There was never a medical finding for that pain; she was just given pills to dull it. The worst thing, though, was that even reading failed to provide any solace or distraction during that dark period. She was unable to concentrate, and flitted from book to book as restlessly as a fly at a picnic.

The Kellers were still living in their house while they shopped around for new jobs. Oddly enough, Stephen did get decent references—his reward, probably, for taking the hit—and Valerie's were said to be over the top. So maybe they'd land on their feet, professionally at least. Angela wasn't even sure they were going to stay together, although she hadn't heard any reliable rumors to the contrary. She longed to see them and dreaded running into them.

Over and over, she imagined walking up the path to the house on Dogwood Drive, as she'd done so many times with such glad expectation, and knocking on the front door. In different versions of the fantasy, different members of the Keller family opened the door to her. Valerie, who had always covered her eyes during brutal scenes in movies, would simply close the door in her face, Angela knew, as if to shut out everything that had happened. If she was unable to discern the best in someone, she couldn't bear to witness and acknowledge the worst. And the glimpse Angela would manage to get of her, of her beauty distorted by grief and anger, would be more terrible than any of the images she still retained of that fateful evening.

When she thought of Stephen coming to answer her knocking, her traitorous heart knocked in response. How could they even look at each other again? In a kind of hysterical amnesia, she already had trouble picturing his face. Her intense desire had been clobbered senseless; his, too, surely. And the old, easy friendship they'd sacrificed was irretrievable. She would be as welcome as a Jehovah's Witness trying to sell him the promise of an afterlife, or the possibility of forgiveness in this one.

And what if Charlotte opened the door? That was something she had actually often done in the past, because she was so quick and willful, even though she'd needed both small hands to turn the knob, and a parent's voice in the background always warned, "Sharly, don't open that door! Ask who it is first!" In the period that Angela forever thought of as "after," but was, even more significantly, before the Kellers finally left town, Charlotte was the only person in the family Angela truly hoped to see. For some reason, she held on to the notion that the child's response to her would provide an accurate estimate of the damage done. Maybe that would give her a measure of peace, if not absolution.

Of course, she didn't knock on their door, and somehow she never ran into any of them until that day years later, when she saw the grown-up Charlotte striding ahead of her on Seventh Avenue in Manhattan. And when they met, face-to-face, five years after that, Angela consoled herself with Charlotte's absence of hostility, and her composure, but no definitive conclusions about the fate of the family could be drawn. As if she'd been interrupted in the reading of a compelling novel, Angela yearned to know the rest of the story.

Then a sudden heat wave in an otherwise temperate summer gave her the opportunity to invite Charlotte out to The Springs for a few days. She wouldn't have to wait until September and Charlotte's birthday for an excuse to see her again. Angela hadn't anticipated the boyfriend, Jimmy, coming along, too, though. Her house was small; it could have easily accommodated another woman, but a couple might seem like an invasion. Charlotte had accepted the invitation without any apparent reluctance. What she'd said was "Oh, great! We've been dying to get out of this furnace."

Angela had intended to offer Charlotte her bedroom anyway. There were still nights when the leg pains woke her and she ended up on the sofa in the living room, so she was used to sleeping there. But her single bed wouldn't accommodate two people—she'd have to make a pallet of some sort for them on the floor, and she had hoped to have some private conversations with Charlotte that would help to fill in the missing years. She didn't say any of that on the telephone, though, for fear the girl would change her mind.

Angela had not lived in close quarters with a man since her childhood. Even her stodgy accountant father had been a notably masculine presence in their Staten Island home. She remembered his shaving things in the bathroom, his heavy tread on the stairs, and the deep timbre of his voice, in counterpoint to her mother's fluty murmurs, coming from their bedroom, which adjoined hers. At least she'd never heard them making love.

Charlotte and Jimmy came out on the train on Sunday afternoon. Angela was waiting on the platform for them in the shimmering, oppressive heat. There was no air-conditioning in her house, but she'd gone to the hardware store the day before to buy an additional floor fan and an inflatable mattress. She just hoped they weren't expecting a swimming pool or ocean breezes.

Jimmy was shorter than Charlotte, and darkly handsome. He looks like an actor, Angela thought, but it wasn't a flattering assessment. They had no luggage other than their backpacks, which they flung into the trunk of the Neon. "We can go to the beach later, if you like," Angela said as she drove away from the station, already trying to please them, to make up for the deficits of her small, creaky car, the unimposing house they would arrive at soon. She hardly ever went to the beach herself, except out of season or early in the morning, before the crowds arrived.

They made themselves right at home, to Angela's delight and trepidation. The screen doors twanged open and banged shut, and in minutes they'd investigated the entire place. Jimmy even stretched out on the inflated mattress on the bedroom floor for a moment or two before springing up to use the bathroom. Angela could hear the strong stream of his urine through the closed door, and over her own raised voice urging Charlotte to help herself to food and drink and books.

But Charlotte was staring at the two paintings on the wall above the bed. How could Angela have overlooked them in her final survey of things before she'd left for the station? Maybe she was so used to them, she didn't really see them anymore. From Charlotte's perspective, though, they must have been glaringly conspicuous.

Stephen had once referred to the portraits, after their affair had begun, as "the odd couple," and Angela remembered thinking that he might have been talking about the two of them. The paintings, of a youngish man and an older woman, were from his Arbus period, when Angela had been his most ardent supporter. The woman wore an absurd feathered and flowered hat—it practically wore her—with a veil that did nothing to obscure her plain features or pathetic vanity. The man, who had low-set ears and a convict's shaved head, glanced sideways, almost furtively, at the woman, as if he were mocking her pretense at ignoring him.

Yet Stephen claimed that there'd been no relationship between his two subjects until Angela had paired them up that way, creating their silent dialogue. The purchase price had been modest, but Valerie declared her a patron of the arts; there was even a dinner party on Dogwood Drive to celebrate the sale. "I consider it a wise investment in the future," Angela solemnly said that night, in a toast, and she recorded the flash of pleasure on Stephen's face.

Charlotte said, "I've only seen slides of these before. They're pretty good, aren't they?"

Angela didn't remind her that she must have seen the paintings hanging in her Wellspring apartment years ago, although they weren't above the bed then. If Charlotte couldn't recall seeing them there, maybe other images from her childhood were similarly buried. She was looking at the portraits, serenely, with a painter's critical eye dimmed by daughterly affection; she didn't appear to be examining them like a detective of the past.

"Yes, I've always liked them," Angela said. "Your father called them the odd couple." *My business is with your father and not with you.*

Charlotte laughed. "That sounds like him," she said, and then the toilet flushed and Jimmy came out of the bathroom, zipping his fly. "How about that beach?" he said.

She gave them towels, a thermos, directions to Maidstone Park, and the keys to the car, but she begged off accompanying them by saying that she had to think about supper. Supper had already been vigorously thought about and partially prepared. Angela had made gazpacho and a pitcher of iced sun tea, and she'd cut up numerous fresh vegetables for a stir-fry. She'd forgotten to ask if Jimmy was a vegetarian, like Charlotte, so she'd bought some lobster salad, too, just in case. Her careful budget was being depleted by this visit.

Now that they were gone and she really had nothing to do, she lay outside in the hammock under the trees and read from Evan S. Connell's *Mrs. Bridge,* the first modern novel she'd assigned to her reading groups this summer. The book, about an upper-middle-class family in the Midwest, was written in short takes, like blackout scenes in the theater, each one reverberating with psychological meaning that manages to escape the protagonist's grasp. Poor India Bridge, under her husband's sway and unable to properly connect with her interesting children, was such a sad character, missing out on her own life like that, making the novel a true cautionary tale.

As Angela lay there, reading and sipping iced tea, she was struck by the altered order of her day. Sundays were usually unstructured, informed only by whatever whim happened to overtake her, to garden or read, or to just drowse and dream. But now she had a clear purpose. In a couple of hours, she'd have to put her book away and set the table. The children were at the beach, and would come home hungry, as children always did after all that sun and salt air. Their towels and bathing suits would be heavily damp and gritty with sand. Angela would have to shake them out and hang them up. *I am like a mother,* she thought, with a thrill of bewildered happiness. This was her old daydream of Charlotte as her own child, she realized, come to sudden, if belated and only temporary, fruition.

When Charlotte and Jimmy did return, though, the illusion was instantly shattered. They were hungry and sunburned, all right, but they were adults, with eyes only for each other, and Charlotte, who had never belonged to Angela, briskly shook out the towels and bathing suits herself, and hung them on the back porch railing. Then she and Jimmy disappeared into the bathroom together and the water in the shower ran and ran while Angela set out their meal, feeling more like a maid now than anybody's mother.

He was nice, though, Jimmy. He held Charlotte's hand during supper, hampering both of them in their attempts to eat, especially during the soup course. And he complimented Angela with genuine enthusiasm on the food. He took back his hand to gobble the lobster salad unencumbered, and Charlotte ate some of it, too, right off his plate. Didn't lobsters have faces?

Jimmy insisted on clearing the table, and he went outside afterward to smoke, giving Angela some time alone with Charlotte, whom she'd wanted to interrogate under a bare, swinging lightbulb but could only casually question in the shadowed living room. As they finished the pitcher of tea, Angela said, "Are you in contact with anybody else from Macon?"

Charlotte looked thoughtful before she shook her head. "Maybe Mom is, but not me. I was really little when we left."

"I know," Angela said.

"The last time she called, I told her that I'd bumped into you."

Angela's breath caught and then whistled out raggedly. "You did?" she managed to say.

"Yeah. She was surprised. Somebody else must have told her you were still in Texas."

Angela waited, but Charlotte didn't say anything else. It was obviously her own turn again to speak. "We lost touch," she murmured, thinking that it was the understatement of the century.

"That's what she said, too," Charlotte told her.

And then the screen door opened and closed and Jimmy came into the room, smelling of Angela's herbal shampoo and the cigarette he'd just smoked. "What's happening?" he asked, putting his hand flat on Charlotte's head, as if to stake his claim on her.

Later, when Angela was lying on the sofa, trying to sleep, turning her pillow over for the umpteenth time to seek the elusive cool side, the sounds from the bedroom began. Their voices first, muted but clearly conspiratorial. Laughter. And then the bedsprings—like the repetitive complaint of some raucous bird, or the usual choir of summer insects—and what must have been Charlotte's head hitting the metal bars of the headboard.

Why weren't they using the air mattress?—it had cost her a small fortune. Maybe they were afraid it would explode beneath them or noisily deflate, like some sexual whoopee cushion. She didn't know how they could bear to touch each other, or to be touched, in all that heat.

Even with the pillow wrapped around her ears, Angela could still hear them, as she must have once heard her parents, unsure of what they were doing in there, but somehow knowing that it was imperative to find out. It was all ahead of her then, the finding out and the doing. How had she ended up on the wrong side of the wall again, her innocence hideously restored, so that she was merely a listener once more, an aging, motherless child?

18.

In Case of an Emergency

Hank called to say that April was in Southampton Hospital. He didn't know what was wrong with her, except that she'd fainted behind her register at CVS and didn't come around for several minutes. Michelle had been waiting for him to arrive when he phoned, and wondering why he was late; they were expected at her brother's house for dinner. Instead she picked Kayla up at a friend's and went to meet Hank in the emergency room. By the time they got there, April had been seen by a doctor, who'd decided to admit her for observation and a series of tests. They were just waiting for a bed to become available.

It occurred to Michelle as they stood in anxious attendance around April's gurney that Hank might still be in love with her in some complicated and permanent way. He held one of her hands and Kayla held the other. The three of them were linked together, just as April was linked to her IV and the cardiac monitor, making them appear like an inviolable family. Maybe it was this stubborn loyalty to their former status that kept him from pledging himself to Michelle.

Not that she thought Hank and April were still sexually involved. That had ended long before they'd even separated. And she didn't think they would ever try to live together again, even for Kayla's sake. But they had all that history between them, of wild early love and difficult marriage, leaving the kinds of scars that probably could never be completely healed by a new love interest. The proof was in this: Hank was the person April had chosen to be notified, as he had been that afternoon, in the event of an emergency. Who had Hank designated on medical forms to be notified if something happened to him?

It was a morbid and unsettling thought that reminded Michelle of her father's disappearance at sea, of the deer that leaped out of nowhere in front of cars during the rutting season, of drunk drivers in any season, and of ordinary mortal illness. Look at April—ringing up Nyquil and Tampax one minute, and stretched out senseless on the floor the next. And all around them, in the other screened cubicles of the emergency room, were other people whose lives had been similarly interrupted.

But who had Hank chosen to be notified? The question haunted Michelle. She was being selfish and obsessive, she knew, decidedly unlovable traits. April, whose heartbeat fluctuated on the monitor—the only show in town—should have been the sole subject of her concern. April was seriously overweight, and suffered from asthma and high blood pressure. She was the mother of the scared, skinny girl hovering at her side, and Michelle truly *liked* her, despite everything. How could she not? *Just let her be okay,* she wished with fierce concentration, in something between a prayer and a telepathic command. She'd even give something up if she had to, in exchange for the favor, although she didn't know right then exactly what that sacrifice might be.

April was especially pathetic in one of those awful hospital john-nies. Her skim-milk skin was already bruised from the needles, and she had to be afraid; yet she was giving Hank patient instructions about calling her boss, checking on the chicken she'd left on slow cook in the Crock-Pot, and making sure that Kayla did her homework. Then she turned to Michelle. "I'll bet I spoiled your evening," she said with sincere regret. "You look gorgeous."

Why didn't she just wear a halo and carry a harp? But Michelle *had* dressed for a festive evening and for admiration. In fact, she'd admired herself considerably earlier, posing in front of her bedroom mirror in the halter top, as she'd posed in front of Lissy's mirror the day that Templeton bitch caught her in the act. And she'd been imagining Hank's reaction to the way she looked. Even in the antiseptic chill of the hospital, and in the midst of her guilty worry about April, she'd caught sight of her own reflection again, in a windowed door, and experienced a little thrill of vanity and a shamefaced but satisfying sense of being in robust health.

They took forever to find a bed for April. During that time, Michelle called her brother and her mother to update them on the situation, and then, at Hank's urging, she took Kayla to the Empress Diner for supper. This wasn't what she'd planned to do in Lissy's shimmery halter top. She was sorry she hadn't changed into something less dressy and a little more substantial before she'd left home; the air-conditioning in the diner was set as high as it had been in the emergency room. Perfect for cadavers, Michelle thought, and shivered.

"I'm hungry," she told Kayla, with false cheeriness, "aren't you?"

"Sort of," Kayla said, playing with the salt and pepper shakers instead of looking at the menu, which seemed longer to Michelle than some books she'd read.

"She's going to be all right, you know," she said, exactly the sort of platitude she, herself, hated. No amount of wishful thinking would guarantee a good outcome.

Kayla didn't even bother answering. She sipped her ice water and tapped on the table, as if she were marking time until she could escape.

When the waitress came, Michelle ordered the fruit salad, while Kayla made neat little hills of salt and pepper along the border of her place mat. "You should eat *something*," Michelle told her. "How about a hamburger?" she added. "I've heard they're pretty good here," although she'd heard nothing of the kind.

"No, thanks," Kayla said. And then, wearily, "All right, I don't care." Michelle remembered deflecting Jo Ann the same way at Kayla's age, agreeing to something, to anything, just to get her mother off her back.

"Medium?" the waitress asked. "Fries with that? Onion?"

In the end, Kayla picked at her food and so did Michelle. The abandoned hamburger looked ragged and bloody, and the fruit salad suspiciously perfect in its glistening syrup. Michelle's cell phone was on the table, and she kept glancing down at it, willing it to ring. Hank had said he would check in with her later, or something to that effect. She pictured him sleeping in a chair alongside April's bed in a secluded, dimly lit hospital room, still holding her hand.

But when they got back to the hospital, he was leaning against the wall outside a fully occupied four-bed room, which was as brightly lit as a restaurant kitchen. One of the other women in there was being attended to by a doctor, and Hank had been kicked out. He told Michelle and Kayla that April was stable. "They think she may have just taken too much of her blood-pressure medication," he said.

Michelle felt enormous relief, as if she'd been holding up the world with her bare, aching hands and could let go, finally, and relax. "See?" she said to Kayla, poking her in the arm, and Kayla happily poked her back, a little too hard. When they were allowed into the room, they all kissed April good night and then drove to the house in Hampton Bays.

The Crock-Pot chicken was perfectly done and still warm; Michelle put one of April's aprons on over her fancy outfit and dished it out. She had only been inside this place once before, a few months before, when she'd brought Kayla home after a weekend visit with Hank, and April asked her to come in and look at something. This was where Hank had once lived with his family, and Michelle had been as curious then as if she was entering a museum dedicated to his former life.

She was also a little nervous about April's invitation. Maybe she was, as Michelle occasionally suspected, simply too good to be true. Maybe her seemingly mild-mannered acceptance of the way things were was merely a façade, and she was going to demand that Michelle give Hank up. Or hit Michelle over the head with a frying pan, like a deranged Kathy Bates character, and hide her body in the basement. But as soon as Michelle followed April inside, she knew how farfetched her imaginings had been.

April had made a pot of tea and a banana bread in preparation for this visit; the paper napkins were folded, origami-style, into swans. And except for a few photographs of Hank and Kayla, back when she was a baby, there were no traces of his ever having lived there. Even at Michelle's house, where he was only a frequent visitor, there was evidence of him everywhere in something he'd left behind, like a single sock or his razor or a few curly hairs in the bathtub drain, or just the lingering briny scent of him.

All that April had wanted her to see that day were some swatches of fabric she was considering for the reupholstering of her sofa. "Hank says you have nice taste," she said, and Michelle felt more surprised and gratified than she'd ever been by a compliment. She knew that if their positions were reversed, she would have been darkly jealous and resentful of April, who was obviously the better person. Michelle still didn't like the idea that Ricky Cavanagh, the boy she'd gone out with right after high school for a couple of months and then dumped because he was a cretin, had survived her rejection of him and gone on to marry someone else.

Hank had never told Michelle firsthand that she had nice taste any more than he'd declared his undying love for her. Maybe he was secretly shy, despite his outgoing personality. Or maybe he was not given to declarations of any kind, except for those spontaneous outbursts during sex. It was the sort of thing she might have asked April, while they drank tea and examined the upholstery swatches, if it wouldn't have been so completely inappropriate.

April had taken her advice about the sofa fabric—the more delicate mossy green print over the brownish maroon plaid that would have lasted forever and never shown a single stain. When Michelle settled back against the cushions on the sofa after supper, she felt comfortable there, almost at home. Hank was in the easy chair, reading the newspaper, and Kayla was at his feet on the rug, doing her summer school homework, or, rather, staring at a blank page in her notebook. A Peeping Tom at the window might have mistaken them, in that ordinary domestic scene, for an ordinary family.

Kayla was supposed to be writing an essay on an American heroine of her choice—and she seemed to have hit a snag; she couldn't come up with a suitable subject. Other girls in her class were going to write about Clara Barton or Laura Bush, and a couple of kiss-ass boys had chosen their own mothers. Kayla quickly made it clear that she considered all of those selections either totally boring or gag-worthy.

"So why don't you write about Michelle," Hank said, from behind his newspaper.

"Huh?" Kayla said, and Michelle sat upright on the sofa. Was he making fun of her?

"Sure," Hank said. "Look at all the things she does for us."

"Like what?" Kayla asked.

"She gave us dinner, didn't she?" he said. "She drives you lots of places, too, and she's very decorative."

"Mom made the chicken," Kayla pointed out.

"She did," Michelle agreed. And to Hank, "Cut it out, will you?" The word "decorative" he'd used was meant to be flattering, she supposed, but it made her feel like some useless knickknack. And his playfulness, which she'd always enjoyed, seemed shallow now, and demeaning.

"Clara Barton had nothing on you," he said. "You're still my American heroine."

"Thanks a lot," she said, surprised by the bitterness of her own tone, and the sudden, unnerving possibility of tears.

"Hey," Hank said. He'd put the newspaper down. "Are you okay?"

Michelle was acutely aware of Kayla, with a pencil clenched between her teeth, watching them. That was the thing about having children around: there was almost always a witness. She felt exposed in the halter top, in her neediness. "I'm fine," she told Hank. "How about Christa McAuliffe?"

"What about her?" Hank asked.

"I was talking to Kayla," Michelle said.

"Maybe," Kayla said, looking doubtful, and then she yawned.

It was contagious. First Hank did it, then Michelle, and then Kayla again. And it struck them all as kind of funny, breaking the tension in the room. "I'd better get home," Michelle said.

"Stay over," Hank suggested. "It's late."

"I really have to go," she said. She didn't have to; Jo Ann must have let the dogs out for their evening run, and she would have to concentrate to stay awake during the drive back. But it seemed improper to sleep at April's place in her absence, especially since Michelle still wasn't certain of her own place in Hank's life.

19.

Buying Happiness

Lissy often felt something like postcoital tristesse after a day of shopping. What had she so fervently desired in the first place? And why wasn't anything ever truly enough? On this rare occasion when her mother was her shopping partner, that feeling of disappointment, even loss, was intensified. As they went from boutique to boutique, like a couple of religious pilgrims, touching the sacred sleeves and hems of hanging garments, Lissy's energy and optimism gradually drained, even as Bernadette seemed to gain momentum and a grim sense of purpose.

Jeffrey had called just before they'd left the house to say that his business in London had been successfully concluded, and that he would take a train to the countryside, to a place called Winchcombe, in the morning, where he would connect with his children. As if they were mature and independent beings, traveling unescorted. He'd failed to mention Danielle at all, a deliberate oversight that disturbed Lissy; she felt compelled to bring her up herself. "Where is Danielle staying?" she had asked, and counted the beats—there were five of them—before he answered.

"Some hotel," he finally said. Lissy heard the rustling of papers. "Here it is. The Marchmont." He tried to suppress a yawn.

It was about three in the afternoon there. He was probably thinking of a nap, and of going into a cool dark pub later for a cocktail. He would pay for it with oversized pink-and-blue play money bearing likenesses of the queen. People around him would be talking with British accents. During Lissy's junior year abroad, she'd inadvertently parroted the way her Parisian hosts spoke, their very gestures—she had practically *become* foreign. It was so easy to slip out of yourself like that, to forgo and forget the familiar in another country, another time zone.

"And you?" she asked Jeffrey. "Where will you be?"

"Me?" he said. "At a little B-and-B, nearby. I'll call you with the number tomorrow."

"So will the kids stay with you while you're there?"

"We haven't really worked that out," Jeffrey said. She could sense the reluctance in his voice, imagine the way he was probably chewing on his lower lip. And she was aware of her mother, downstairs, pacing, impatient to go into East Hampton for shopping and lunch.

"I see," Lissy said, with far more certainty than she felt. She didn't see anything, really, except for the words "Jeffie, you miserable prick," scrawled in Danielle's excited hand on one of her letters, and a disquieting picture in her head of Jeffrey in a fuzzy Cotswold setting with his family. A moment later, she envisioned her father and *his* preferred family in a similar bucolic scene in yet another part of the world. Lissy's mother called up the stairs, "What are you doing up there?"

Within the hour, they both clutched shopping bags like trophies of a hunting expedition. It occurred to Lissy that men didn't shop together, just as they didn't conduct the kind of intimate conversations women were always lording over them. "We tell each other *everything*," they gloatingly informed the men, who couldn't imagine such candor or closeness any more than they could imagine sharing a dressing room, or zipping each other up and then stepping back to admire and be admired.

But that famous female camaraderie hardly existed between Lissy and Bernadette. There were no heart-to-hearts in their history, and so far during this visit they hadn't talked about any of the things that mattered urgently to Lissy, like the state of her marriage, or those chronic concerns that pulsed quietly in the background of her mind: her father's second life in an alternate, tropical reality without her, and the loss of Evie.

Then, in The Oyster's Secret, a brand-new shop on Newtown Lane, mother and daughter emerged simultaneously from separate dressing rooms wearing the same lavender linen sheath. It seemed like a setup in a sitcom, Lucy and Ethel playing for a charge of canned laughter, but it was purely accidental. Lissy was already trying her dress on when a saleswoman brought it in a larger size to her mother, but she felt complicit in what seemed like a cruel mockery of Bernadette, and caught out in her own brazen youth and beauty, by the way the fabric draped perfectly across her breasts and hips and how the color suited her blondness.

Her mother, staring at her, seemed to be peering into a sardonic mirror, one that ridiculed her true dumpy self, and hid the ravages of aging and roller-coaster dieting and plastic surgery and years of rancor. "Oh," Lissy said, brightly, helplessly, "that looks really nice on you. Are you going to get it?"

Bernadette didn't legitimize those pathetic, counterfeit remarks with a response, and she didn't do what Lissy longed for, and knew that other women's mothers might have done in the same circumstances—smile with amusement at the silliness of the situation, compliment her daughter on her appearance without jealousy or malevolence, and even offer to buy the sheath for her, or something else, some trinket that represented maternal approval and affection.

Of course, neither of them bought the sheath, although Lissy had coveted it for a moment before she stepped out of her dressing room, and Bernadette's gray mood darkened considerably after their unfortunate twinning. Lissy wasn't very hungry, but the only diplomatic gesture she could think of was to suggest that they go to lunch. Eat and make up. There was a new brasserie in Amagansett called Triomphe that Joy had raved about, so they put their bounty in the trunk of the car and headed farther east, while Bernadette harped on Lissy for having left the keys in the ignition while they'd shopped. "The car will be stolen one of these days," she said, but it was more like the laying on of a curse than a mother expressing concern for her daughter's possessions.

"That doesn't happen around here," Lissy said lamely, remembering that Jeffrey had given her similar warnings in more loving tones. "Everybody leaves their keys in the car." Bernadette only shook her head in disgust, and they didn't exchange another word all the way to Amagansett.

You walked through a marble archway into the restaurant. That was only an architectural play on the establishment's name, so why did Lissy feel so oddly alerted, practically atingle, as she stepped through it? The place was bustling—the usual noontime Hamptons scene—women, mostly, but some men at their midweek leisure, too, tanned and booming, and children perched on the little thrones of their booster seats, playing with croissant and baguette crumbs. Lissy surveyed the room, but there was no one she recognized, no one to interrupt these arduous hours she was spending solely in her mother's sour company.

The role Bernadette was supposed to have played, as an obstruction between Lissy and Patrick, seemed to have been written out of the script. He hadn't phoned again since she'd hung up so abruptly on him, and she found herself obsessively checking for missed calls, and even making sure every once in a while that the telephones were still in working order.

As they looked at their menus, Lissy toyed with the insane idea of confiding in her mother, as if the right words could miraculously regenerate some deadened nerve, a sentiment they'd once shared. Woman-to-woman. I'm worried about Jeffrey and Danielle, she might begin, and then there's this man . . . Or: Did you get any warning before Daddy left? Did you love me before then? Did he? Instead she ran her finger down the list of entrées and said, "The Niçoise is supposed to be excellent here, Mummy. Joy says they use seared local tuna. Or we could try the Dover sole."

They ate in loaded silence for a while, until Lissy felt she couldn't bear it another second. She put her napkin to her lips, as if to stifle herself, and then she lowered it to her lap, clasped her hands there, and said, "I need to ask you something."

Bernadette appeared to shrink in her seat, like the Wicked Witch of the West melting into a puddle in *The Wizard of Oz*. Soon there might be nothing left of her but her crumpled Lily Pulitzer dress and those tiny, hoof-like pink leather scuffs. *Don't you dare go!* Lissy wanted to shout, but she continued in her usual conciliatory tones. "It's all right," she said softly. "I just wanted to talk to you a little bit about Evie."

Bernadette poked at the ruins of her salad with her fork, at the mound of tiny olive pits, the wilted shreds of lettuce. "What about her?" she said.

"Well . . . you know," Lissy managed to say before a wave of tears began to rise in her throat. It was like going under in the ocean, the salty sting, that sense of being overwhelmed. Oh, great, now she was going to make a scene. The room shimmered around them; she was the only one in full focus, and everyone but her mother was looking at her. It was just an illusion, of course, and after she'd swallowed hard a couple of times, her composure returned. "I never really asked you about how she died."

"Yes, you did, and I've told you," Bernadette said. "It was her appendix."

"But why did she die of it? People usually don't, do they? They have operations and then they get better."

"Because it was too late. Because she was taking care of you."

"What do you mean?" Lissy asked, terrified of the answer.

"I mean, she didn't want to leave you alone, so she took a couple of aspirin and put her hot-water bottle over the pain."

"Where were you?" Lissy said, desperate for an accomplice to this unremembered crime.

"I don't know, I was out. It doesn't matter where *I* was."

That was unarguably true: Evie was hers, not her mother's. But she had to know the rest of the story, even though her hands had slipped between her clenched thighs by then and she was filled with dread, as if she were listening to fresh, terrible news. "Was she dead when you got home?"

Bernadette considered the question. "No," she said at last. Then she popped a couple of the olive pits into her mouth and sucked on them before spitting them into her hand and tossing them back onto the plate. "No, she lived for a couple of days."

"Did I go to the funeral?" Lissy asked. "Or did you send her back to Scotland?" *My bonnie lies over the ocean, my bonnie lies over the sea.*

"What?" her mother said distractedly. "Why are you asking about all this now?"

Why indeed? Lissy's curiosity, her persistence, seemed a little perverse, even to her. But before she could think of what to say next, the waiter came and took away their plates and flourished the dessert menus, effectively putting an end to the conversation.

That didn't mean she could stop thinking about it, though. Evie's wrinkled bedsheets, the smooth clammy flesh of the hot-water bottle.

And something someone said back then that had seemed so important. But what was it?

"Let's get two desserts and split them," Bernadette said. She had always had a sweet tooth, as if she could pave over her misery with mounds of sugar. And Lissy wearily agreed. "You choose," she said.

Back at the house, she checked once more for telephone messages. There were only two, the first from a tree-spraying service—something about birch-leaf miner and gypsy moths—and the other from the man who cleaned the chimneys. Bernadette gathered her purchases and went upstairs to lie down until supper. A few minutes later, Lissy carried her own shopping bags up to her bedroom. Soon there was a cloud of tissue paper on the floor and, on the bed, a heap of things—shirts and shoes and bracelets and beach sarongs she'd never really needed and no longer wanted.

What had Angela called material possessions again? The wallpaper of the soul. But Lissy remembered feeling smugly satisfied that day with the trimmings. And she had once read a quote in a fashion magazine: "Whoever said money can't buy happiness didn't know where to go shopping," and had laughed contentedly, and repeated it at a dinner party later. God, why could she remember *that* now, verbatim—and even that it was Bo Derek who'd said it—but not whatever it was she'd been told or had overheard right after Evie's death, the determining event of her life?

Bernadette was probably snoring away down the hall by now—she'd been nearly comatose all the way home—and Lissy was growing sleepy, too. She shoved her new belongings onto Jeffrey's side of the bed and stretched out on her own pile of pillows.

When she began to awaken, stiff-limbed and headachy, she was plunged back in time. She might have been in the confines of her childhood bed, from which she could see the archway that led to Evie's room, and when she looked through her mind's eye she saw that space filled with the silhouette of a woman's figure, and then another's. One of the women was her mother, the other her Grandmother Ellis. Lissy was still coming groggily awake when she heard a voice, her grand-mother's voice, saying clearly and sternly, "How *could* you?" But to whom was she speaking, and what did she mean?

Lissy emerged into complete consciousness then, fully grown and in the present moment, on the wide expanse of the bed she shared with her husband, who was so conspicuously absent. She moaned a little, about that, about her aching giant self, and about the dream-like memory that was rapidly receding, like a barely missed train. She sat up and tried to conjure her grandmother again, in one of those di-aphanous floral-print dresses she favored, with that feathery crown of white hair, and her particular but faint tea rose scent. The whole scene was gone by then, though, irretrievably. And Lissy was *here*, right now, feeling heavy with homesickness. But you're home, dummy, she chided herself, and felt only slightly better.

She went, barefoot, into the hallway, and listened for sounds of life. It was blessedly silent; her mother was still asleep. I've got to get her out of here, she thought. Then she tiptoed back into her bedroom and closed the door and stared at the telephone, daring it to ring.

20.

Remembering Joe

The Firefly Theater was up three musty flights of stairs in an abandoned-looking building in the meatpacking district, and Angela was flushed and winded by the time she reached the top landing. A group of younger people thudded past her, laughing raucously at something, while she leaned against the banister and tried to regain her breath.

The ticket to the play and an invitation to the party afterward had arrived in her mailbox a couple of days earlier, a happy surprise among the usual junk. After she'd dropped Charlotte and Jimmy at the train station that afternoon the week before—their arms laden with the books Angela had pressed on them, flowers from her garden, and bags of local corn and tomatoes—she hadn't expected to hear from them again, or at least not so soon.

People always promise to keep in touch, as those two had so politely, sweetly done, and don't really mean it. According to Charlotte, her own mother had concurred with Angela that they'd simply "lost touch," as if nothing bad had ever happened, and only a gesture of some sort was required to reunite them.

Angela had enjoyed having Charlotte and Jimmy with her in The Springs, and they seemed to be sincerely grateful for her hospitality and that brief respite from the city heat. But she also knew how improbable connections between the generations were, except in cases of family love and obligation. And whatever fantasies she'd had about her relationship to Charlotte were hers alone. She was no one to the girl, really, except some vague figure from the past, from her *parents'* past, and old now, anyway. In Angela's own youth, she recalled ruefully, the elderly all wore cloaks of invisibility.

This place must have been a factory of some kind once. It had a raw, industrial look, with exposed brick walls and a maze of ceiling pipes. There was a makeshift stage in the center of the room, a rough wooden platform, really, around which a few rows of various unmatched folding chairs were arranged. There was no curtain. *Fire Trap* seemed like a more apt name for the theater; there didn't appear to be any other way out besides the stairs.

Angela took a seat in an almost empty back row and opened the program she'd found in a pile on a stool at the foot of the staircase. It had to have been printed directly from someone's computer, like the ticket, and then crudely folded. The one-act play was called *Remembering Joe,* and it was co-written by two members of the cast. In fact, everyone involved in the production was part of the Firefly Players. Jimmy was not only playing one of the main roles—he was also the stage manager and lighting consultant for this production.

Charlotte was listed, too, as the set designer, although the "set" was only a pair of weary armchairs turned toward each other, with a rickety table between them. Still, Angela experienced a kind of proprietary thrill at seeing Charlotte's name in print. Years ago, just before Christmas, she'd accompanied Valerie to Charlotte's nursery school to listen to the children sing a round of carols and a couple of obligatory Hanukkah songs. Their voices were piping and hesitant at first, but grew surprisingly strong after the first round of applause.

Angela remembered how Charlotte had kept her gaze fixed on her mother while she sang, as if to pin her in place, and the ripple of envy she'd felt at the intensity of their attachment. This was during the heat of her affair with Stephen, when so much of her personal currency was invested in her own attachment to him. Had she actually felt less guilty and even more entitled that day because Valerie had Charlotte so irrevocably to herself? It had to have been a kind of madness, she thought now as the houselights dimmed and the actors took their places on stage.

When the lights went up, two people, a man and a woman, were sitting, nude, on the armchairs, reading sections of *The New York Times.* One of them, Angela realized, with a considerable jolt, was Jimmy, who seemed no more self-conscious in the altogether than he had coming out of her bathroom, zipping up his fly. She glanced around and saw, in the semidarkness, the startled profiles of a middle-aged couple nearby—other indulgent parents, probably, who would also pretend sangfroid at the children's naughty game. *Other* parents? What was she thinking?

The play was idiotic, really. There was no conceivable reason for the nudity, except perhaps to provoke, or because of the dearth of a costume designer in the Firefly ensemble. Jimmy and the voluptuous young woman seated in the other armchair chatted and droned in Pinteresque garble for what seemed like hours about someone named Joe, who was either dead or had never existed. It was the sort of tedious performance that let you wander off into your own mind, coming to every once in a while to feebly try and find your place in the story.

Angela, who believed so strongly in the power of narrative to inform one's life, drifted off into the kind of reverie Emma Bovary
might have had after ingesting one of the romance novels she lived by.
Maybe it was just the title, *Remembering Joe,* that was the springboard
for remembering Stephen, or maybe it was the casual nudity, or the
absence of absorbing content in the play itself. Whatever had stimu-
lated or released her, she went off like a stage hypnotist's shill into the
past.

It was early in the affair and it was snowing—how the senses can
re-create the blur and scent of a winter's day; the way a scarf, unwound
from a lover's throat and wrapped around your own, could transfer his
warmth; and the salty perfume of that first taste of his skin. They'd
traveled, in their separate cars, to a motel thirty miles from the campus. There was a heightened sense of risk because of the icy roads, and
she had to drive slowly, as if in a dream, with Stephen driving only a
few yards behind her, trying to keep her in view.

They both knew that this trip could end disastrously, in an accident that would be difficult to explain. And there was even the chance
that they would be unable to get home at all again that day if the
storm intensified. On the way there, though, she had allowed the rapture of anticipation to overcome any anxiety. Sexual pleasure had become an obsession by then, her raison d'être.

But Stephen was worried about being able to be back in time to
pick Charlotte up from some lesson—gymnastics or ballet or Suzuki
violin—she had so many precocious extracurricular activities. And Valerie had meetings scheduled all afternoon and couldn't fill in for him.
So he was distracted and not inclined to be leisurely in bed. Angela remembered that they were out of sync that day, like dancers moving to
different musical beats. He rushed her and she held back, trying to
keep him there. It made for a sweaty tension between them, which offered its own perverse pleasures, but wasn't what anyone could possibly call loving.

And then, when they were leaving, without the usual treat of having dozed for a little while in each other's arms, another motel door opened, opposite theirs, and a family emerged into the swirling snow. There were three of them, a young mother and father and a little girl about Charlotte's age. The girl waved a mittened hand, and the mother smiled and waved, too, companionably, as if they were all bound together by the awful weather, and the possibly treacherous journey ahead. Stephen and Angela might also be married, for all they knew, with a child or two of their own waiting for them to come home safely.

Then the father began to clear the windshield of his family's station wagon with an ice scraper, and Angela saw that Stephen was about to do the same, first to her car and then to his own. The couple would quickly figure things out, she knew, from the separate cars. The dinky motel, which must have been the nearest port in an impending storm for them, even had a weakly flashing neon sign about day rates.

Why did she care what these strangers thought of her, when she was so daring, even reckless, among people she actually knew? But she did care, with a feeling close to panic or heartsickness, and she turned back toward the door to the motel room, which had locked shut behind them. And the key, naturally, had been left inside. "Stephen," she called, and he set his scraper down on the hood of her car and came over to her.

"Did you forget something?" he asked, and when she only shook her head, her huddled back still turned to him and the departing family, he seemed to understand what had happened. "It's all right," he said. "It doesn't matter." And he put his hand comfortingly on her shoulder, and waited with her under the shallow overhang in front of their room until they heard the slamming of car doors and the revving of the station wagon's motor.

A third person, clothed, had come on stage and was standing in a circle of blue light. Joe, or more likely his ghost, judging from the actor's waxy pallor, although Angela had completely lost track of the play. There was quite a bit more of it, though, which she sat through in some cramped space between memory and the moment. Then, a burst of applause, as startling as gunfire, erupted from the sparse audience, and Angela belatedly joined in, wishing, against all reason, those untalented and misguided children well.

The party was to be at Charlotte and Jimmy's apartment. Angela had driven into the city and now she found herself going downtown with what was surely an illegal number of passengers. The actor who'd played Joe, and hadn't bothered to wash off his greasepaint death mask, sat next to her with a girl bouncing on his lap, and there were four more people in the back of the Neon, all of them giddy with celebration, or something they were on.

Angela had never been young in quite this way, as part of a thrumming, howling pack of baby wolves. Until Valerie and Stephen had taken her on and into their gregarious lives, she'd been as solitary and self-contained as she'd become again after they were gone. Finding herself in the midst of these kids was a little overwhelming, but she marveled at and even envied all their radiating energy and heat.

Still, it was a relief to see that a few other older people had been invited to the party, too. There were a couple of scruffy, leftover hippies who lived next door and greeted everyone as "man," and that pair she'd noticed in the audience and had correctly surmised were the parents of one of the Firefly Players. Their daughter, Titania, had been on stage with Jimmy, as naked as the day they'd welcomed her into the world and named her with such wanton ambition. They had a suburban look, too dressed-up and manicured for the occasion, and their conviviality, which had to be at least partly forced, touched Angela. The father, Dan, was a radiologist; the mother, Eileen, did something in public relations. That was the first thing established in Angela's conversation with them—what everybody did for a living. Then Dan went off to get them all some wine. "Well!" Eileen exclaimed in the hubbub, offering Angela a faint smile before glancing helplessly at their surroundings. How did we end up here? she seemed to be saying.

The apartment might have been an updated stage set for *La Bo-hème*. There was the requisite kitchen bathtub, the threadbare, thrift shop furniture, and two cats weaving their way among the legs of the guests. One of Stephen's paintings, an early, ironic self-portrait, hung on the wall over the sagging sofa. Angela remembered it from the master bedroom on Dogwood Drive, and she had to focus on keeping her balance. What if Charlotte had actual photographs of him on display, too, and of Valerie? She was afraid of being caught off guard again, so she looked slowly and cautiously around.

That's when she noticed what had to be Charlotte's work, surprisingly small and quiet abstract canvases hung in clusters around the room. Angela excused herself and went to look closely at a group of them. They were as different in concept and execution from Stephen's work as possible. Delicate pointillist dots swarming together here and there like clouds of gnats, as opposed to his generous painterly strokes, his witty, stylized portraiture. Charlotte's work seemed inspired by nature—perhaps microscopic life—rather than Stephen's colorful fables and fairy tales. Angela felt a pang of disappointment; she had expected the girl to be as bold in her art as she was in her being. But maybe her subtlety was a kind of bravado. She decided that she would buy one of the paintings and hang it next to Stephen's, as a kind of quiet postscript.

"Kids," someone said in her ear. It was Dan, with a plastic tumbler of red wine in each hand.

"Thanks," Angela said, and took a sip of her wine, which was as harsh as she'd expected.

"So which one of these geniuses is yours?" he asked, and she located Charlotte at a safe distance before she pointed and said, "That one." Then she indicated the paintings. "She's an artist."

"Oy," Dan said, making an effort at twinkling good humor. "Where did we go wrong?"

"I don't know that we did," she said with deliberate calm.

"They're living authentic lives, at least. They're artistic and independent." She took another, longer, swig of the wine, as if to wash down her words, even though it burned her throat.

"Sure, except for a little subsidizing," he said, still trying for a playful mien, but clearly feeling irritable, even angry.

"Weren't you subsidized in medical school?" Angela asked him.

"How can you compare that to this?" he said hotly. "I was going to earn a living, I had student loans I knew I'd have to pay off."

He was right, of course. Titania and Jimmy, and maybe Charlotte, too, were only playing at life. If Charlotte truly were her child, she'd likely have the same conventional concerns about her future. But she felt willfully wicked. "Charlotte's gifted," she said. "That requires a certain amount of faith on her part, and on the part of others." When he didn't respond, she said, "Her father was an artist, too."

She'd played the death card now, in addition to that flagrant misrepresentation of herself. Could this radiologist see right through her, the way he saw the innards, the very bones of the patients he x-rayed and scanned? He'd seen it all, no doubt, but his solemn expression showed that he still had some respect for mortality, if not for the immortality of art. Before he could clear his throat, though, and offer some standard sympathetic remark, Angela made her way across the crowded, buzzing room toward Charlotte and Jimmy.

"Well done," Angela told him. "I'll always remember Joe." Stephen, Rodolphe, Vronsky, whoever. Jimmy almost knocked her down with a grateful hug.

And to Charlotte, whose small firm hand she pressed between her own palms, she said, "Thank you, my dear. Say hi to your mom for me, won't you. Don't forget. And let's not lose touch."

21.

An Inauthentic Life

It had been raining for two days, and the heat was so oppressive that the Page Turners were going to hold their meeting inside that afternoon, in the perfectly climate-controlled atmosphere of the Snyders' library. Lissy was still upstairs in her bedroom, getting dressed, and the other women were yet to arrive. The pale leather love seats and chairs that Michelle had grouped together for the occasion seemed to hold out their cool and silken embrace. She dropped the feather duster she'd been listlessly wielding and quickly tried one inviting seat after another, like Goldilocks on uppers. They were all just right.

Hank had a leather chair, too, in his living room, an oversized, mahogany-colored recliner, on which, in its full extension, they'd made love a couple of times when Kayla wasn't around, but that leather was much coarser and less supple. You tended to stick to it during the acrobatics of sex, and it always left a kind of new-car smell on your skin. Michelle sighed, thinking about Hank and about sex, about her longings and her misgivings, as she flicked at the imaginary dust around the room.

Lissy came downstairs, finally, giving off vibes of her usual cheery anxiety, and soon the rest of them came in and took their places. Michelle reentered the library, on cue, without the feather duster this time, and offered to take individual drink orders. Everybody wanted iced tea, though, just as she'd predicted. She had already prepared a large pitcher of it, so jammed with stems of mint and slices of lime it looked like swamp water.

There were five of them in attendance that afternoon, including Lissy and the leader. The bitch in white who'd caught Michelle in Lissy's bedroom that day was missing again; maybe she'd finally run off with her scuzzy boyfriend. (Everybody in town knew about them now, except maybe her husband.) The others all carried paperbacks with a photo on the front cover of that older actress, the one married to Paul Newman. As Michelle was leaving the room, she heard the leader, Angela, say, "What do you think, everyone: is India Bridge a tragic heroine?"

In the thoughtful silence that followed, Michelle loitered just outside the doorway, listening. The strange combination of those two words had caught and held her. "Heroine" had a kind of built-in glory that "tragic" seemed to take away. It sounded almost as weird to her as when someone said "pretty ugly" or "jumbo shrimp."

"Yeah," one of the squeaky-voiced blondes said, at last. "She's tragically dull."

"She lets her husband run the world," another one said.

"I don't know . . . ," someone else—Lissy?—began. "She does have this . . . inner life . . ."

"Yes?" Angela said. Michelle imagined her sitting forward in her seat, the way old Mrs. Eckstein, her own high school English teacher, used to do when she wanted to yank the words out of some dumbbell's mouth.

"I mean she *almost* asserts herself a few times, doesn't she?"

"Like when she wants to initiate sex with her husband, but then doesn't."

"And when she thinks about going into analysis, and he talks her out of it."

"Don't you want to shake her?"

Michelle was getting bored; it was like overhearing gossip about people she didn't know. She was about to leave when one of the women said, "And what about him, *Mr.* Bridge? He won't even tell her that he loves her," and Michelle leaned back against the wall and continued to listen.

"He's such a stiff. They both are."

"Well, it was different in those days, and they lived in Kansas."

"That's not exactly outer space. And it was the twentieth century, not the Dark Ages."

"And her friend Grace Barron speaks up."

"Yeah, and then she kills herself."

"She and Emma Bovary."

"I really like her, though." Lissy, again. "And I feel sorry for her."

"Who—Madame Bovary?"

"No. Mrs. Bridge."

"Why?" Angela asked.

"Because," Lissy said. "Because she seems decent at heart, but weak, as if she can't escape her husband's spell."

"She follows his rules, without holding his convictions."

"Even in the voting booth."

"But still . . . ," Lissy said, just before Angela broke in, proclaiming, *"She lives an inauthentic life,"* with the authority of someone having the last word in an argument.

There was a long, expectant pause, and then Lissy said, shrilly,

"Oh, where is that girl with the tea?" and Michelle scurried away down the hall to the kitchen.

. . .

Later, after everyone was gone, Lissy went upstairs to lie down. She always seemed to need to recover from her book group, as if she'd just worked out too strenuously at the gym. Michelle was in the library, straightening up. She had taken away the tea things and was moving the leather chairs back to their usual, separate stations when she noticed that someone had left a paperback book tucked behind a cushion.

It was a copy of that novel they'd been discussing, *Mrs. Bridge,* its pages curled and its covers bent out of shape, as if the reader had been trying to destroy it. There were underlined passages and penciled comments in the margins. "Get a life, girl!" and "Give me a break!" appeared on one page. Michelle hated when people wrote in books, sticking their own two cents' worth into somebody else's story, although she had once drawn a handlebar mustache on a portrait of Dolley Madison in a sixth-grade history text.

She sat down on the chair she'd just moved, slipped off her shoes, and put her feet up on a hassock and began to read. When the telephone rang about thirty pages later, she jumped as if she'd been caught sleeping on the job. Lissy must have answered on one of the extensions upstairs, cutting off the second ring, and Michelle went back to the kitchen, still carrying the book. It belonged to that bubblehead, Joy; her name was written inside, too. Did she think someone would try to steal that sorry-looking thing?

Michelle put the book on the worktable, alongside the single earring she'd retrieved from beneath another cushion, and the usual loose change. She finished putting the dishes away and swiped one more time at the spotless counters with a sponge. But when she heard Lissy on the stairs, she opened her own purse, which was sitting on a stool, and dropped the book inside. Lissy came into the kitchen and paid

Michelle, who made a point of showing her the recovered earring and coins—a testament to her honesty—and left.

She had never lifted anything at work before. It had always been a matter of pride, because there were so many temptations, and it was easy to rationalize that rich people wouldn't miss a couple of bucks here or there, or one of a few dozen sweaters or scarves. That she messed with their belongings never bothered her conscience. Curiosity wasn't a crime. There was no harm done, really, and it was a built-in risk they took for needing all that caretaking, for leaving so much private stuff just lying around.

But of all the things to have taken, when she'd passed up diamonds and furs! It was just a cheap, scribbled-in book, not even a hardcover, and it wasn't Lissy's, a fact that held some peculiar importance for Michelle. But she felt a funny buzzing in her chest, like an interior alarm going off, as she went through the back door, clutching her purse, and walked to her car.

She was on the couch at home, still reading, with the dogs like bookends beside her, when her mother came in from work, whistling, and then stopped and said, "Didn't you start the potatoes?"

"I forgot," Michelle said, tossing the book onto the coffee table. "I'll do them now."

Jo Ann continued to stand there staring at her, her arms folded across her chest.

"What?" Michelle said.

"Isn't Hank coming over?" Jo Ann asked.

It was Tuesday, it was after five, of course he was coming over; their lives were run by the calendar and the clock. But Jo Ann must have noticed that Michelle hadn't showered or changed her clothes, as she usually did before seeing Hank, those little rituals of their endless courtship. "Yeah, so?" she said.

"What's the matter with you?" Jo Ann said. "You look like you just woke up from a hundred-year nap."

Michelle only shrugged and went into the kitchen to scrub the potatoes and set the table.

Hank, when he showed up, right on time, thought that she seemed a little off, too. And like some asshole sitcom husband, he wondered if she had PMS.

"That's it!" she cried scornfully, ducking his solicitous hand. "It's only *woman* trouble." *Right, and maybe that's what Mrs. Bridge suffered from all those years, too.* Michelle dumped some pork chops onto the cutting board, and when Pete and Bill rushed over to check them out, she shoved them away. "Move!" she ordered sharply when they stalled, and their tails sank and their eyebrows twitched with injured surprise.

Hank whistled for them as he went out to light the barbecue, and Michelle watched through the window while he drank some beer, moved the coals around, and played with the dogs. He was nothing like that tyrannical workaholic, Mr. Bridge. And Michelle hardly resembled wussy Mrs. Bridge. She was more like that Mexican artist, someone fiery with passion, who took real chances. Except that Hank seemed to be calling all the important shots in their relationship, and she seemed to be going right along with him, not speaking her own mind. Which meant, in the long run, that she was living an inauthentic life.

But she knew that if she ever said that sort of thing to Hank, it would sound like some inauthentic bullshit. He would either burst out laughing, or look as confused and hurt as the boys had when she'd reprimanded them for their excitement about the pork chops, for merely living their own authentic doggy lives.

So after supper was done, she revived the PMS scenario, claiming a headache, and begged off going back to Hank's house with him. He seemed skeptical and disappointed, but he went home alone anyway without making a fuss. He even said, "Feel better, Mushy, okay?" and gave her a little kiss on the bridge of her nose. Jo Ann went up to bed, and Michelle let the dogs out before returning to the couch and *Mrs. Bridge.*

She kept hoping against reasonable hope that the course of the story would change, that *true* heroism would eventually prevail. "Listen to me, Walter," India Bridge might say to her husband, in any one of the few short chapters left, "things have to be different between us from now on." Michelle preferred novels with happy surprises in them anyway, which made them less like real life.

But the next thing she, and Mrs. Bridge, knew, Walter Bridge had dropped dead—at work, of course—and with everything that mattered still unsaid between them. Michelle couldn't read another word. She felt as clogged and weepy as if she really was about to get her period.

No wonder the book looked so beat up; she wanted to throw it across the room, herself, and then into the trash. But she would probably just bring it back to Lissy's the next day and "rediscover" it under a cushion in the library. It was hardly worth spoiling her clean record over.

Then she heard the dogs whining and scratching on the porch and she let them back into the house. It had finally stopped raining that afternoon, but their coats were still damp, and they smelled awful, as if they'd been rolling in something dead. "Get away from me," she told them as they circled her legs. "You stink to high heaven."

But they were such fools for love, so completely incapable of holding a grudge. Even as she banished them to the basement for the night, their tails waved like windshield wipers, and Bill's lip was still curled in a tentative, hopeful smile when she shut the door in his face. If they could only read, she thought, bizarrely, the balance of power would surely shift.

22.

Knock Knock. Who's There?

Her mother went home at last, and still he didn't call. The telephone had become an instrument of torture; she wished that it had never been invented. One day she was going through some papers on her desk and found his business card—A TOUGH ACT TO FOLLOW—and called him. When his voice-mail announcement came on—"This is Patrick, aka Doctor Delirium. Leave a message and one of us will get back to you"—she hung right up, as if she were letting go of something hot.

But she picked up the phone again later that afternoon and left a hasty, badly rehearsed message. "This is for Patrick," she said. "It's me, Lissy. Please call." And then instantly regretted it. Her voice had been too breathy, for one thing, and she was sure she'd sounded needy. She should have addressed his alter ego, anyway, the one she'd known professionally, so if she had a change of heart before he called back, she would have a graceful out.

A couple of days later, Jeffrey called her from his B&B in Winchcombe, to confirm that he and the children would be arriving at Kennedy the following Monday. Lissy's disappointment at hearing his dear, distant voice, after she'd picked up the phone so expectantly, shamed her. Only when she learned, by inquiring, that Danielle was still in Winchcombe, too, did she feel a little less guilty.

The last day of her mother's visit had been rife with tension. Bernadette complained about everything—the excellent food, her ergonomic mattress, a nonexistent draft—and Lissy kept thinking of Evie, of that hauntingly cruel story of her death. The hot-water bottle, her own comatose, ignorant self. That mysterious sentence she'd heard, or dreamed, her grandmother say. *What have you done?*

It was strange that when she allowed thoughts of Patrick to enter her consciousness, she believed that Evie might have given her guidance in this matter, or at least consolation, as she had done in so many other matters during the turbulence of Lissy's childhood. Bad dreams, turncoat friends, the friction she could sense building between her parents like an oncoming electrical storm. Lissy had counted on Evie's magical incantation, "No matter, my girl," and to hear her say that things would work out somehow, that she wouldn't even remember whatever it was that had agonized her so, in ten or twenty years. That turned out to be true in some cases, and untrue in others, but the comfort afforded at the time was unassailable.

There was certainly no maternal comfort forthcoming then or now. Bernadette simply wasn't capable of it, and Lissy could only wonder, with the tiny drop of charity she managed to muster, what had been done to *her* as a child, and how far back in family history blame could be cast. It made her dizzy to contemplate, as if she were peering down into a multilayered grave, and terribly sad.

She'd gotten her mother to leave finally by faking the onset of a cold. Bernadette had a morbid fear of germs; she had never been a bedside mother and certainly wasn't going to become one at this late date. "You're not getting sick, are you?" she said accusingly when Lissy sneezed. And she averted her face from a farewell kiss, just as she had when she'd been greeted on her arrival. Of course, Lissy actually did catch cold a few days later—she'd never gotten away with lying—and by the time Patrick called her back, late on the night before Jeffrey was to return, she had developed laryngitis. Her voice came and went with capricious suddenness.

"Is that you?" he asked. "You sound like a little frog. I'll have to kiss you and make you human again." So there was to be no preamble, no charade of innocent friendship. She could only answer him with a gasping croak.

He had been away, he said, in Maine, to see his father, who'd been ill but was better now. He had given up on hearing from her, and hadn't even bothered to listen to his messages until he'd returned. But now he was here, and when could he see her?

"This isn't the best time," she whispered hoarsely, and she guessed that he imagined her husband in the next room, and that the thought probably excited and scared him as much as it did her. "Let me get back to you, okay?" she said, and then she kept coughing and wheezing over his protests, as if she'd swallowed a harmonica. So he had to let her go, finally, and she was off the hook, at least for the moment.

The last time Lissy had seen the children, shortly before they went abroad, she and Jeffrey had taken them to lunch at Ruby Foo's, and then to FAO Schwarz. It wasn't a successful day. At the restaurant, Miranda, who had insisted on Chinese food in the first place, pulled everything she deemed suspiciously "hairy," like bean sprouts and celery, from her chow mein, using a single chopstick as a spear, and dropped it onto the tablecloth. Miles hummed while he ate and kicked at a table leg, getting Lissy's shin more often than not. And he read aloud from a book of alphabetized knock-knock jokes, doing all the parts himself, until Lissy wanted to rip the book from his hands instead of echoing Jeffrey's indulgent chuckles as she did.

But even he began to lose patience after a while. Miles was up to the *E*'s by then—"Knock knock. Who's there? Ewer. Ewer who? Ewer getting sleepy!"—and people at neighboring tables were giving them dirty looks. "That's enough now, Miles," Jeffrey said. "Eat some of your sesame noodles." But Miles said, "Wait, Dad, wait. Listen to this one," and Jeffrey sighed and said, "Okay, one more, but that's it."

Then, later, when they were crossing Fifth Avenue, Lissy tried to take Miranda's hand, only to feel the painful flick of the girl's surprisingly sharp fingernails on her palm, forcing her to let go. At FAO Schwarz, Jeffrey rewarded them both for their bad behavior with a pile of extravagant purchases.

They were much taller now than Lissy remembered. They must have grown, as children tend to do when you're not watching. But she refrained from remarking on how big they'd become, because she knew what an annoying cliché that was, and because she hated to acknowledge, even to herself, that they appeared less manageable than ever in their pre-adult stature.

And it wasn't just that. Their features had emerged more clearly from the pudding of their baby faces, and she could almost predict how they would look eventually, and what would become of them. She saw Miles as handsome in a sleek, ferrety way (like his mother), and working as a stand-up comic at some obscure club in Alphabet City, his whole repertoire built around his anger at the corporate world, his father's world, the hand that continued to feed him. Jeffrey would be in the audience every night, applauding madly, laughing at himself with tears shimmering in his eyes, the way they did when Miles appeared in a nonspeaking role as a slave in the lower school's production of *Big River*.

It was clear that Miranda would be ruthlessly beautiful, with men collapsing at her feet, and Lissy envisioned her in a courtroom, charged with the murder of her second or third husband, or of some salesclerk who'd been foolish enough to be rude to her. The victim's DNA would be under her fingernails, but Jeffrey would win her an acquittal with the best defense team money could buy.

Jeffrey looked different to Lissy, too, in a way. His face was a little fuller, sort of jowly, or maybe he'd just gotten a bad haircut over there. But had he always had that habit of tapping her arm when he spoke to her? Out of the blue, she remembered that scene in *Madame Bovary* when Emma's husband tries to kiss her shoulder, and she shuddered. God, maybe she was just reading too much.

The first thing the children did when they came into the house, even before they used the bathroom, was to call their mother, who, it turned out, had been with them on their flight from London, and was back in Manhattan now. Apparently, she'd asked to speak to Jeffrey, because Miranda handed the phone over to him with a sly smile, saying "Mommy wants you." They were all in the kitchen and Lissy stayed right there, eavesdropping shamelessly.

She could hear Danielle's staticky soprano, like an outraged cartoon character's, without comprehending a word she said. And Jeffrey might have been speaking in code for all she could glean from his end of the conversation. *Yes. No. Well, I can try. Uh-huh, it was. I'll think about it. Yeah, okay, you, too.* Suddenly he looked up and blew a kiss to Lissy across the kitchen, and she blushed and turned away.

They got through dinner somehow, and Jeffrey supervised the children's baths. Then he went into the room Miranda and Miles were going to share, to read to them and tuck them in. Lissy had taken pains to prepare separate rooms for their stay, with a couple of her own old Rainbow Brite dolls propped on the dresser for Miranda, and a nonpartisan selection of sports posters tacked up for Miles, because she wasn't sure which teams he favored, or if he actually even liked sports.

One Sunday the summer before, she and Jeffrey had played a game of catch with both children in Central Park, and Miles kept missing the ball, and eventually threw it past his sister into a stand of trees, from which it was never recovered.

According to Jeffrey, it was Miles's idea to share a room with Miranda; he'd said, cryptically, that she "needed to be protected." Jeffrey was amused and touched by such brotherly concern, but Lissy couldn't help thinking: Protected from what? From whom?

They both had to be exhausted from the flight—children suffered from jet lag, too, didn't they? But they didn't fall asleep, and they kept calling out for something—another story, one more glass of water, a stuffed animal that had been left behind in England. And Jeffrey kept saying "That's it, guys, I really mean it this time," only to trudge back into their room again and attend to their latest wish or command.

But he was finally overcome by fatigue, and he fell in a sprawl across his and Lissy's bed with his clothes still on, as if he'd been clubbed. He was fast asleep in moments. She removed his shoes, covered him with a throw, and fit herself carefully into the narrow space left beside him. They had been apart for almost two weeks, the longest separation of their marriage, the longest time ever that they hadn't made love.

Of course, he was exhausted, and she wasn't exactly in the mood, either, but she was acutely awake. Although she'd regained her voice that morning, she still had remnants of her cold, and there was all that residual tension from her mother's visit, from her phone call with Patrick, from the knowledge of the children lying restlessly only a few yards away. But she shut her eyes and let herself drift down the spiral of lazy, disconnected thoughts that usually led to sleep. And she was almost there when she heard Miles call out, "Dad! Hey, Dad, you'd better come in here!"

Jeffrey didn't stir, so Lissy put on a robe and went down the hallway to the children's room. By the meager light of the glow patch Jeffrey had plugged in at the baseboard, she saw Miles sitting upright in one of the twin beds. His blanket and pillows were in a tangle on the floor, as if he'd wrestled them there. Miranda seemed to be asleep in her bed, although, oddly, her eyes were slightly open. Her mouth was open, too, and every few seconds she emitted a little noise, somewhere between a mumble and a snort.

"What is it, honey?" Lissy asked Miles. She picked up one of the pillows, fluffed it, and placed it behind him.

"I didn't call you," he said. "I called my dad."

"I know," she said, "but he's asleep. You should be, too. Aren't you tired?"

"I never sleep," he said, and a little chill ran through her.

"Did you need something?" she asked.

"I need to talk to my dad."

"About what?"

"About nothing."

"Well, I guess it can wait until the morning, then," she said, and bent to retrieve the blanket.

"Knock knock," Miles said.

"What?" She stood up and folded the blanket.

"Knock *knock*."

She waited for him to answer himself, as he'd done that day at Ruby Foo's, but it appeared that he expected a response from her this time. "Okay. Who's there?" she asked gamely.

"Alfredo," Miles said.

"Alfredo who?"

"Alfredo the dark!" he shrieked.

It took her a moment or two to get the pun, and another to realize what he was trying to say with it. She sat down on the end of his bed. "Miles, are you afraid of the dark?" she asked.

"No!" he cried. "*Al* is!"

She almost said "Al who?" but checked herself in time. "That's a good one," she offered belatedly, instead, and he lay back against the pillow. He didn't look all that tall lying down. She thought of giving him a hug, but settled for patting the mattress in the vicinity of his feet and dropping the blanket across him. "I'll leave the door open," she said, and before she went back to bed she switched one of the hall lights on.

23.

A Table for Two

Angela had forgotten all about the dinner she'd won in the raffle at the Fisherman's Fair until she came across the pot of blackberry jam she'd bought there that day. If she had remembered her prize during Charlotte and Jimmy's visit, she would have taken them to The Battered Clam one evening. It was just the sort of fast Hamptons "scene" Angela avoided, but they might have been amused by it.

On an impulse, she reserved a table for two there at nine forty-five—past her regular bedtime, but all she could get, even on a Monday—and then asked Irene Rush if she'd like to join her for a free dinner at a local zoo. After the slightest hesitation, Irene accepted. "Good, then," Angela said. "Why don't I pick you up?"

So now here they were, in the kind of clamor she had last heard a millennium ago in her high school's cafeteria. She and Irene, who usually had such quiet talks among the ancient trappings at the shop—about the social turmoil in *Barchester Towers,* or the health of their respective tomato plants—found themselves practically shouting across the little table about whether they should share the *fritto misto* and order a bottle of Chianti.

The food was delicious, if somewhat rich for the hour, and there was such unexpected pleasure in having company during dinner, something Angela supposed she'd been too anxious to appreciate when she was hosting Charlotte and her boyfriend. It didn't even matter that it was so difficult to conduct a real conversation in all that racket.

She was touched that Irene had dressed up for the occasion, in a vintage print dress that suited her rangy figure as much as her usual jeans did. And Angela marveled at how someone living alone had managed to work her hair into a French braid. She had always stuck to a short, brushable bob herself, and never wore anything that zipped or buttoned up the back.

By ten thirty, the crowds had thinned and the noise had greatly abated. They could hear each other now, but they sipped their espresso in companionable silence for a while. Then Irene said, "How are the book groups going?"

Angela told her that there were only one or two interesting people this year, including a poorly read but appealing young woman in her Sagaponack group. "She has good instincts," Angela said, "but I think she may be dyslexic."

"But then why did she join a *book* club?" Irene asked. "That's sort of masochistic, isn't it? Like an anorectic deciding to become a food taster."

Angela smiled. "Denial?" she said. "Overcompensation? Those are the only two words I remember from Psych 101. But I think it's brave of her. And in any event, the books are holding up well. Reports of the novel's death are greatly exaggerated."

She asked how Irene had gotten into the antiques business, and Irene said that after she'd left Social Services, she fell into the habit of going to auctions, and of being an early bird at local yard sales. "I started accumulating things I didn't need, and often didn't really want. Your hand goes up and you've bought it—that Prussian army officer's helmet, a boxful of horn buttons, those tintypes of someone else's grim ancestors. I couldn't kick the habit. This was the only sensible way out." And she put one hand to her flaring throat, as if she'd just made an important, regrettable confession.

"There are worse habits," Angela said. She was thinking of her own accumulation of books, and that she should really weed them out before they overtook her house. She might even be able to place some of them on consignment in Irene's shop, and this was probably a good time to ask. But she was surprised to hear herself say, instead, "Like not being able to let go of the past."

It was her turn to blush, or rather to pale. Perhaps it was the sudden hush in the big room that had invited such a confessional remark. Or maybe it was just the wine talking—she had been feeling uncommonly relaxed, and Irene appeared looser and more forthcoming, too—except that neither of them had had much more than a glassful of the Chianti.

Irene seemed just as surprised by Angela's openness, and she waited, with her hands folded on the table, giving Angela a chance to back down, to change the subject. And she could have, easily enough. Why, even amassing piles of old books could be interpreted as a way of clinging to the past.

But Angela took a deep breath and went on. "I had a falling-out with some married friends years ago," she said. "The man is dead now, and the wife lives pretty far away. I was thinking of trying to reconnect with her, you know, maybe to set things right."

"I see," Irene said, although she couldn't possibly see anything from the sketchy little history that Angela had drawn. Where was the affair in her bland narrative—all that passion and deceit? Where was Charlotte? And that absurd euphemism, *"a falling-out"*! It was like saying, after a bloody war, that two countries had had a disagreement and one of them wanted to kiss and make up.

But if she went any further, she might go too far, and they could begin to exchange confidences like a couple of giddy high school girls. Once, when they were walking on the beach, Irene mentioned that her marriage had been early and brief, and Angela hadn't intruded by asking any questions, and now she was being afforded the same courtesy.

The veil of her characteristic reserve fell over her again, like a shroud. "It will all work itself out, I'm sure," Angela said briskly, cutting off the discussion, and looked around for the waiter, so she could signal for the check and turn in her winning ticket.

But before the waiter showed up, a stocky man in a black shirt emerged from the kitchen, lumbering and blinking like a bear coming out of a cave after hibernation. "That's *him*," Irene said in a stage whisper.

"Who?" Angela asked.

"Guido Masconi. He owns this place. I've seen his picture in the *Star* a couple of times."

He looked like someone who would get his picture in the papers. "Ah," Angela said. "Well, then maybe I should go thank him for our dinner." But she made no move to do so.

"There's all this talk about him," Irene continued.

"Oh?"

"People tend to gossip while they browse in the shop," Irene said, almost apologetically.

"What do they say?" Angela asked.

"That he's having an affair with some woman named Ardith Templeton. They're both married."

"*Ardith?* Really? She's in one of my groups," Angela said. "Or at least she used to be. She hardly shows up anymore."

"Maybe she's using you as a cover."

"What?"

"Sorry, just a stupid joke," Irene said.

"But, no, it's more than possible. She reminds me a little of Gatsby's Daisy—you know, headstrong, and with a fatal bent." As I once was, she thought.

"And the other women in the group never said anything about her . . . and *him*?"

"They may have, I don't know." They were always gibbering away about something or somebody before she got the meetings going, a cacophony of noise, like musicians—piccolo players—tuning up before a performance. She didn't really listen; she was already lost in the universe of the book they were about to discuss.

"They say her husband has a terrible temper, that he keeps an arsenal of guns."

"My goodness," Angela murmured.

"And *he* looks as if he's packing something, too," Irene said.

They both laughed, and then Guido Masconi turned and went back through the swinging doors into the kitchen, and their waiter came to the table with the check.

*   *   *

It had been dark out when they'd driven there, but it seemed even darker on the way home. The moon had hidden itself behind invisible clouds, and there were fewer headlights illuminating the road. Angela felt more cautious behind the wheel on the return trip, because it was almost midnight by then, that witching hour for drunk drivers and footloose deer, and because she was more keenly aware now of having a passenger in her custody. So she drove slowly, and with what others might think of as comical, spinsterish care.

"This was lovely," Irene said as they approached her place. "Thanks for inviting me, Angela."

"My pleasure," Angela answered, as it truly had been for most of the evening. She watched as Irene went up the flight of stairs at the side of the shop, waving before she opened her door.

At home, Angela turned on all the lights, unlike her usual parsimonious self, and her stacks of books cast familiar, reassuring shadows everywhere. Even in complete darkness she knew her way around them, and which piles held the Brontë sisters and which the Hawthorne and Thackeray novels she'd been meaning to reread. She probably wouldn't give any of them up until they became a safety hazard, or she became a headline in the tabloids, like those infamous, eccentric Collyer brothers, who were both found dead so many years ago behind the wall-to-wall trash in their house.

Was she becoming peculiar, too? It was only a casual, transient thought as she brushed her teeth; it was gone before she got into bed. After all, there was a major difference between chosen, dignified solitude and an abnormal withdrawal from society. She had just shared a pleasant meal with a friend. She was engaged in meaningful, enjoyable work, and there was Charlotte, who had invited her to a play and a party, and to whose mother Angela had sent greetings. Say hi for me, she'd said, and stay in touch.

What a strange phrase that last was, because it meant to phone or write or e-mail, nothing actually *tactile*. When had she last been touched by anyone but herself? Of course, Charlotte and Jimmy had both hugged her the night of the play, and a few weeks before that she'd gone to the walk-in clinic in Wainscott because of a rash she'd worried might be Lyme disease, but wasn't. That nice young doctor had felt for the pulse in her ankles, and rested one hand lightly on her shoulder while he listened to her lungs through his stethoscope.

She should have been groggy by now, after the wine and all that heavy food, but the interruption of her routine must have disturbed her body's rhythms, its sleep and waking cycles. And her legs had begun to ache. She would have to get up and take a couple of her pain pills; maybe they would help her fall asleep. Didn't the insert say that they might cause drowsiness?

Or maybe it was insomnia they'd warned about; she couldn't remember. In any case, she had to put on her nightstand lamp after she'd gotten back into bed, and pick up a book, the one closest to hand, which turned out to be *Can You Forgive Her?* How had it made its way again to the top of that teetering bedside pile?

When Angela was a child, her mother had a friend, a Mrs. Gladstone, who liked to find guidance at random in passages of the Bible. She would shut her eyes and open it to any page and then put her finger blindly on a line of text. If it didn't seem particularly relevant to one of her personal concerns, she'd give it another shot, or two, or three, until she found the magical phrase she'd sought, something juicy and rapturous from the Song of Solomon, or plainly directive in Proverbs: "Discipline your children and they will give you rest; they will give delight to your heart."

She was a foolish, kindly woman whose undisciplined children did not give delight to her heart, or to her pocketbook. What made me think of her? Angela wondered. Then she closed her eyes, opened the book on her lap at random, and stabbed at the right-hand page. Her finger had landed on one of the lighter and less dynamic passages in the novel, about the peripheral Mr. Cheeseacre and his courtship of Mrs. Greenow. And it didn't in any way speak to Angela about her own life. Like poor, deluded Mrs. Gladstone, she tried again a couple of times, still coming up empty, first with some political digression, and then with Mr. Cheeseacre again.

She had no idea what she'd been looking for, and this arbitrary poking at printed words, out of context, was hardly what she'd ever meant about literature teaching one how to live. But what if the answers were only to be found in the living itself? That question hung there like a quivering drop of water that refuses to fall, so she put the Trollope back where she'd found it, and turned off the light.

24.

Maybe

Summer school was over and Kayla needed a haircut, some extra spending money, and something to keep her occupied until the regular school term began. April was busy making up the hours she'd lost at CVS when she was out sick, so she asked if Michelle would mind taking Kayla to a salon called Scissorhands in Flanders on Saturday. "She says that's where all the kids go," April said, doubtfully. "Just see that she doesn't get anything extreme, like a buzz cut or some spiky goth look."

That was exactly the sort of thing Kayla might do when she was feeling restless or moody—she'd once shaved her eyebrows and forearms out of sheer boredom—and a few days ago her two best friends had gone off on a camping trip with their families, and wouldn't be back until after Labor Day. "And Michelle?" April went on to say. "Make sure she gets a snack or something, okay?"

Michelle had been planning to confront Hank on Friday night about their idling relationship, but she decided to put that on hold until the following night, and she agreed to spend one of her precious free days in the company of his fourteen-year-old daughter. In truth, she was relieved by the delay; she hadn't been looking forward to the encounter with Hank.

And she didn't really mind being with Kayla. She had once read a story in the newspaper about a woman who'd divorced her husband, but couldn't bear to separate from his family—his parents and grand-mother and sisters—whom she continued to meet with on the sly. The husband tracked them down, using a private detective, and forced them to take his side. Jo Ann thought the whole thing was hilarious, but it didn't seem that strange or funny to Michelle. She likened her-self to those polygamous wives on that TV show, who become emo-tionally attached to their husband's other wives and children. Except that she wasn't married at all.

"So what do you need money for?" she asked Kayla when they were on their way to Flanders, thinking that it could be for anything from clothing and jewelry to a navel stud and a fake ID.

"I want to get an iPod," Kayla said.

"Didn't your dad get you one of those for Christmas?"

"He got me a *shuffle*," Kayla said.

"Isn't that an iPod?"

"Duh. But it doesn't have near enough bytes. It only holds, like, two hundred and forty songs."

That sounded like plenty to Michelle, who could listen to the same couple of Springsteen albums all day. But she could still remem-ber being fourteen, and how the newest thing—in her time, the semipermanent mendhi tattoo and the Laura Palmer half-heart necklace—became essential and then obsolete in about a split second. "How much would a better one cost?" she asked.

"Well," Kayla said, ticking them off slowly on bent-back fingers, "there's the shuffle, and then there's the nano, and then there's this new, totally awesome kind that's even got *video*. That one, the one I want, is around three, four hundred dollars."

Michelle whistled. "You're going to have to save your allowance for about a decade." She paused, and then she said, "I know! Why don't I give you a haircut, myself, and you could pocket the money?"

"Do you remember what happened to Pete and Bill?" Kayla asked.

She was referring to Michelle's only previous barbering experience, earlier that month. The dogs hadn't looked *that* bad, aside from a minor nick or two and a couple of bald spots. "Well, now I've had practice," Michelle said.

"No, thanks," Kayla said. "I still have to be seen in public." In her case, that pretty much meant the mall and the beach.

"You could try finding an odd job or two," Michelle suggested.

Kayla seemed to flinch. "Doing what?" she said warily.

"I don't know. Maybe you could help out at the house where I work."

"You mean like be a *maid*?"

"No, I meant my other job, as a movie star."

"Ha-ha," Kayla said, mirthlessly.

"There's always babysitting," Michelle said. "I did it all the time at your age." And she had a sudden flash of herself snooping in drawers, of finding the Polaroid of half-naked Peggy Waller, and that pamphlet with the woman and the pony. Maybe babysitting wasn't such a hot idea, after all.

But Kayla seemed to consider the possibility for a moment or two before she said, "I'm not all that crazy about kids, actually."

"Me, neither," Michelle said, giving her a sidelong glance like a nudge, but Kayla was oblivious to the innuendo.

At Scissorhands, Kayla meekly submitted to a conventional trim from a guy with a Mohawk, but then Michelle treated her to a few Day-Glo magenta streaks, something else she and Hank could be at odds about that night. At least there wouldn't be any witnesses. Kayla was staying home to watch a reality show with her mother—as if there wasn't enough reality in their lives—and Jo Ann was going to Eddie and Kathleen's for supper.

On the way back to Hampton Bays, Kayla couldn't stop admiring herself in the rearview mirror, crowding Michelle, who kept elbowing her away as she drove. As soon as they pulled up to the house, she realized that she'd never gotten Kayla that snack. It wasn't that big a deal. April was just being overprotective again. The girl still wasn't a great eater, but she seemed to have stopped purging, and she wasn't about to waste away. "See you around, kiddo," Michelle said, and waited for a typical Kayla comeback, like "Yeah, in around a million years," or "Not if I see you first," before she flung herself from the car.

But instead Kayla threw her arms around Michelle and said, ecstatically, "My mom is gonna *freak!*"

How thin and bird-like she was, her shoulder blades so sharp they might have been about to sprout wings. Her newly washed, lightning-struck hair smelled like lemonade, like summer. "Clean your plate tonight," Michelle said, "and maybe she'll get over it."

Michelle would always remember that Saturday as being divided sharply in half: the time with Kayla, and the time with Hank. In between she played a couple of hands of solitaire, with "he loves me" or "he loves me not" built into the outcome, and, of course, she lost both times. Dumb superstitious crap. Then she took a long cool bath, as if to soak away the heaviness she felt in her bones and around the sluggish pump of her heart.

She'd probably had the longest fake PMS in history, and Hank wasn't stupid, just unwilling to deal. A little sympathy and a little abstention were a lot easier for him to handle than a long talk. But a long talk was what he was in for; he'd even been warned—*Come over, we*

have to talk. And she'd put the boys out back, so they wouldn't interrupt, so they wouldn't become an amusing distraction.

He came by just after six, trying to hide his apprehension behind
a hangdog smile. At least he didn't rush her with a kiss or an embrace,
his usual style. He stood in the doorway to the kitchen, which she'd
decided was the most neutral place in the house to do this. Not that
she had made herself embraceable. She was sitting at the table, her
hands clasped primly in front of her, her bare feet hooked over the
rungs of the chair. *Stay away from me,* in body language.

"What's going on?" he said, by way of a greeting. He was still in
the doorway, pressing out against the sides of the frame as if he wanted
to widen them.

"Sit down," she told him.

"This sounds serious," he said in an unserious way, but he came in
and sat down opposite her, putting his own hands only a few inches
from hers on the table.

She tried not to look at them. She could hear the dogs scrambling
up the back steps and onto the porch. They must have heard his voice
or picked up his scent, and would begin whining and barking soon to
be let in, and at him. "Hank," she said. "Where is this thing going?"

At least he didn't pretend not to know what she was talking about.
"I thought we were doing fine," he said. "I thought we were good."
And Pete and Bill started moaning in the background, as if he'd given
the wrong answer.

"Yeah, if we were seventeen," Michelle said, and then remembered
that was how old Hank and April had been when they'd begun.

Maybe he was having the same thought, because his eyes lowered
and he didn't answer. She waited, and he said, "There's nobody else, if
that's what you're thinking."

She hadn't been thinking that, but now the idea came roaring
through her head like an express train. Why would he ever bring that
up, only to deny it? He was a natural flirt. All sorts of women—check-
ers in the supermarket, the blue-haired crowd at the Ladies' Village

Improvement Society, even her own mother—were charmed by him. She remembered that the pretty girl behind the counter at Snow Flake had once said, "Here you go, Hanky-Panky," as she handed him their ice cream cones.

And sometimes a couple of those rich young wives, like Lissy Snyder's friends, went along on a fishing day trip on the *Kayla Joy.* It was easy to imagine one of them needing help in landing a catch. At home they all needed help breathing. Although she didn't really like being on the water, Michelle had gone out with Hank a few times, too, and once, when she'd hooked a thirty-pound striper, he had stood behind her with his arms pressed tautly over hers, and they'd reeled it in together. It was fun, and kind of sexy. "I wasn't thinking that," she said sullenly.

"Then, what?" he asked, loudly enough to be heard over the dogs, who were barking now.

"Do you love me?" she shouted back. Mrs. Bridge's own words, the only brave thing she'd done in her whole stupid, inauthentic life. And of course her husband quickly put her right back in her place.

"Come on, Mush," Hank said. "You know I do."

"How do I know that? Through ESP? You never say it."

He looked genuinely bewildered, she'd give him that. "What do you mean?" he said. "Of course I do!"

"No, you don't."

"Well, then I'm saying it now. I love you, I love you, I love you!" He sounded angry and sort of robotic. Like an angry robot. The dogs were reduced to whimpering. You'd think they were the ones being yelled at.

"Well, don't say it that way," she said.

"*What* way?"

"Like I *made* you say it. Oh, but I did, didn't I?" she despaired.

"Jesus," he muttered.

"I heard that," she told him. "Jesus probably did, too."

"What do you want me to say? Just tell me and I'll say it."

"It doesn't work that way," she said. "You have to make up your own lines." And she thought of the vows that Eddie and Kathleen had written by themselves for their wedding ceremony. Mostly cornball stuff—about holding hands throughout life and always sharing the remote—that made people laugh while they were wiping their eyes.

For the first time since she'd known him, Hank seemed to be at a loss for words. Michelle watched the second hand of the clock on the wall behind him go full circle around the dial before he spoke again. Then he sighed and said, "Well, maybe we need to think about moving up to the next step." She waited—tick, tick, tick, tick. "You know, like maybe moving in together."

That, she supposed, was what she'd wanted him to say all along, but much sooner, and of his own free will. She might have been holding a gun to his head. And the way he'd said it—with all those *maybes*—like he hoped to be talked out of it.

"Or *maybe* we ought to take some time off from each other," she said sharply. And he recoiled in his seat, as if that imaginary gun had accidentally gone off.

"I don't want that. That's not what I want, Michelle," he said.

It wasn't what she wanted, either. But it wasn't up to her, was it? She realized then that the boys had quieted down. A squirrel or a chipmunk might have caught their attention, or maybe they were just listening outside the door to see how things would turn out.

But Michelle already knew the end of the story, the way she did when she cheated, by flipping through to the final page of a novel, because she was in a hurry to find out what happens.

25.

¡Vamanos!

Ardith Templeton and Guido Masconi had both disappeared, presumably together. The news sizzled through the wireless Hamptons' air, reaching Lissy repeatedly on the morning of the final Page Turners meeting. It was almost all she could think about as she surveyed the gazebo, which was dry and comfortable on this glorious day, and festooned with strings of tiny chili pepper lights.

The children were splashing in the pool with Jeffrey; Lissy could hear them screaming the way children do in swimming pools, so you could just as easily think they were drowning as having a wonderful time. A leaf blower howled in the distance, the buddleias were drawing their usual crowd of butterflies, and a small plane that trailed a streamer heralding a polo match soared overhead. But where were Ardith and Guido?

Lissy was here, cozily settled on her considerable property and in her familiar life, while Ardith, wherever she was, had clearly chosen sexual adventure at the risk of losing everything else. She had so much to lose: the town house on East 70th Street, the glass-walled Gwathmey on Georgica Pond, the condo in Telluride, the weeks at Canyon Ranch, the magic plastic whose bearer was entitled to every white designer outfit ever created, her unofficial position as first lady of the East End's junior corporate society—everything Angela might blithely dismiss as the "wallpaper of the soul"—and it would all, but for a few pathetic token possessions, be lost. Larry, so brutal in business, so well connected legally, would see to that.

Was it worth it? Lissy felt coolly superior to Ardith and madly jealous of her, alternately agitated and washed with relief. She paced outside the gazebo, swatting at imaginary mosquitoes, nibbling at imaginary hangnails. Oh, why did those brats keep screaming? Thank heaven Jeffrey had taken time off from the office for the rest of their stay. He would keep them busy and mostly out of Lissy's hair, and be there as a moral sentry for her, in case she ever needed one, which was highly doubtful. What she'd had was a harmless flirtation, a momentary lapse of judgment. Nothing had happened that she would need to feel sorry about later. And nothing was going to happen.

The only regret she had was the lost possibility of a friendship with Ardith. Lissy knew now that they could never have been friends, because she wouldn't have made the cut. She wasn't nervy or smart enough; she wasn't *original.* If she *had* begun something romantic with Patrick, it would have been only a weak imitation of Ardith's more daring affair, without Larry and his famous temper, and Guido and his purported links to the mob. Lissy would probably have ended up in some sleazy motel, with butterfingered Dr. Delirium dropping her on the way to an unsavory-looking bed.

She walked out of the woods and down to the pool area, shading her eyes in the sunlight. There was a bright pink whale bobbing on the water, something Jeffrey had bought and inflated with a bicycle pump for the occasion of his children's visit, and it was big enough to accommodate all three of them. In fact, the float was obscene in its swollen mass, its cartoonish aspect. Miles was wearing a yellow life jacket and Miranda a pair of water wings, even though both children had had extensive private swimming lessons. They might have been aboard the *Titanic* instead of a grinning rubber whale. "Come on in, sweetheart," Jeffrey called to Lissy, "the water's great!" His voice was as hoarsely strident as the kids', and his shoulders and bald spot were raw with sunburn.

Lissy picked up the tube of sunblock from the poolside table and was about to toss it to him when Miranda leaned over the edge of the whale and tried to splash her, soaking Jeffrey instead. He splashed her back, and then Miles became involved, and that awful screeching began again. Family fun. Even with her fingers in her ears, Lissy could hear them all the way back to the gazebo. She'd have to ask them to hold it down or to go somewhere else before the Page Turners were in session.

At the house, Michelle was putting the finishing touches on a tray of empanadas and a bowl of guacamole. Two pitchers of margaritas were waiting in the refrigerator. Lissy hoped that these refreshments, the chili pepper lights, and the piñata she'd had especially prepared and delivered by Fiestas on Wheels would give the meeting a festive Latin touch and enhance their discussion today of *Love in the Time of Cholera*, by Gabriel García Márquez.

"*Buenos días,* Señorita Cutty!" she said brightly as she walked into the kitchen. It was a line she'd cribbed, and paraphrased, from Mrs. Bridge's recorded Spanish lesson. Michelle just looked at her as if she were insane.

When Lissy had gone to Canio's Books several days before to buy her copy of *Love in the Time of Cholera,* she'd learned that the author's proper last name was García Márquez, not simply Márquez as she'd said it to the salesclerk. The woman had been so sweet and diplomatic about it. "Ah, yes, García Márquez," she'd murmured, when Lissy inquired, "one of my favorites, too," and guided her to the appropriate shelf.

It was a very long book, especially after the sparer *Mrs. Bridge,* and Lissy sighed when she opened it at home—so many words crawling in a caravan across the Sahara of the page toward meaning. She was determined to finish the whole thing, though, and she resorted to some tricks she remembered from her reading tutor at Betsy Ross: running one finger along each line of text as she read, the way the bouncing ball leaped across the lyrics of a song on the movie screen in assembly; holding a straightedge ruler under a sentence to set it off and reduce the distraction and discouragement of all the other sentences to come; and carefully sounding out each word, until Michelle heard her and came in from the bathroom she'd been cleaning to see if she was being summoned.

But there were the festivities to attend to as well, a demanding chore that Lissy enjoyed much more than reading. She was especially pleased with her own idea of having a custom-made piñata filled with literary favors—bookmarks and bumper stickers inscribed with various slogans and quotes, including HONK IF YOU LOVE TOLSTOY and A BOOK MUST BE THE AX FOR THE FROZEN SEA INSIDE US. As an afterthought, she'd ordered a Harry Potter piñata, too, as a treat for Miles and Miranda. She was still trying to win them over, or at least to have Jeffrey see that she was trying.

She believed that she was making some progress with the boy, who deigned to speak to her once in a while, if only to regale her with further knock-knock jokes or say things like, "My mom makes better toast." The girl continued to give Lissy the silent treatment. Like opposing magnetic forces, their eyes never quite met, and the only physical contact they'd had so far was the near-splashing at the pool.

In *Love in the Time of Cholera,* a man persists in his love for the same woman for more than fifty years while she's married to someone

else, and while the population around them is decimated by cholera
and war and ordinary death. That's what the summary on the Google
site said, anyway—and that Gabriel García Márquez celebrated the illusion of immortality that true love brings. But the novel, starting
with the suicide of a secondary character, took its sweet time getting
to the heart of the story, making Lissy feel even more frantic in her
failed attempts to get through it.

Jeffrey hung the piñata for her from a tree near the gazebo before
he took the children into town for lunch and a movie. As soon as the
book group assembled, Lissy called for Michelle to bring out the refreshments. She didn't even bother waiting until the discussion had
begun; this was to be a celebration of an end to summer reading as
well as a regular meeting. And none of the other Page Turners seemed
that inclined toward literary analysis, either. While Angela waited
with her copy of *Love in the Time of Cholera* open on her lap, and her
eyes cast down at it, Joy and Debby started right in on the local scandal.

Then Michelle came up the path, carrying a tray with a pitcher of
margaritas and an array of stemmed glasses with salted rims. She
wasn't wearing the darling sombrero Lissy had provided for her, and
there seemed to be a residue of salt on her upper lip. Lissy might have
said something, but the girl seemed particularly sour.

"These aren't spiked, are they?" Brenda said in mock alarm. "Why,
it's not even two o'clock." But everyone, including Angela, took a
glassful when Michelle passed the tray around, and the moment she
was gone, the gossiping resumed.

"They say she left without a note, without a word," Joy said.

"And nobody's seen her *or* Guido for ages!" Debby exclaimed.

Angela looked up from her book. "I saw him last week," she said,
and took a sip of her margarita.

They all stared at her, as if a plant had inexplicably spoken; she'd
never joined in on one of their non-book-related conversations before.

"Where?" Joy asked.

"At The Battered Clam."

"What were *you* doing there?" Lissy said before she could stop herself. But it was hard to imagine her staid, elderly book club leader at the hip and youth-driven Clam.

"Having dinner, as one does in restaurants," Angela said drily.

"Oh, I didn't mean—" Lissy began, but Joy interrupted her.

"What was *he* doing?" she asked Angela.

"Coming out of the kitchen for a minute, maybe counting the house." She paused. "He looked like a caveman."

Somebody whooped, and Brenda asked, "Are you sure it was last week?"

"Monday night, to be exact," Angela said.

"So he must have had Ardith stashed somewhere by then, because she's definitely been gone much longer than that."

"She could be dead, for all we know," Deb ventured, looking a little pale, and Brenda said, "Larry's been seen, too, on the target range at the gun club."

"I heard he's taking anger-management therapy in the city," Joy added.

Lissy picked up the pitcher Michelle had left on the table and topped off everyone's glass.

"Ahem," Angela said, holding up her book and waving it, and the Page Turners reluctantly opened their own copies of *Love in the Time of Cholera*.

Angela began by asking how they felt about the novel's central premise.

Brenda raised her hand. "*More* magic realism," she said, so bitterly that her friends all looked at her as if for the first time. She pointed out that the lovesick hero, Florentino, has more than *six hundred* important affairs and several one-night stands while he waits to be reunited with Fermina, his so-called true love. And Angela said, serenely, how much more remarkable that made the reader's sympathy for his quest.

Lissy began to mull over the direction of her own sympathies and her legitimacy as a reader, and what might be going on in Brenda and Brad's marriage, letting the continuing discussion float around and past her.

In what seemed like a short while, Michelle came by again, balancing the second pitcher of margaritas, the guacamole, and a platter of the empanadas, and they all eagerly dug in. There was some further, halfhearted book talk after that, and then Lissy stood, clapped her hands, and announced that it was party time. *"¡Vamanos!"* she sang out, a word she'd coaxed from Pedro that morning while he was trimming the hedges.

She'd had blindfolds and long sticks waiting in the gazebo, and Joy helped her carry them to the tree nearby where Jeffrey had hung the piñata. Angela held back, but Debby and Brenda each took one of her arms and led her outside, and they insisted that she go first. When she demurred, Lissy cried, "Oh, but you have to, Angela, it has a *literary theme!*"

"You get three tries," Joy said, and Angela was handed a stick, and allowed herself to be blindfolded and spun around. She looked so old and frail to Lissy as she stood there, unsteady from the spinning, and maybe the margaritas, and tried to get her bearings. "This way," Lissy said, turning her gently in the right direction and then ducking as Angela wildly swung her stick. She flailed two more times before she hit the target and the piñata burst open, spilling its contents everywhere.

It must have been defective to break that easily, Lissy thought, but the other women screamed and applauded, and then dived for the scattered favors while Angela pulled off her blindfold and watched them. Debby had retrieved a miniature broomstick and Joy held what looked like a wizard's hat. Brenda was staring at the winged, gold-colored ball cupped in her hands. "What's this supposed to be?" she asked, and Debby said, "I guess that's the Golden Snitch. And I've got the Nimbus 2000."

"What?" Lissy said, feeling confused and a little drunk. She'd picked up a plastic lightning bolt and a pair of novelty eyeglasses.

There was a plastic owl on the ground near her feet. Where were the bumper stickers and the bookmarks, the quotes from Kafka and Joyce Carol Oates?

"It's from Harry Potter," Deb explained. She had nephews who were old enough to read. "Why did you get Harry Potter?"

• • •

Miles and Miranda became very upset when Lissy explained about the mixup. Their piñata was supposed to have been a surprise, *her* surprise, but Jeffrey had told them about it, holding it out like a carrot on a stick all afternoon, so they would behave at lunch and the movies. Miranda began to bawl, the way she had at their wedding, and she just got louder at Lissy's offers of the abandoned Harry Potter favors.

There was nothing to do but let them at the other piñata, which Jeffrey hung from a lower branch of the same tree. They both refused to be blindfolded or to take turns, and they wielded their sticks together with what seemed like a vengeance. Lissy couldn't help thinking *That could be me* when the piñata tore open at the third or fourth double whacking, and the scraps of paper fluttered down.

She'd thought the children would be disappointed when they saw the adult-oriented prizes they had released. But Miles scooped up a bunch of bookmarks and immediately began to quiz Lissy: "Who said 'Fill your paper with the breathing of your heart'? Who said 'The human race has one effective weapon, and that is laughter'? Who said 'Always forgive your enemies; nothing annoys them so much'?" Miranda just hurried off toward the house, clutching her loot.

And later, when Lissy and Jeffrey went into the children's room, with their arms linked, to check on them, like young parents in a magazine ad, they were both out like lights. While Jeffrey picked up Miles's blanket from the floor and laid it back over him, Lissy leaned over Miranda, who was temporarily tamed by sleep. This was the only time she could get this close to the girl. Lissy dared to move a silken strand of hair back from her face with excruciating care. The mouse belling the cat.

And then, for a disorienting moment, she was gazing down at her own child-self, fast asleep when her daddy left forever, and while Evie died and was taken away in the night. But, of course, it was only Miranda in the bed, guarded even in slumber, with her eyes slightly open like that. There was a bumper sticker plastered across the chest of her Little Mermaid pajamas that said BOOK SLUT. Would they be able to laugh about that together someday in the far-distant future?

In Gabriel García Márquez's novel, a man's unrequited love survives half a century of separation, and worse; and that very night, in some unknown hideaway, Ardith Templeton was settling for a five-minute fuck that would probably frazzle whatever was left of her brains. Lissy thought of Angela being spun dizzily around under the trees, of Michelle siphoning sips of the margaritas in the kitchen, of Pedro brimming with his own language as he silently clipped the hedges, of Brenda's cynical outburst about unlikely, enduring love. It was all so mysterious and wondrous and terrifying.

Back in their own bedroom, Lissy lay in the cradle of her husband's arms, trying to calm herself in preparation for sleep, and to understand how anyone in the world, with or without the assistance of literature, ever knows how to live.

26.

The Heart of the Day

Love in the Time of Cholera had always evoked more thoughts of mortality than of undying love in Angela. Life is short, eternity long, etc., etc. Maybe it was natural melancholy on her part, magnified even more, lately, by aging and regrets about the past. Whatever the reason, she phoned Charlotte right after her final meeting with the Page Turners and asked for Valerie's address. She would write to her, while she still had the nerve, the letter she should have written long ago.

But Charlotte told her that Valerie was on a tour of Spain and Portugal with her local library group, and wouldn't be back until the middle of September. Her mail was being held at the post office until then, Charlotte said, so there really wouldn't be any point in writing to her now.

Angela had already started composing the letter inside her head, revising it as obsessively as Virginia Woolf was said to have done with her manuscripts. "Dear Valerie, it has taken me all these years to summon the courage . . ." "Val, I can hardly imagine you reading past this first line . . ." "My dear, will you allow me to say what is in my . . ." "Valerie, please hear me out . . ."

"Did you give her my message before she left?" she asked Charlotte. *Say hi to your mom for me.* When had she started speaking that way, like someone with a limited vocabulary and even less imagination?

"Of course I did," Charlotte said. "Didn't I tell you? She said to say hi back to you." That didn't sound like Valerie, either. Maybe everyone was reduced to juvenile speakease these days. Or maybe the situation was too awkward for sincere language. But Angela's spirits lifted a little, even at that ineloquent response. It was the beginning of communication, and there was no evident animosity in it.

The next day, she paid a visit to Irene at Things and, as usual, went right to the shelf of books. There was nothing she particularly desired there—just a few of those ubiquitous Elbert Hubbards, a novel by Mary Roberts Rinehart, a couple of thrillers (the kind that Valerie used to like), *The Joy of Cooking,* and some children's books. "Slim pickings," Irene remarked as Angela crouched in front of the shelf. "They were left on my doorstep last week, like a carton of kittens. Better than drowning them, I suppose."

"Did you ever read this?" Angela asked, holding up a copy of *Harry Potter and the Sorcerer's Stone.*

"No. Everyone says that she's wonderful, that the books are born classics, but I've just never cared for fantasy."

"Not even Oz or Wonderland?" Two of Angela's own early refuges from Staten Island.

Irene shook her head. "I could never work up a willing suspension of disbelief in talking rabbits and melting witches."

"Too bad," Angela said, "that sort of thing can be useful." And then, "I'm going to take this." The book, apparently the first one in the famous series, had belonged to a boy named Jason Blatt. He'd inscribed his name in ink, in chubby, careful block print, right under J. K. Rowling's, as if he'd been her co-author or her translator instead of a mere reader. The book didn't seem abused—it hadn't been dropped into Jason's bath, and there were no other markings in it, or food-stained pages—but it had that pleasing, broken-in look of a much-read volume.

The piñata favors at Lissy Snyder's the day before, with their quirky, invented names, had intrigued Angela—the Golden Snitch, which seemed to neatly juxtapose elegance and lowlife, and the Nimbus 2000, like an unsuccessful and dated car model. Now the title of the book's opening chapter, The Boy Who Lived, was an invitation to read on. When she'd finished the whole thing, and if it was as good as advertised, she would put it aside for Charlotte, in case she hadn't read it.

So many of her idle thoughts and plans involved Charlotte, and, recently and more cautiously, Valerie. When she allowed herself to daydream, this was what Angela imagined: she would write the best letter she could—all those epistolary novels she'd read over the years must have taught her something about that particular form, and Valerie would write a letter back, in her own unaffected voice, and in her handwriting—like those notes she used to leave on Angela's desk at school: *Come at eight. Bring the blue platter, and yourself!*—a letter of understanding and conciliation. It would most likely take several letters back and forth, and even some telephone calls, before that entente could be reached, but there was a patience built into Angela's new sense of urgency.

She'd entertained a few possible scenarios to follow these exchanges, but the favored one involved a trip to Indiana, where she'd never been. Charlotte would accompany her, and Angela pictured them on a plane to Indianapolis. They would hold hands at takeoff and landing, and in between they would sit side by side, reading. Angela saw *Villette* in her own hands, and the book of Grimms' fairy tales that she'd bought at the Fisherman's Fair in Charlotte's. She never permitted herself to go past the final image, of the plane touching down; it was as if a reel of film had frozen in a projector, but she was still ashamed of such blatant, sentimental fantasizing, and especially of how gratifying it was.

Another customer, a woman in her fifties, came into Things and asked Irene if she happened to have a recording, preferably a forty-five, of Eddie Money's "Baby Hold On." After the woman left, empty-handed, Irene laughed and said, "Can you believe it? Some people seem to think this little shop is a repository of their past, the way their mother's basement was, until she cleaned it out and threw everything away. They're so specific in their requests, and so surprised when I don't have what they want."

"Does that mean you don't have my high school yearbook?" Angela said, glancing around at the crowded tables and shelves.

"Why would you want that?" Irene asked. "Didn't you hate high school?"

"Of course I did. I didn't fit in, except with some oddball teachers. And then I became one myself." She'd said all that offhandedly, but she could feel her heart beating.

After a moment, Irene said, "I felt out of place, too."

"In high school?"

"In high school, in college, in my marriage." She shrugged. "In my skin."

Angela looked toward the door. She wondered if other customers would wander in then, but this wasn't a busy, drop-in location at any time, and it was the middle of the week and a beach day. "But you found yourself," she said. She'd phrased it somewhere between a statement and a question, so that the necessity of a reply would be Irene's own call.

"Yes," Irene said. "I think so."

Angela pretended to look through a box of old picture postcards.

"Me, too," she said. "This is a good place to be, isn't it? An island, but not a desert island, and with an escape route to the mainland." As if they'd been discussing geography or real estate.

And then she found herself staring at the tinted photograph on one of the postcards under her hand, of Clove Lake Park on Staten Island. Not far from the place where she had grown up, and gone to school, and longed to leave. The card would have required a two-cent stamp in its day, but it hadn't been written on or sent to anyone. How had it found its way here—perhaps from Angela's own mother's basement? She tucked it into the Harry Potter and went to the counter to pay for them both. Maybe she would write to Valerie on the back of the postcard. *Wish you were here.* Not that Staten Island—or Long Island, for that matter—would have any particular meaning for her, but it would be as if Angela were reaching out from an earlier, more innocent time and self.

She took a few bills from her purse and said, "Do you remember my telling you about that old friend I wanted to contact?" Irene nodded and Angela said, "Well, we've been in touch, actually. And I think we may be able to repair things between us."

"Good for you," Irene said as she handed her the change. "You must feel better about it."

"I really do," Angela said.

But when she was home again the feeling of buoyancy began to fade. What she had told Irene was only the product of wishful thinking, one of those lies you tell to pump yourself up. That whole story of reconciliation was in her head, and she'd let herself become lost in it, as a foil against memory. No wonder she couldn't ever go past a certain point in her reverie, to the part where Valerie actually entered the picture.

It was lunchtime, and Angela had thought she was hungry, but when she opened the refrigerator, nothing tempted her. So she took the Harry Potter novel out to the yard and lay down with it in the hammock. It was what Stephen used to call "the heart of the day." He was referring to the quality of light in his studio in the early afternoon, the best time, he'd often said, for him to paint. And sometimes he had sacrificed that precious light and his work to be somewhere else with her.

The light in Angela's backyard was dappled by the trees, as it always was in the full of their season, but there was enough of it to read by. She'd cut the grass that morning, and its fragrance still lingered. The family of birds that made their home in her yard—red-breasted nuthatches, according to the bird book—twittered and shook the leaves overhead, but when she looked up she couldn't see them. They were alive and hidden, like the past, or the future. She opened the book on her chest and put one foot down on the grass to make the hammock rock. It was like pushing out to sea in a rowboat. So this is summer reading, she thought, without a trace of cynicism.

The book was excellent. Harry Potter, the boy who lived, had all the characteristics of a Dickens hero. He was orphaned, downtrodden, and at the mercy of malevolent adults and other, even darker forces. But Harry had the inherited power of wizardry on his side, in addition to a sense of humor and ordinary human courage. In one wonderful scene, he risks crashing into a barrier at a train station to make his way to a seemingly nonexistent platform. The sort of predicament you find yourself facing in dreams, usually with a less happy outcome, or a last-minute jolt back to wakefulness.

Angela placed the book, still open to the page she'd left off reading, across her chest again, and shut her eyes. Would *she* risk crashing into a barrier of reason if she took her fantasy further than that same, safe cutoff point? She knew that she was forcing the analogy, looking for the kinds of connections that might have appeared in some Macon freshman's paper on meaning in metaphor, just to prove once and for all her tired thesis, that literature teaches one how to live.

But behind her closed eyes, she made the leap and let herself finish the story. She and Charlotte stepped off the plane in Indianapolis. They had to descend a flight of metal stairs and walk a few yards to the terminal. Angela walked inside ahead of Charlotte. It was an hour earlier than in New York, still the heart of the day. Valerie, who had driven more than fifty miles to get to the airport, was waiting at the baggage claim area for them. Angela had worried all the way there that she might not recognize Valerie in her incipient old age, especially in a crowd, without having witnessed her metamorphosis. Charlotte might have to step forward and draw them together.

But Angela knew Valerie at first sight, the way she had known Charlotte that day on Seventh Avenue, as if she'd seen one of those police artist sketches that project missing children into their future faces. She looked like Valerie, that's all, and her arms were opened wide.

27.

Meat Hunger

After all that time, Michelle was without Hank, and she felt shaky and lopsided, like a table that requires a matchbook under its shorter leg for stability. That stupid book. If she had never read it, they might have gone on forever the way they'd been, and that would have been better than this. Who ever said anyone's happiness depended on living an "authentic" life? Well, that old lady Angela had, but what was so great about *her* life? From what Michelle had overheard at Lissy's, all she ever did was drive her crappy little car to and from her crappy little house, where she lived alone, except for a gazillion books. If a man ever looked right at her, she'd probably die on the spot.

Michelle didn't like the way she was being looked at, especially by her mother and Kathleen and Eddie. It wasn't exactly pity she saw in their eyes—they wouldn't have dared to show that—but there were flickers of worry, as if they believed she might not survive on her own. And she knew they were talking about her behind her back. She'd even caught Jo Ann on the telephone once, saying, "Yes, but you know how mule-headed she can be." Then, when she realized Michelle was in the room, she'd started rattling off a recipe for a three-bean salad. Kathleen was probably on the other end.

To her face, though, they were supportive and philosophical, if not what anyone would call cheerful. Her mother observed, unconvincingly, even gloomily, that "things always work out for the best," and Eddie muttered, "That asshole. You're better off without him." God knows what he and Hank said to each other when they were out together on the boat all those hours. Kathleen offered to take Michelle shopping and give her a foot rub, and she went on about those poor cancer patients at the hospital, as if *that* was supposed to make her feel better.

The worst of it was that everybody seemed able to see directly into her head, and even into her wretched heart. Michelle had always prided herself on her impenetrable cool, her independence. On her very first report card, Ms. De Angelo had written "Michelle displays quite an independent spirit!" By the time she was in high school, the remarks tended to be less appreciative and more direct. "Michelle needs to address her attitude problem," or, in red ink, *"Uncooperative!"* And her mother often advised her not to be so "gosh-darn stubborn." Whatever anyone called it, it had become her trademark. When Hank came up against that side of her, he usually caved and said something like, "I just love it when you're cruel, Mush."

For the first week or so after the breakup (because that's what it was, really—not just a time-out or a trial separation), she was more at peace with the dogs than with people. They could sense her mood, too, but they didn't feel called upon to comment on it. She took them out running on the beach, early in the morning or late at night, when dogs were allowed to be there. And she encouraged them to get into bed with her.

But after a while, Bill's sighing and Pete's restless legs would get on her nerves, and she'd kick them out, punch her pillow a few times, and try to get some sleep. And she began to crave human company; it was something like the meat hunger she'd developed the few times she'd tried to become a vegetarian, and as much against her better judgment. It wasn't just anybody's company she wanted, though.

The less Lissy Snyder said to her, for instance, the better—even her diary had become too boring to read. And when Michelle worked an outside catering job, she couldn't stand all the whispery gossip in the kitchen or the dining room. They'd be carrying on about Brangelina one minute, and Ardith Templeton and that guy from The Clam the next. She suspected they talked about her, too, when she wasn't there, at least in the kitchen. Local East Hampton was a small, close-knit community, and word had quickly gotten around about her and Hank.

One day a woman named Patti Floyd she'd known in high school, and still saw occasionally in town or at the beach, called and asked if she wanted to go to Pinky's, a bar in Montauk, that night. Patti had been married twice, and she had a little boy her parents were helping her to raise. She did hair at an Amagansett salon, and she changed the color of her own as often as other women changed their minds.

Michelle wasn't crazy about the bar scene; it was too much about sex and loneliness, which were both on her mind a lot anyway, and drinking with strangers had never been her thing. But she'd seen Jo Ann looking at her funny again earlier, and the thought of staying home one more night, avoiding her mother's attention and watching shows about other people's sex lives and loneliness, was more than she could bear. So she agreed to go out with Patti, who said "Great!" and to pick her up around nine.

Michelle was instantly sorry. She remembered belatedly that Patti had always been a drinker, even back at East Hampton High, when she'd needed to get smashed to make it with one of her boyfriends. She probably wanted a designated driver that night as much as a companion.

Michelle was even sorrier the moment they walked into all that desperate noise at Pinky's, the cranked-up music and too-loud voices, the same old same old of hanging out and hooking up. And she was a little paranoid about running into Hank. He wasn't a barfly, either, but she was here, wasn't she, and he docked in Montauk. She was relieved not to see him, or anyone they knew—although she wasn't sure why she cared about that. It was a free country and she was single, a reminder that pierced her breast like a poisoned dart.

Patti was cruising. She had left Michelle's side soon after they'd picked up their drinks. She was dressed for the hunt in that diaper-sized skirt and fuck-me platforms. And she'd hinted enough about it in the car on the way here—how she hadn't gotten laid in ages, and that men were such pigs, but what could you do, they were the only animals on the farm. Then she'd laughed, that annoying little goose honk of hers, and Michelle didn't really mind when she took off, downing her schnapps chaser, and got lost in the crowd at the bar.

Michelle carried her beer to a tiny table in a corner with only one chair next to it, which was as good as wearing a sign that said LEAVE ME ALONE. But apparently it wasn't good enough, because after a while some guy swung another chair up to the table and straddled it backward. "So where've *you* been hiding, sweetcakes?" he asked. He was good-looking, if you liked that thick-necked, muscle-bound type (which she once, admittedly, had), and here he was, as far east as you could go without falling into the Atlantic, dressed up like a cowboy.

"I'm waiting for somebody," Michelle said, looking right past him.

"Oh, yeah?" he drawled, riding his chair a little closer. "And who might that be?"

"Not you," she said, and she got up and walked away.

She'd forgotten she could be that mean, and how exhilarating it felt. Hank had softened her brain, had turned it to real mush. Now she was starting to be herself again. But coming to this place was still a mistake, and after she'd brushed off a couple of other men, who weren't even that bad, only nothing like Hank, she just wanted to go home. She looked around for Patti, certain she'd never be up for leaving this early. Maybe she could get herself another ride, though. She was probably planning to ditch Michelle, anyway, as soon as she settled on one of the hounds sniffing around her.

Patti's hair was currently a bright metallic red, making her as easy to spot in a crowd as a cardinal in the backyard. But she was nowhere in sight, and Michelle wondered if she'd gone home with somebody already, without saying anything. If she was high enough, she might just do that. Michelle checked the ladies' room, which was empty, and then went outside, where the smokers were congregated. She bummed a cigarette from one of them and stepped away into the side parking lot to smoke it.

When she was about to put the cigarette out, she heard a car door slam, followed by Patti's unmistakable honking laugh. She was making her way over the gravel, and when Michelle caught sight of her, she had the backseat equivalent of bed hair, her teensy skirt was twisted around so the zipper was in the front, and she was staggering a little.

A couple of seconds later, there was the beep-beep of a horn and the flashing lights that meant someone was locking a car. Then Michelle's drugstore cowboy, of all people, appeared a few feet behind Patti, whistling tunelessly and patting himself down, checking out his wallet or his equipment.

Michelle didn't know why she felt so angry and grossed out. They were only two poor fools who'd gotten it on in the back of a van or the cab of a pickup, something she'd done herself, but not for years, not since her mother finally accepted the fact that she was grown and that whatever she did she was safer doing under their own roof.

"I'm going," she called to Patti. "Roy Rogers can take you back." And she started to walk away toward her car.

"No, Michelle, wait up!" Patti yelled. "I'll go with you." The guy had already gone past her, on his way back to the bar. Wham, bam, thank you, ma'am.

Michelle didn't answer, but when she reached the car she got inside and just sat there with the motor running, waiting for Patti to catch up.

She was carrying her killer shoes, and she plunked herself down beside Michelle, saying "Whew!" the way she always used to when she'd nearly missed the school bus. Her beery, sexual perfume filled the car. "So, did you have fun?" she asked.

"Not as much as you, obviously," Michelle said coldly.

Patti smiled and leaned back. She was still slow on the uptake of an insult. And in less than a minute, she was asleep with her jaw dropped open.

There was some ground-hugging fog on the Napeague Strip, and Michelle, who felt acutely sober, drove with her hands gripping the wheel as if she thought it might get away from her. But her anger was gradually shifting from Patti, who was merely a pain in the butt, to Hank, who had so seriously let her down.

She would get over it, she knew; you got over almost everything after a while, or at least grew used to it. It was just a matter of time; *time heals* was another one of her mother's tired lines that often turned out to be the truth. She was starting to feel almost kindly disposed toward Patti, when she came to and announced that she was going to be sick.

Michelle put on her flashers and pulled over onto the shoulder opposite Lunch. Patti immediately stumbled out of the car and crouched down, retching. Michelle came out, too, and leaned over, holding Patti's hair back from her face. "Let it out," she said, "Let it all out," which was what her father used to say to her when she was throwing up, as if you could stop the gush once it started, even if you wanted to. But she remembered how his words, and his hand bracing her head, had comforted her.

When they pulled up to Patti's place, a two-room cottage off Copeces Lane, she said, "Come in for a minute, okay?" She was still pretty buzzed, despite the vomiting, and now her breath really stank. When Michelle hesitated, Patti grasped her arm and said, "Come *on.* I just want to show you something."

Patti's mother had been asleep on the sofa, and she struggled to her feet and into her shoes. "Hello, girls," she said, "did you have a nice time?" As if they'd just come from the junior prom; she was as clueless as her daughter. She told Patti that the baby had been as good as gold, and asked that Michelle remember her to her mother.

After she left, Michelle said, "What did you want to show me? I'm really beat." Patti beckoned and she followed her through beaded curtains into the other, smaller room, where Patti shared a bed with her son, Kieran, who was about four years old, not really a baby anymore. He was a skinny blond kid, and he looked a lot like his father, whose framed photo in Marine Corps blues sat on the dresser. Sonny Floyd had enlisted right after September 11, and he was on his third tour of duty in Iraq. People said it was just to get away from Patti.

There was a lamp on in the room, with something pink thrown over it, so everything had a rosy glow. The boy, curled up in a pair of Pull-Ups in the middle of the bed, reminded Michelle of the infant Jesus in the church crèche. Patti sat on the edge of the bed and slid him over to make room for herself.

Michelle said, "What is it? What did you want to show me?" She'd already come up with a few possibilities herself. Patti was known to peddle pot; maybe she wanted to give Michelle a couple of joints as a thank you for the ride, or as an introductory offer to a potential new customer. Or she could be into selling knockoffs of designer watches and handbags. Who knows, maybe she was going to pull out the latest Clairol Color Chart for Michelle's consideration.

Patti lay down next to Kieran and shut her eyes.

"Hey!" Michelle said, but only the boy stirred in his sleep.

Michelle poked Patti's shoulder, twice, and nothing happened. "Hey," she said again, but flatly this time, without any real hope of rousing Patti. It didn't matter; if there had been anything she'd meant to show Michelle, she'd probably forgotten what it was the moment she'd brought it up.

In her own bed later that night—practically the next morning— it came to Michelle that Patti might have just wanted to show her how she lived. It was such a weird, scattered thought, the kind that runs through your head when you're right on the edge of sleep. But she couldn't let it go. Was Patti making a bid for sympathy, or merely showing off, with her hero husband's photo on the dresser and her cute little kid asleep in the bed? Was she saying *See, at least I'm not alone, like you?*

As soon as she awoke, even before she brushed her teeth, Michelle picked up the telephone and called April. "Oh, how are you doing?" April asked. There was enough friendly concern in her voice to indicate she knew all about Michelle and Hank. But she was much too polite to be the one to bring it up first.

So Michelle was spared any further commentary about her failed love life, and was able to get right to the business of her call. "I was wondering," she said, "if Kayla is still looking for something to do. Maybe she'd like to hang out with me and the boys for a couple of days."

28.

A Hostile Takeover

They'd finally made love, after confirming that the children were asleep, and locking their own bedroom door anyway, just to be on the safe side. But it wasn't like the rollicking time they'd had the night before he left for London, when she had worn the black underwear she'd bought with Patrick in mind. And it certainly wasn't like the night they'd become engaged and blazing tears had stood in Jeffrey's eyes as he came. In fact, he didn't come at all on the downy, lavender-scented bed behind the bolted door, and afterward they made all the pathetic noises loving couples make in similar circumstances.

"It's okay, honey, it happens."

"I'm sorry, sweetheart, it must be the jet lag. I'm still so damn tired."

"Of course you're tired, and it's really, really nice just to be held."

And it *was* nice, in its way, but it wasn't completely satisfying, and it certainly didn't help her fall asleep. Reading, she supposed, might still do the trick. So after Jeffrey had turned over and shut off his lamp—he wasn't going to hold her all night, apparently—Lissy reached around on the floor for one of the fat, juicy fashion magazines she'd bought that afternoon as a sort of book club graduation gift to herself.

The fall fashions were already on display in the shiny pages—and even a few little season-jumping fun furs—as well as the editors' fall choices in movies, books, television, and the hot new restaurants. What to wear, what to see, what to eat, what to do. A far cry from what Angela had called the "moral ambiguity of fiction" that was supposed to let you make considered, individual decisions. Lissy settled back against her pillows and surrendered herself to direct commands.

Then she turned the page and there was Danielle, wearing nothing but a blue fox capelet and a pair of silver Manolo Blahniks. Lissy gasped. But on closer examination, she saw that it wasn't Danielle at all in that attention-grabbing, full-page ad, just a sleek, bony look-alike, with skinned-back hair and that same imperious gaze. When had models started looking like that, with longer noses and almost manly jaws, instead of conventionally pretty, with small, even features, like . . . well, like herself? Taste in beauty appeared to be as arbitrary and fickle as fashion itself.

I'm so awake now, she thought, and she glanced over at Jeffrey's sleeping bulk with a mixture of affection and resentment. The poor guy needed his sleep; he had such a busy schedule planned for the next day. He was going to take Miranda and Miles to the Montauk Lighthouse, and then go seal-watching with them from the beach near there. If there was still time, they'd go on to the Marine Museum in Amagansett. He was becoming a regular Hamptons tour guide.

Of course he'd asked Lissy to join them, pointing out that these were local attractions she'd never visited, either. But she had begged off, as she did with almost everything involving the children, except for meals and watching television, and sitting on the sidelines while they paddled, screaming, around the pool. She wasn't comfortable tagging along on their excursions, and she suspected they had a much better time without her.

Now she felt terribly alert, as if there were a lion in the house, a sleeping, caged lion, maybe, but still something wild and unpredictable that didn't belong there. She turned the pages of her magazine to the calming beauty section that told you that shimmery eye shadow was in again, that black was the new black, and how to plump up your lips without resorting to medical procedures.

Her mother, she knew, lived by the gospel of these publications. That thought chilled Lissy, and for the first time she wasn't that interested in preventing cellulite with a breakthrough French formula, or trying the essential oils discovered in the tomb of a beautiful, ancient Egyptian queen. Bernadette was aging badly—her thighs looked like large-curd cottage cheese—and that poor queen had been essentially dead for thousands of years.

Lissy flipped back to the model in the blue fox capelet. Was that Jeffrey's true type? Was that who he envisioned when he was making love to Lissy, and *still* failed? Once the cascade of thoughts began, she couldn't stem it. There was England, where they'd been a cozy little family again, out of her line of vision; there were the letters still imprinted on Lissy's brain, although she'd shredded and flushed so many of them: *Dear Jeffie, you sexy bastard.* And all the phone calls since the children arrived, allegedly for them, but with Jeffrey always getting on to say something banal or cryptic, or both, Lissy could hardly tell anymore. Knock knock. Who's there? Danielle. Danielle who? Danielle Snyder, his first and only true wife and the mother of his children, you stupid blond slut!

Well, this was madness, now she'd never get to sleep. She'd have to start counting sheep, or her blessings, until she ran out of fingers and toes to count them on. Or regress to the way Evie used to help her let go on wakeful nights. *There's the man in the moon, my girl, looking down on all of us. Here is Evie, watching only you, my girl. There's Teddy on the shelf, guarding the dollies. And way up in Tuxedo, there's Granny Ellis, tucked into her own bed under the very same moon . . .*

Jeffrey was awake so early; the room was still pink with dawn, and he was out of bed, opening the drawers of his highboy as quietly as he could. Lissy had hoped they'd try again this morning, refreshed by sleep and—in her case—relieved of unreasonable, obsessive thoughts, but he was already dressed, and not in the shorts or jeans he'd have put on to visit the Montauk Lighthouse and the Marine Museum. He was wearing his deep blue shantung shirt, her favorite, and a pair of black linen slacks. And he was probably rummaging in the drawers for his cufflinks.

"Jeffrey," she murmured. "What are you doing?"

"Shhh," he said. "I didn't mean to wake you." He came to the bed and leaned over to kiss her forehead.

She reached up and pulled him down on top of her. His jaw was smooth; she could smell his faintly citrus aftershave. "Hey," she said. "Where are you going? We have some unfinished business here."

Another chaste kiss, this one just to the side of her mouth, and then he pulled himself upright and sat on the edge of the bed. "You won't believe it," he said, "but I've got to go into the office."

She almost *didn't* believe it. He was on vacation; his precious children were with him for only a few short, precious days—that was how he kept putting it, anyway—and everything at the firm was supposed to be under control in his absence. Two of his partners were on duty, and numerous, well-trained assistants were in place, too. "Why?" she asked. "What's the matter?"

"Paul called. There are rumors of a hostile takeover—it may be an international cabal. And we've all got to sit down and strategize."

She hadn't heard the phone ring. And all that sudden, dramatic language: *a hostile takeover, an international cabal.* She imagined armed men in the uniforms of a foreign army crashing their bayonets into the Midtown office suites of World Trade Consultants. "Why can't you just have a conference call?" she said, aware of sounding more querulous than curious. She reminded herself, guiltily, that she should really know more about what he did at work.

He stood up. "Because I'm the *CFO,* for God's sake. I *have* to be there. Where are my cufflinks?"

"They're in the leather box on top of your chest. When will you be back?"

"When the meeting's over," he said. She heard him phone in a reservation for the helicopter. Then he came back to the bed, fastening his cufflinks, and with his jacket over his arm. "Listen, sweetie, I'm sorry. And I'll call you later, as soon as I have a better sense of all this. Do something fun with the kids, okay?" And he was gone.

The kids—talk about hostile takeovers! And she'd be alone with them for the first time. Even Michelle, who'd been mopier than ever lately, had the day off, a day that now stretched interminably ahead of Lissy. But she had no intention of chauffeuring Miles and Miranda around in the broiling sun to any "local attractions." She'd just have to do some strategizing of her own.

By the time the children awoke and came downstairs in search of Jeffrey, she was showered and dressed. "Daddy had to go into the city," she announced, because there was no way of softening that news, and no point in delaying it. Miranda's face crumpled immediately. She ignored the fresh orange juice that Lissy had poured and set before her.

And Miles was as incredulous as Lissy had been earlier. "But, but," he said. "But he *promised* we were going to the *lighthouse.* But he's on *vacation.*" He downed his orange juice as if he were pouring a soothing potion over his wounded heart.

"We'll do other stuff," she said. "We'll swim, we'll play cards."

"Do you know Wimpo?" he demanded. "Do you know BS?"

Were those real card games? "No, I don't," she said. "But how about Go Fish, or War?"

"All right, War," he said with a sigh, as if he'd just agreed to go into actual combat.

"It'll be fun, you'll see," she said. "Let's finish breakfast and clear the table. We can play right here."

The game of War, she remembered, could go on for hours, as the cards shifted from one player to the other and then back again. A hand or two could kill a good part of the day. She and Evie had played War on rainy weekends, or when she was kept home from school with a cold. Lissy had always, miraculously, won in the end, and Evie had pronounced her a lucky duck. It had taken her years to figure out that she'd been allowed to win, knowledge that came to her long after Evie was gone, along with the realization that she wasn't that lucky, after all.

While she was negotiating with Miles, Miranda had been crying, but quietly, rather than in her usual histrionic style. And she seemed genuinely stricken, plucking at the neck of her pajamas like that. She never touched her glass of juice or her scrambled egg, but when she took a few surreptitious bites of buttered toast, Lissy felt extravagantly pleased. The girl didn't leave the table afterward, and Lissy hurried to get the cards. She cut them into three equal-looking piles and, without saying a word, set one in front of each of them.

Of course Miles counted his right away. He was as good at math as Jeffrey had always boasted. "Three into fifty-two is seventeen and one third," he recited. "That means somebody has to get eighteen cards. It should be me because I'm the only boy, and I just have fifteen."

Lissy skimmed the top three cards from her own pile and added them to his. Then she placed her hand in readiness on her remaining cards and said, "Okay, everybody. One, two, three . . . go!"

And each of them, even Miranda, flipped over one card. And when she saw that her king was high, she raked the others' cards in with the practiced ease of a croupier.

She turned out to be the lucky duck among them, confiscating Miles's and Lissy's aces and the remaining kings in one triple war after another. It was going to be the shortest hand in the history of the game. And then what?

And then Lissy heard the opening chords of Beethoven's Fifth, but so dimly she thought she might be hallucinating. Jeffrey's cell phone! She jumped up from the table and toward the stairs, where the sound grew slightly louder. By the time she got up to the bedroom, it had stopped. It didn't take her long to find the phone, though; she just followed her instincts to Jeffrey's highboy, where it lay right next to the leather box. He'd never forgotten it before; he must have been really upset about the work thing.

She picked it up and saw that there was a brand-new text message from his secretary, which she opened. *Dear Mr. Snyder, Just to let you know the signed IRAs came in on the Prestige account. Enjoy the rest of your vacation! Lisa.* Jeffrey had taken the helicopter into the city; he would have been there for a while by now. Why was she writing to him as if he were still at home?

Lissy scrolled through his recent calls, and aside from the one from Lisa, there had been no others that day, not from Paul Jacobs or anyone else. But on the previous day, there'd been four received calls from Danielle, the last one shortly before their aborted attempt at lovemaking. He hadn't taken any of them in Lissy's presence.

"Oh, my God," she said, and had a flash of Larry Templeton killing the fly at the beach with his cell phone. Jeffrey's streamlined Palm Treo suddenly felt like a lethal weapon, and her sweaty fingerprints were all over it. She rubbed it against her T-shirt so vigorously she might have been trying to erase its contents. It was freezing in the house, and her belly clenched and cramped. "Oh, my God," she said again, before she went to her desk and searched out Patrick's number. She used Jeffrey's phone to make the call.

He answered so quickly, he might have been sitting right there with his phone in his hand, willing it to ring, the way Lissy had vainly willed hers to when her mother was visiting. Bernadette was supposed to have rescued her from her worst impulses, and now it seemed as if

Patrick was about to gratify them. I'm just getting even, she thought when he said "Hello," and "Oh, it's you," in a molten voice. It was only an eye for an eye, which was petty, maybe, but biblical, too.

They arranged to meet at noon at a motel near the airport. Neither of them said anything about lunch or a drink or used any other euphemism for what they were going to do. Her heart was beating like something trapped and frantic, in her chest, her throat, her mouth. She threw open drawers and closet doors, pulling out so many items of clothing the place quickly looked ransacked, burglarized. The black underwear, of course, and a filmy white summer dress, like something Ardith might have worn. You could see right through one layer to the next—was that vulgar, rather than just daring? What did it matter—everything would be ripped off in seconds.

It was only after she'd showered again, and dressed, and brushed her hair so hard it stood up around her head in a static-charged, perfumed cloud, and came tripping down the stairs, that she remembered the children. She ran into the kitchen, expecting to find them frozen in the tableau she'd left—was it more than half an hour ago? But they weren't there, or in the den or the library or on the sunporch.

She called their names as she rushed outdoors, shielding her eyes against the assault of sunlight. And she thought: *They're in the pool, they've drowned, I'm going to be punished, I'm going to get what I deserve, even though I haven't done anything yet.* But the thought—as her mother, that mind reader, always said—was as good as the deed.

The filter hadn't kicked in yet that morning, and the surface of the pool was serenely blue and still, unbroken by so much as a stray leaf or the body of a mosquito. When Lissy turned and looked toward the house, the children were at the window of their bedroom, looking back at her. Miranda waved.

29.

Charlotte's Web

Dear Valerie,

This has been such a long time coming, and yet suddenly I couldn't wait one more day, even another moment, to write to you. As I'm sure you remember, I was not always an impulsive person, and yet I had a dire failure of self-control, and even of common sense and decency, all those years ago. You were my great good friend and I betrayed that friendship. Can that ever begin to be forgiven?

My heart was lightened by our brief exchange through Charlotte, who is all I'd expected her to become. There's so much more to say, Val, but I'll hold off until I hear from you again.

Yours,
Angela

Let her letter be waiting there for Valerie's return with all the other held mail, significant in its square white envelope among the corporate bids for charity, the bills and magazines and catalogs. Angela's relief, as she signed her name, was instantaneous, as if an abscess had been lanced, and by the time she called Charlotte for Valerie's address, she was almost giddy. But as soon as she'd made her request, Charlotte said that she was late for something and practically out the door; could she call Angela back that afternoon?

Angela had her own errands to run: books due at the library, milk and eggs and butter to buy, and, eventually, a trip to the post office before it closed, but she stayed home, as foolishly expectant as a girl waiting to hear from the boy she has a secret crush on. And the day ran slowly out in ticking silence. Only the birds chattered, and, at one point, there were the sounds of a truck backing up to deliver a small mountain of mulch to the house across the road. Angela couldn't even read in her antsy state.

She would have called Charlotte again sooner—the young can be more forgetful than the old sometimes, because their lives and minds are filled to flood level with plans, with infatuated thoughts of one another—but she didn't want to seem intrusive, to spoil the fine balance of their friendship. So she waited until it was too late for the library, and then the post office—until it began to grow dark, and most of the air had leaked out of her elation.

Jimmy answered the phone this time and told her to hold on, he'd get Charlotte. Then his hand must have muzzled the receiver, because Angela could hear a lot of urgent whispering without being able to make out anything being said. When Charlotte came on, Angela apologized, instead of the other way around. "I'm sorry to bother you again," she said. "I just wanted to get your mother's address."

She thought that the line might have gone dead, and she said, "Hello? Charlotte?" And finally Charlotte sighed and said, "Listen, Angela, we really have to talk."

"Go ahead," Angela said over the whooshing, like the ocean's surf, in her ears.

"Not like this," Charlotte told her. "Not on the phone."

They agreed to meet the next day in the city, and when Charlotte didn't invite her to the apartment, Angela suggested the coffee shop across the street. She wanted it to be someplace familiar, and where good things had transpired between them. And she decided to bring along the book of fairy tales she'd bought at the Fisherman's Fair for Charlotte's birthday. You didn't need a formal occasion to give someone you care for a gift.

* * *

They had the same peeling red booth. Angela arrived first and claimed it. It was where Charlotte had blithely said, when asked about her mother, "Hey, you guys should be in touch." Now she slid into her seat across from Angela and pronounced, without even the prelude of a greeting, "She hates your guts." Angela waited, breathing, and Charlotte went on. "And she made sure he was just as unhappy as she was."

"Tell me," Angela said.

"That day, after the gallery? It started in the car. She kept punching him in the head while he drove. His glasses fell off, and we almost went off the road into a ditch." She touched the bridge of her own glasses, as if to protect them. "I think she forgot I was there."

"Sharly," Angela said, but she kept her hands to herself.

"They never really got over it, or past it. But they stayed together, you know, the way people do, as if they *had* to. We moved around every few years. He didn't get tenure anywhere."

The pity Angela felt was for herself, too, for those lost years at their table, in the protection of their purview; for being deprived of the changing child, for whom she might have bought her first bicycle or ice skates, and her first copy of *Charlotte's Web*, although Valerie would have been the one to read it to her, the two of them weeping a little over the mortality of spiders.

The waitress came with menus and water and went away. "And you?" Angela asked. "How did you feel about all of it?"

"I didn't actually get it for a long time. I mean, I got *something*—you'd have to be in a coma not to—but I had no real idea of what'd happened. Then it was like those 3-D pictures you stare at for hours with your eyes out of focus, and suddenly you see the dinosaur or the vase of flowers." She sipped her water, and shrugged. "I must have just gotten old enough to understand."

"Weren't you angry with me, too, then?" Angela asked. "Didn't *you* hate me?"

"Sure. But I hated everybody in those days. I was a *teenager*. I was stuck in a jerkwater town in *Indiana*."

"Wellspring, Texas, wouldn't have been a big improvement, believe me," Angela said, and was appalled by what must have sounded like a callous, dismissive joke.

Charlotte didn't appear to be offended. "It was me who said it, you know," she said.

"Said what?" Angela asked, although she already knew the answer.

"In the gallery. I pointed and said, 'Angela!' and everybody looked."

"Charlotte, that's crazy—they would have seen it anyway, they would have known. And you were just a baby."

"Yeah, I suppose so."

The waitress came back, with her pencil poised above her pad, but Angela waved her away. "The last time we were in this place, you said that your mother and I ought to be in touch," Angela said. "Why did you say that if you didn't mean it?"

"But I *did* mean it! It was sort of like making a magic wish, though, that everything that happened would be undone, and we'd be the way we used to be again. I loved you," she said miserably. "I loved when you came to the house."

"Me, too," Angela said, and she reached across the table and took Charlotte's hand. It was like capturing a bird. "Would you tell me about your father?" she said.

Charlotte knew what she meant. "He was sick for two years. They thought they got it with the surgery, but then it came back, worse than before. He decided not to do anything else about it, although she wanted him to, but then he changed his mind at the last minute and it was too late."

Angela tried to imagine that, and then tried not to. "Was he able to paint during any of that time?"

"A little, I think. And he kept a sketchpad with him in bed, even toward the end."

"Your mother doesn't know that you've seen me, Charlotte, does she?"

Charlotte shook her head. "I was never even allowed to mention your name."

"Oh, my dear," Angela said, and she released the girl's hand. "You were right not to tell her." Charlotte seemed uncertain. "No, you did the right thing. It would have just hurt her more. Again. She wasn't always like that about me, you know. She was lovely and generous. . . . You remember that, don't you?"

Charlotte was huddled on her side of the booth, as if she were trying to make herself small again, before the burden of memory and comprehension.

Angela picked up her menu and opened it. "Let's have something to eat," she said.

*   *   *

She called Irene as soon as she got back to The Springs and asked if she could come by for a little while that evening, but she declined the offer of supper. "I just need to talk," Angela said, a paraphrase of what Charlotte had said to her the night before.

Irene's apartment seemed like an extension of her shop, with its overflow of found objects. There were several needlepoint cushions and a beautiful, mended paisley shawl on the velvet sofa, and Angela sank back against them, resisting the temptation to lie down. Irene sat opposite her on a straight-backed Shaker chair. "What's going on?" she asked.

"I did a terrible thing," Angela said. "I stole from a friend."

"What are you talking about? What did you steal?"

"Her happiness, more or less."

After a moment or two, Irene said, "You mean you had an affair. Was it with her husband?"

"Yes, a very long time ago. Everyone was badly hurt by it." But that seemed like the least of it to Angela now.

"Was she the friend you said you'd fallen out with, the one you'd contacted again recently?"

"Quite a falling-out, wasn't it?" Angela said. "And I never contacted her. That was only another lie I wanted to believe." And she began to tell Irene everything, or everything that mattered, about her isolated, shy, and supercilious self, and how she had been rescued and reclaimed by Valerie and Stephen, about the pleasures of their household and of their little daughter. "I wanted it all for myself," Angela confessed, "like some jealous, selfish child who hasn't been taught to share."

"You said that it happened a long time ago."

"But it never completely went away," Angela said. "What I'd had, what I did, what I lost. And then I saw Charlotte again."

She had come to the turning point in the story. How many times had she instructed her students to identify the crucial turning point in a story? The untried girls at Macon would have chosen the moment she and Stephen had begun their affair, or that day at the Paradise Gallery when they were found out. And they wouldn't have been completely wrong, because those events altered the outcome of the lives of everyone involved.

But Irene seemed to understand that the more dramatically interesting and morally complex turning point was when she'd reconnected with Charlotte and gladly resumed the desire, the quest, for something that didn't belong to her. No wonder they both liked Trollope, with all his narrative threads. "What are you going to do?" Irene asked.

"That's the thing," Angela said. "I don't know." She thought about her fantasy of the airport reunion, as trite and unreal now as that recurrent scene in movies where the lovers move in slow motion toward each other, with outstretched arms, across a meadow. She thought of her plans to buy one of Charlotte's paintings, and remembered how, after she'd purchased those two of Stephen's, Valerie had affectionately referred to her as a patron of the arts. She thought of Charlotte struggling to reconcile her love for her mother and for Angela all this time. And she remembered the book of fairy tales she'd never removed from her bag at the coffee shop. *My business is with your father and not with you.*

Irene said, "Oh, but I think you do."

"It's so difficult," Angela said, almost wailed.

"I know," Irene said. Then she came and sat beside Angela, who finally looked back into her eyes, and at the pale, faintly freckled skin of her face and throat, the skin she had once felt so uncomfortable inhabiting.

Her embrace seemed to catch Angela in midfall, if not really by surprise, and when they kissed, tentatively at first—like the tasting of something new—and then with growing ardor, she knew that this was yet another, more promising turn in her unfinished story.

30.

A Death in the Family

Human company was not all that it was cracked up to be, not Kayla's company, at any rate. The female bonding Michelle had counted on, and that she'd felt between them during fleeting moments in the past, probably wasn't going to happen during this visit. The girl had become such a crab; no wonder April was so willing to share her. And unlike her mother, Kayla wasn't guided by discretion or tact. "What happened between you and my dad?" she demanded as soon as she'd dropped her backpack on the floor.

"Nothing," Michelle said. "We're taking a break, that's all." Kayla snorted. Michelle might as well have tried lying to her about the birds and bees, too.

"There's nothing to do around here," Kayla complained a

little later, as if she'd been shanghaied to The Springs on her way to Disney World. She refused an offer to be driven to the beach, saying, whining, that it was too hot, and she didn't even take it seriously when Michelle suggested she do some chores, like weeding or emptying the dishwasher. Only the two of them were at home—Jo Ann was working—so there was no one to pass her off to.

She followed Michelle upstairs and watched her make the beds while she tried on several of Michelle's things, pronouncing most of them, and herself, ugly. "I'm so *fat*," she groaned a couple of times, although she practically disappeared when she stood sideways.

Then she said, "Can I have this?" and Michelle turned to see her wearing the halter top Lissy Snyder had given her. She hadn't worn it since the night April was in the hospital. Kayla could have used a couple of towels to fill it out. "You can *borrow* it," she said, but Kayla was already on her way downstairs in her continuing search for something else to do.

Only the dogs provided some temporary relief from her maddening boredom, serving as impromptu pillows, wrestling partners, garbage disposals for the tuna sandwich meant for her lunch, and confidants. She lifted their silky ears to whisper into them, making them shudder and yip. Before long, they crawled into the shadows under the front porch to get away from her and to cool off.

Then she was on Michelle's heels again, grumbling about the heat, and opening and closing the refrigerator door without ever taking anything out. Michelle was thinking of just giving up and bringing her back home when Lissy called, looking for a babysitter for her husband's children. It was kind of an emergency, she said, and Michelle thought, Yeah, an emergency pedicure, I'll bet. But she saw a solution, in Lissy's problem, to her own dilemma. "I'm kind of busy," she said, "but my . . . my, uh, *niece* is staying with me, and she's available."

She was all set to start singing Kayla's praises as a responsible, experienced sitter—she'd seen Jeffrey Snyder's kids and they weren't babies, they didn't need professional minding—but Lissy wasn't about to ask for references. She didn't even ask how old Kayla was, just if she could be there in the next fifteen minutes.

That's when Michelle's own sense of responsibility kicked in. She thought of that great big house and all its goodies, the deep, sparkling swimming pool and gorgeous gardens, Kayla's curiosity and her carelessness. "It would be better if you could bring them here," she said, and Lissy didn't argue; she just asked her for directions.

"Well, congratulations, you've got yourself a job," Michelle told Kayla a moment later. "And close that refrigerator, you're letting all the cold air out."

Kayla's eyes narrowed. "What kind of job?" she asked.

"Babysitting. For that woman I work for."

"But I already told you, I don't really like kids."

"You don't have to. I don't like cleaning, either. But I like the money."

"How much?" Kayla said.

Michelle hadn't asked, but from the way Lissy sounded, they could probably name their own price. "I don't know. Plenty, I would guess."

"Do I have to play with them?"

"No, just tie them to a chair and torture them."

Kayla gave her a dirty look, and then stooped to check out her reflection in the oven door.

"Maybe you ought to take that top off before they get here," Michelle said.

"Why?"

"Because it was hers, the mother's. The stepmother's. Whatever."

"You mean you *stole* it?" Her eyes glittered with interest for the first time since her arrival.

"No, birdbrain, she gave it to me."

"Like a hand-me-down?"

"Of course not. It was brand-new; it still had the tags on it."

"So why do you care if I wear it?"

It was a fair question, but Michelle wasn't in the mood to try to figure out a reasonable answer. "Do what you want," she said, and when Kayla put her head into the refrigerator again, she asked her to see if there was enough juice in there for the kids.

It occurred to Michelle, while they were waiting for Lissy to show up, that she might have asked Kayla to stay with her under false pretenses, and that the girl had sensed something insincere in the invitation. Maybe that's why she was being especially difficult. Was it really Hank that Michelle was seeking, if only just a genetic piece of him? Or was she setting some kind of trap?—*I've got your kid, come and get her.* But she wasn't that pathetic, was she?

Before she could think over that latter, unsettling possibility, there was a squealing of brakes, and when she looked out the window she saw the Snyders' black Lexus SUV at the curb in front of the house. Then the driver's door opened and Lissy slid out on spindly heels. What was she wearing? Something white and see-through, with black underwear. She looked totally slutty.

Michelle headed for the front door as Lissy hurried up the steps and approached it from the other side. She'd left the motor running. "Hello?" she called through the screen, shading her eyes with one hand, and rapping sharply on the door frame with the other. "Anybody home?" Kayla, of course, had conveniently disappeared. And where were the children she was supposed to watch?

The boys ambled out from under the house and shook their coats free of debris as they slowly approached the car. That's when Michelle saw the two little heads peeping over the window in the backseat of the SUV. "You found us," she told Lissy, who said, "Michelle! Oh, good, I wasn't sure I had the right place. I didn't see any numbers out front."

She turned toward the street and called, "Miles! Miranda! Come on, we're here!" How did she expect them to hear her with the windows rolled up like that?

"They're friendly, aren't they?" Lissy asked nervously about the dogs, who stood near the car, panting and wagging in welcome.

"They haven't eaten anybody yet," Michelle said, opening the screen door and stepping out onto the porch. That's when she saw a flurry of activity inside the car, one of the kids scrambling over the seat to get in front—headfirst, feet in the air—and the other one jumping up and down in the back, as if she were on a spring. "Hey!" Michelle yelled, but it was too late. The SUV had started to roll down the street, picking up momentum on the incline as it went, with Pete and Bill in pursuit.

"Oh no, oh God! Stop! Somebody help!" Lissy cried, and she tottered down the steps, losing one of her shoes on the way. Michelle went right past her, flying almost, but she felt as if she were running in place.

The car didn't travel that far before it turned a little—the kid must have been trying to steer—and headed off near the bottom of the road toward a stand of birches. When it veered, Pete didn't, and Michelle saw him go under the wheel only seconds before she heard his yowling, the worst sound she had ever heard, and then the light smack of the SUV hitting the trees.

The children's screaming was muted by the windows, but when Michelle flung open the driver's door, it became loud and lusty, as if they'd just been born into the world. They both leaped out as Lissy came limping toward them, and went into her arms.

Michelle lay facedown on the ground, trying to see and to reach under the car, where there was a terrible, merciful stillness and silence. Bill struggled at her side, pushing his head against her hip and whimpering. After a while, she sat up and held him with one arm and ran her other hand over his head, his heaving flanks, and his drooping tail. He didn't seem to be hurt. She continued to sit there, holding on to him. And then Kayla was next to her, too, crying wildly, looking like a child dressed up for Halloween with her striped hair and Lissy's ballooning halter top.

A few neighbors had come out of their houses to see what had happened. Two men were looking at the car; one of them took out his cell phone. The Mexican woman who lived around the corner walked carefully toward Michelle, carrying a brimming glass of water. Another woman knelt next to Lissy and the children, speaking to them. It was like that part of a movie when the camera pulls back, so that you can see the whole scene at once, and you aren't inside anyone's head.

Lissy, tearstained and barefoot now, approached Michelle, whispering "Sorry, sorry," and then a taxi took her and the children away. Michelle made Kayla go into the house with Bill before the wreckers came and lifted the SUV off what was left of Pete. She crouched to look at him: a bloodied golden bathmat. Roadkill. With one finger, she touched a feathery part that might have been his tail. Her beautiful boy.

By evening, everyone was there. Hank and April came together to fetch Kayla, who clung to one of them and then the other like a scrap of Velcro. He put his hand on the top of Michelle's head and she leaned into him for a long moment, the way Bill had leaned into her. But when he left with his family, she didn't watch them go.

Eddie started to sob the minute he came into the house, and Kathleen and Jo Ann, and even Michelle, had to console him. Every once in a while, someone asked Michelle if she was okay, and she kept saying yes, yes, and she was. All that time, Bill paced restlessly from room to room, as if he were waiting for somebody else to arrive, something else to happen.

Finally, it was just the three of them. Jo Ann filled Bill's food and water bowls, and she made sandwiches and tea for Michelle and herself. It was possible to eat and drink. When it was time for bed, Michelle went upstairs, and Jo Ann lifted one of the rarely used leashes from the hook on the back door and took Bill outside.

They came into her room later, letting in the light from the hallway. She rubbed her eyes and propped herself up on one elbow; she could hardly stay awake. "He did his business," Jo Ann reported, and the clank of dog tags and the reek of fur pervaded her senses as Bill clambered up beside her, and she let go.

31.

Wallpaper

At bedtime, the children swore her to secrecy, to not telling their father about what Miles had done. "Please," he begged, and Miranda bounced on her bed the way she had in the car, loyally echoing, "Please, Lissy, pretty please." She'd actually said her name! It was as simple as that. Lissy had even been able to make her oath of silence conditional. "First you must tell me what you've learned from all this," she said as she tucked them in.

"Not to ever, ever touch anything in the car again," Miles said, with one hand splayed over his heart, as if he were pledging allegiance to the flag.

"Ever, *ever*," Miranda said.

Lissy had already concocted a few possible scenarios in

her head to explain away the minor damage to the Lexus: a pothole, swerving to avoid a squirrel, the sun in her eyes, but she'd worried, unnecessarily it seemed, about keeping the kids quiet.

As for Patrick, her desire for him was erased by the events of the day almost as easily as she'd erased all the voice-mail messages he had left for her from the airport motel. Getting even no longer seemed like such a compelling notion. That anxious and unhappy little boy asleep upstairs, for whom she'd had to leave a bedside light burning, had inadvertently saved her from something that would surely have ended badly, too, just as he had saved his father's life on September 11.

She had gotten away with murder, so to speak, although no one but an animal had died. The children might well have, if the impact had been stronger, if the airbags had deployed. Her breath became ragged when she let herself think about that. She'd even shaken out those pink pills she'd stolen from Angela's house, and wondered if she could have killed herself with them—would she have had the nerve? Would they have done the trick?—if something had happened to the children. Then she'd flushed the pills down the toilet.

As it was, Miranda and Miles were unhurt. They'd had an adventure that would find its way into their collective memory as something very bad, but good, too, somehow—a future dinner-party anecdote, a narrow escape. Those images and sensations—Michelle, lying prone on the road; the agonized sounds of the dog; the rough kiss of bumper and tree—would all probably change or disappear over the years, according to whatever else happened to them. For now, though, they wouldn't talk about it; they wouldn't give her away.

And Jeffrey had his own day, his own actions, to answer for. Everything that had happened to her, and that had almost happened, was attributable to him, if you really thought about it, if you wound the hours back to the morning, when it all began.

So when he returned from the city late that night, she was on the offensive, tensely poised at the edge of one of the stools at the island in the kitchen, in her ivory silk kimono, waiting for him. She hadn't picked up the phone when it rang earlier, and he'd left a message that his "meeting" had run really late, that he would try to make it home before midnight. Like Cinderella, he arrived just on the stroke.

"Listen, Jeffrey," she said as soon as he walked in. "I know where you've been, so don't bother lying again, okay?"

He sat down at the table, where he'd laid his briefcase and then his cufflinks, and said, "Okay."

It was not the response she'd expected, and she felt her shoulders and her spirits sag. She was a little frightened. "I thought we were happy together," she said, sounding more plaintive now than angry or self-righteous.

"What do you mean?" he said. "Of course we're happy."

"Then why did you go to see her, to be with her?"

"Because she was threatening stuff about the kids, about custody."

"And she used *sex* for that?" It was the most shocking thing she could imagine.

"What are you talking about?" he said. "Oh. Oh, no. Is that what you thought? Jesus. I wasn't *with* her, Liss."

"You weren't? Not in England, either?"

"Sweetheart," he said. "She's not my type, not anymore. And Danielle would never use sex as a bargaining chip." He gave a bitter little laugh. "She hardly ever even used it much for fun."

"So what was this about, then?"

"It was about money, of course. The way everything is."

How much? was her immediate thought. "Wallpaper," she said, almost to herself.

"What?"

"That's not true. Everything *isn't* about money." She vaguely remembered saying the same thing to him at least once before.

He looked at her in her silk kimono, in her gleaming, nuclear-age kitchen, and smiled indulgently. Then he came to where she was sitting and kissed her hand, the inside of her scented, pulsing wrist. "Oh, no?" he said. "Since when?"

It was not an argument she was prepared to take on. She wasn't even certain what she believed. Hadn't she just wondered how much he'd agreed to give Danielle to ransom his children? As ugly a thought as what a confession might cost her.

And that afternoon, she'd toyed with the idea of giving Michelle a raise, if she ever came back to work for them. Then she had considered buying her a puppy, after a decent interval, of course. Something pedigreed and blond, like the one she'd lost, delivered to her doorstep in a basket, with a red ribbon tied around its neck. An out-of-season Christmas present, a replacement dog.

She had never had a dog herself, because her mother didn't like them. And Lissy had always been uneasy around other people's pets, an offshoot, perhaps, of her general incompatibility with nature. Or maybe it had something to do with what one of her therapists had called her "fear of attachment."

But now she was swamped by a wave of wretchedness. Something that had been alive—a breathing being—wasn't anymore because of her careless, impetuous behavior. Those awful images she'd imagined drifting from the children's heads had become fixed in hers. And she recognized Michelle's grief as genuine and important, something that probably couldn't be stanched with cash or whatever else it could buy. Money really wasn't everything. Maybe that was what *she* had learned from all this.

On the other hand, Lissy cherished her beautiful kitchen and her beautiful kimono, and all the other objects of her pleasurable, privileged life. Wasn't it possible to keep the wallpaper without giving up the soul? Like the moral issues raised by the novels she'd tried to read this summer, that thought made her sleepy. "Come," she said to Jeffrey, taking him by the hand. "Let's go to bed."

32.

Other People's Lives

MONTAUK MAN MURDERED

Guido Masconi, owner and manager of the Battered Clam, a popular dining spot on Fort Pond in Montauk, was shot to death in a Center Moriches motel room he was sharing with Ardith Templeton, of Sagaponack and New York City. According to the police report, Masconi's wife, Doris Marie Masconi, a television actress known professionally as Delora Deane, entered the room at the Beachcomber Motel on Rt. 27 where Mr. Masconi and Ms. Templeton were asleep at 5:20 A.M. on Wednesday, carrying a .22-caliber revolver registered to her husband.

After shooting Mr. Masconi in the head at close range, Ms. Masconi aimed the weapon at Ms. Templeton, who had awakened and was trying to flee the room. Ms. Masconi fired twice more, hitting a lamp and grazing a TV, and Ms. Templeton was able to escape and summon help.

Ms. Masconi confessed immediately to the shooting, yelling "That will teach him to screw around!" She told police that she had learned to handle a gun on the set of the CBS series *Original Sin*, on which she played Starry Knight, a sex-crazed, homicidal rookie cop.

Neither Ms. Templeton nor her husband, Lawrence P. Templeton, the noted financier and real estate developer, could be reached for comment.

Angela put down the paper she'd been reading at the breakfast table. "Did you see this?" she said. "It's amazing."

"What is?" Irene asked. "That she used his own gun? That she missed Ardith? That *her* husband didn't do it?"

"All of the above," Angela said. "I mean, why do we bother reading fiction?" But even as she said it, she was thinking that the never-ending marvel of other people's lives was precisely what she had always loved in literature.

Then Charlotte and Valerie came to mind, as they still did at least once a day, and she wondered once more what each of them was doing right then. Several days had gone by and Charlotte hadn't called, as Angela had hoped and dreaded she might.

She'd diagrammed and parsed their final conversation in the coffee shop many times, looking for hidden psychological content. "She hates your guts," Charlotte had said; there was certainly nothing hidden in that. And then, "I loved you. I loved when you came to the house." The past tense, used with apparent sorrow and regret.

Angela had truthfully portrayed Valerie as "lovely and generous," prodding Charlotte to remember that, a way of turning her back over to her rightful owner. I'm like Stella Dallas, she thought ruefully, the last fictional heroine she would have ever chosen as a role model. Her first choice would be Brontë's Lucy Snowe, who didn't think she would find love, either, or that she particularly deserved to, but never stooped to steal it from someone else.

When Angela had been with Stephen, and even in those recent weeks with Charlotte at hand, her joy had been excessive, unbalanced, a kind of emotional vertigo, and always shadowed by darkness. That state of being which people probably meant when they claimed to be dying of happiness.

Now her aging, flawed, distracted self was wholly loved and capable of loving back. Her balance and sanity restored, and not without passion—wasn't it better this way?

That night, when they were reading in bed, she heard Irene draw in her breath and emit a resigned sigh. She'd probably just come across a passage in her book she wanted to share, and then had wisely resisted the urge.

Irene had once told Angela that reading aloud in bed was something she'd regularly done during her short marriage and that Howard Rush had pretended to appreciate, until one evening when he threw off the covers and shouted, "For God's sake, I can read that myself!"

That was the beginning of the end for them. Little by little they both put aside other pretenses, and eventually Irene was able to admit to Howard, and fully to herself, that she didn't want to be with him, or with any other man.

For Angela, reading had always been the last threshold of privacy, the one place she could go alone without the danger of feeling lonely. In this regard, she was secretly sympathetic to Howard Rush.

Now she looked at Irene, half lying next to her, still intent on her open book. Lamplight pooled on the curve of her bare shoulder as her breath rose and fell.

Angela closed her own book, mentally saving her place for later. She turned to Irene and touched her, lightly, as if to confirm that she was really there. "Read something to me," she said.

33.

The Middle of Nowhere

When Michelle took Bill outside the morning after the accident, Pete's remains were gone, and the part of the road where he was killed appeared to have been hosed down. Maybe a neighbor had taken care of it, or someone from Animal Control. Michelle felt relieved and bereft, and also a little cheated. Bill, on a leash again, sniffed around the area, peed a few times in the bushes off to the side, and then went docilely back home with her.

They stood in front of the house while several cars went by, but he didn't tug at the leash or show any other interest in taking off after one of them. He had been a follower all his life, a sidekick, and he didn't have Pete to lead him into the chase anymore. Michelle let him off the leash and went back up the stairs and into the house. He was right behind her.

In the evening, Hank called and asked her what she wanted to do with Pete's body. "It's gone," she said. "Somebody took him away."

"Yeah," he said. "That was me and Eddie. We've got him in a tarp out in the pickup, and you have a decision to make. I spoke to the people at Animal Control, and you can either . . . uh, dispose of him, or have him cremated."

She hesitated, and he said, "I'd go with the cremation if I were you, Mush. It's a little expensive, but otherwise Pete may be headed for the landfill." When she agreed, he said he'd see that it was done, and get back to her afterward.

A week later, Michelle and Hank were out on the *Kayla Joy* with the bag of ashes. It was still dark out, a couple of hours before his regular morning run. She had met him down at the dock in Montauk, and they'd shared a thermos of coffee, and a minimum of conversation, in the pickup before they'd boarded the boat.

Michelle was what Eddie mockingly called a landlubber; she had never liked the roll of the waves under the hull, that sense of being out in the middle of nowhere. She didn't get seasick, exactly, but as they pulled away, she looked back in the direction of the shore she could barely make out under that sliver of moon with a feeling of unease. "It'll get calmer in a little while," Hank said, as if he could read her thoughts.

"I'm fine," she told him.

The cremation had cost almost three hundred dollars, and she'd declined Hank's offer to split the bill with her. Pete wasn't his dog, and she wasn't Hank's girlfriend anymore. Besides, Lissy Snyder had sent her a hefty check, for "expenses," enclosed in a note of condolence, along with an elaborate basket of food from Loaves & Fishes.

Michelle's first instinct was to return the money, and then she changed her mind. Why *shouldn't* Lissy pay for Pete's cremation? It was her car that had hit him, and she could afford it. Her note was sappy, but at least she hadn't offered to buy Michelle a new dog.

Hank dropped anchor about five miles out to sea. The horizon was rimmed in pink by then, the way it usually looked in the picture postcards they sold in the souvenir shops. The water, gentler now, as he'd promised, was tipped with silver. "So we're here," he said.

Michelle opened the sealed bag—it was a little tricky, but she'd figured out how to do it back in the pickup—and put her hand inside. The ashes felt something like the gritty sand she'd always let sift through her fingers when she lay on the beach.

"Go portside, away from the wind," Hank told her, and then, when she was at the railing, "Should we say anything?"

She shook her head, not trusting her voice. If she could speak, she might have said, "What are we doing out here?" Or, "How I do even know this is really Pete?" She had the eerie notion that her father was nearby, just under the lapping water, which she immediately dismissed as stupid and sentimental, but couldn't quite shake off.

She threw out the first handful herself and then passed the bag to Hank, as if she were offering him some peanuts. He threw out another, larger handful—how much there seemed to be!—and then she took the bag back and upended it, letting the rest of the ashes drift down into the water.

The sky was slowly growing rosy. They rocked in place; Hank hadn't picked up the anchor. When she looked at him, he was just standing there, a few feet away, looking back at her. "Mushy," he said. "I'm such a jerk."

"Yeah, you are," she said.

"I don't want to always be that way, though."

"Good luck with that, then," she said.

"No, listen, will you. I want to marry you."

She laughed, but it came out like a hiccup. "What?" she said. "Is this like a pity proposal?"

"I'm the one who's pitiful," he said.

"Yes," she said.

"Yes, what?" he asked.

"Yes."

34.

Lost and Found

The Gormans' fifteenth anniversary party was to be Lissy's last hurrah of the season, a sit-down dinner for fifty of the couple's closest friends, to be held at their sprawling Bridgehampton cottage. Lissy had arranged for a highly touted Chinese chef to come in from Manhattan and prepare a traditional Cantonese banquet, and she'd hired two musicians, a flautist and a harpist, from Juilliard's summer program, to play softly in the background. She'd asked them to find music that sounded sort of Asian, but still had a melody.

Janet and Sidney Gorman had two little girls named Willow and Ivy—adopted, Lissy had heard—who weren't to be included in the festivities. They were only three and four years old, and this was strictly a grown-up affair. But they would be allowed to appear once at the beginning of the evening to see every-thing and to be seen.

The guests were due at six, and Lissy had arrived an hour earlier to check on the preparations. She would slip out unobtrusively as soon as she was sure that the party was smoothly under way. The Gor-mans were upstairs getting dressed, and everything seemed to be going as well as expected downstairs.

The bartender, who looked a little like a younger Woody Harrel-son, had set up in the gallery off the entrance to the house. He had ice tongs, Lissy noted approvingly, and the rows of wineglasses were sparkling. She pretended not to notice that he winked at her as she went by, or how her heart fluttered. In the kitchen, the chef was giv-ing rapid-fire orders in a singsong dialect, and his helpers were chop-ping and slicing as swiftly and deftly as that man selling Ginsu knives on late-night TV.

The Juilliard students, in long skirts, were warming up in a corner of the screened porch, where two long tables had been elaborately laid with red brocaded cloths, bowls of summer chrysanthemums, and oversized golden chargers, like Chinese gongs. And the rafters had been hung with paper lanterns and miniature wind chimes, some of their clappers taped into silence in case of a sudden, brisk breeze.

Lissy had found the lanterns and chimes in a funky little shop in East Hampton called Things, where Angela Graves, of all people, was seated on a stool behind the counter, reading. This was probably a sec-ond job for her, now that the book club season had ended. She ap-peared sage-like on her high perch, with the book open before her like a sacred text, and Lissy had an urge to consult her about matters that had been on her mind. She might ask if the "other" that one was sup-posed to contemplate could ever be a dog, whether a reading problem doomed you to a kind of moral limbo for life, and if Angela thought that Lissy had changed in any perceptible way since they'd first met.

The moment for such personal questions went by, though, and instead she asked if there happened to be any decorative Chinese objects in the shop, and Angela closed her book and said, "I believe there actually are some around here someplace." And they only made small talk after the purchase, about the cooling weather—how quickly the summer had flown!—and the way the leaves would begin to turn color soon.

Lissy felt proud of herself for having attended so carefully to every small detail for this evening, like those inspired decorations. Some of her other parties, while not exactly flops, had definitely suffered from a few amateurish touches. Patrick's bumbling magic act, for instance; that sadistic mime; and the time she'd ordered twenty-five capons for a family reunion and they'd arrived, shortly after the guests, un-cooked—she could have sworn she'd said they were to be roasted. The day was saved, finally, with an emergency delivery, at her own expense, of platters of smoked fish. Then there was the fiasco of the piñatas at the final Page Turners meeting.

But now she was really getting the hang of party planning, and was on her way to becoming a true professional. Maybe next summer she'd take on an assistant or two and advertise her services, rather than just depend on Jeffrey's connections for referrals, although she wouldn't refuse his financing. She might call her company Let's Party! or, more simply, Celebrations. She'd always been good at coming up with names.

Things were sweet between Lissy and Jeffrey, the way they'd been at the very beginning. Somehow, she had managed to pass the stepparenting test. The children had even asked to stay with her and Jeffrey for part of their Christmas vacation, and Danielle—her palm suitably greased, no doubt—had agreed. When Lissy had a baby of her own, in two or three years, they might all blend into a family of sorts. A very lucky outcome, when you thought about everything that might have gone wrong, and almost did.

She was not half as lucky as Ardith, though, who'd been miracu-lously restored to her place in Hampton society, not to mention in her marriage, as if she'd never left her post. She was still ahead of Lissy on all counts, because she'd dared to have her fling, and then someone else conveniently got rid of her lover for her before the bloom wore off. Larry, the famous fly-slayer, was all bluster, as it turned out, and the scandal had simply rendered Ardith, in her virginal garb, even more interesting and more in demand than ever.

The Gormans came downstairs, looking handsome and animated. She wore a red silk cheongsam and a gardenia in her ash-blond hair, and he had a black mandarin jacket on over his summer whites. "Beautiful, just beautiful," Janet kept saying as she walked around, inspecting, with Lissy close behind her. And Sidney patted Lissy's arm and said "Great job!"

She stepped back into the kitchen when the guests began to arrive, so that she would be discreetly hidden. Pans were hissing on the stove, and there was Chinese chatter all around her, but she could still hear the clinking of ice—like a counterpoint to the lovely, strange music from the porch—and excited greetings at the door as people came in, although they'd all probably seen one another at some other party the night before. It didn't matter; this one was going to be a big success, the one they'd talk about all winter.

Lissy was about to go out quietly through the back door when she heard Janet call, "Eve! Bring the girls down now, please!" There was an expectant hush among the guests; you would think they'd never seen children before. But Lissy found herself drawn in, too, and she went back to the kitchen, where she'd have a good view of the staircase.

"How adorable!" she heard one of the women cry, and there was a little burst of applause as the children came haltingly down the stairs, holding hands. They were Chinese, Lissy was astounded to see, as if they'd been chosen to suit the motif of the evening. But, of course, it was the other way around—the party's theme was a celebration of their native culture.

They must have been babies when they were brought here—was anything familiar to them in this trumped-up American Orient? Their nanny, a plump, grandmotherly Caucasian, trailed behind them, carrying a large, gift-wrapped box that had to be an anniversary present from them to their parents. How far these tiny girls had journeyed to find their new life, just as Lissy's father had done to escape from his old one.

Lissy felt a thrill as the little procession descended, and a peculiar connection to those dark-haired children in their matching, butterfly-printed pajamas. Then the littler one tripped on a lower step and the nanny reached out and grabbed her arm to right her. "Be careful, my girl," she said in that marvelous, known voice, in the Scottish burr she had never lost, and Lissy fell into a swoon.

The party was interrupted, if not quite ruined. Lissy came to on the kitchen floor, surrounded by curious, concerned sous chefs, and with a doctor guest in mint-green slacks kneeling at her side. Her head was resting on a small cushion. "You fainted," the doctor said, holding her wrist. "Don't sit up yet." Beyond him, she could see the crowd of guests peering at her, the unintended main attraction of the evening. The children and Evie had disappeared, as if she had only imagined them.

She hadn't imagined them, of course. After the party resumed, and she was brought upstairs to lie down for a while in a spare bedroom, Evie came to her with a wet cloth for her head. Her charges were in bed down the hall, she told Lissy, whom she instructed to be quiet and rest. But Lissy couldn't. "Do you remember me?" she asked, and Evie laughed and said, "Why, I never forgot you."

Which might or might not have been true. It didn't seem to matter. The main thing was the story she told, of how unhappy Lissy's father, that coward, that hero of his own survival, had been in his marriage. "He *had* to get out," Evie said, and Lissy thought, *Yes, but he could have taken me with him.*

For a little while after she'd had that dream/memory in which her grandmother had said, to someone, "How *could* you?" it occurred to Lissy that her mother might have killed Evie, or had her killed—an insane, intolerable idea. But all she had done was fire her, in a wild tantrum in the middle of the night, and then told Lissy that cruelest of lies the next morning.

"Why didn't you ever get in touch with me?" Lissy asked, and Evie said that she had, that she'd sent postcards and birthday cards that must have been withheld.

Together they pondered why Lissy's grandmother had never told her the truth, and concluded that she may have believed a seeming death would be easier for a child to bear than another defection. As they talked, Lissy could hear the children in their bedroom, calling "Eve! Eve! Come here, we need you!"

When Evie rose to go to them, Lissie got up to follow her. But she stopped in the doorway of their room as Evie went inside, saying "What's going on in here, my girls?"

"We can't sleep, we need a story," one of the children said. And while Lissy looked on, as if she were watching a movie of her own life, Evie took a blue book down from a shelf and opened it to the first page.

A Reading List

Villette
Charlotte Brontë

Mrs. Bridge
Evan S. Connell

Madame Bovary
Gustave Flaubert

Love in the Time of Cholera
Gabriel García Márquez

Frida: A Biography of Frida Kahlo
Hayden Herrera

Harry Potter and the Sorcerer's Stone
J. K. Rowling

Can You Forgive Her?
Anthony Trollope

Acknowledgments

With deep gratitude to Nancy Miller
and Henry Dunow.

About the Author

HILMA WOLITZER is the author of several novels, including *The Doctor's Daughter, Hearts, Ending,* and *Tunnel of Love,* as well as the nonfiction book *The Company of Writers.* She is a recipient of Guggenheim and NEA fellowships, and an Award in Literature from the American Academy and Institute of Arts and Letters. She has taught writing at the University of Iowa, New York University, and Columbia University. Hilma Wolitzer lives in New York City.

About the Type

This book was set in Garamond, a typeface originally designed by the Parisian typecutter Claude Garamond (1480–1561). This version of Garamond was modeled on a 1592 specimen sheet from the Egenolff-Berner foundry, which was produced from types assumed to have been brought to Frankfurt by the punchcutter Jacques Sabon.

Claude Garamond's distinguished romans and italics first appeared in *Opera Ciceronis* in 1543–44. The Garamond types are clear, open, and elegant.